Shadow Lane
Volume 1 & 2

The Romance of Discipline

by
Eve Howard

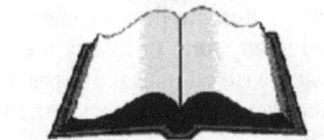

CCB Publishing
British Columbia, Canada

Shadow Lane Volume 1 & 2: The Romance of Discipline, Spanking, Sex, B&D and Anal Eroticism in a Small New England Village

Copyright ©2009 by Eve Howard
ISBN-13 978-1-926585-24-6
Second Edition

Library and Archives Canada Cataloguing in Publication
Howard, Eve, 1953-
Shadow lane : volume 1 & 2 : the romance of discipline, spanking, sex, b&d and anal eroticism in a small New England village / written by Eve Howard – 2nd ed.
ISBN 978-1-926585-24-6
Also available in electronic format.
I. Title.
PS3608.O82S53 2009   813'.6   C2009-903091-8

Cover artwork by Tarsis: www.briantarsis.com

Shadow Lane Volume 1 & 2 were originally published in episodic form in *Shadow Lane* and *Stand Corrected* magazines, Copyright © Shadow Lane, between 1987 and 1990. Blue Moon first edition published 1993, 1994 Copyright © Eve Howard.

Publisher: CCB Publishing
               British Columbia, Canada
               www.ccbpublishing.com

Dedicated to

Steven, Bill and Dave

William and Damaris

Shadow Lane

Volume 1

The Romance of Discipline,
Spanking, Sex, B&D and Anal Eroticism
in a Small New England Village

ৡ

Contents

Chapter One

Susan and Laura

Laura felt that she and her younger sister had lingered too long on their walk. Shadows had begun to fall in the forest and soon it would be dark. Laura's brow was wrinkled as she purposefully strode along, pulling Susan by the hand. The mischievous girl began to laugh at her serious sister.

"What's the matter, Laura?" Susan teased, "Afraid we might get spanked?"

When Laura made no comment, Susan said, "I wish I had someone thrilling and masterful like William in my life!" Laura responded with a small smile. She put her arm about Susan's slim waist as they walked. It was good to have a sister who shared one's sexual proclivities.

"Let's stop at Hugo Sands' house on the way!" Susan cried, breaking from Laura's embrace with sudden excitement.

"But that will make us late," Laura protested, for her husband liked dinner served promptly.

"Not if we only stay for a minute. I want to tell Hugo I'm leaving for art school tomorrow," Susan pressed.

"Then visit him after dinner, alone."

"Laura, you know he's never happy unless you're there too."

"Don't say that!" Laura pulled her sweater tightly about her against the early autumn chill.

"Please, Laura," Susan persisted, "let's stop. You know what it would mean to me to see Hugo before I left. I have the most brutal crush on him."

"Susan, you're not going to college in Nepal. You can visit Hugo whenever you like."

"Laura, don't be selfish. You know the only way I can please Hugo is by bringing you to him."

"Susan, you're going to get me in trouble with William!"

"There's his house. Come on, just for 10 minutes? Please?"

Hugo Sands was a dealer in antiques, the publisher of an esoteric journal, and a figure of glamour in the tiny coastal village of Random Point.

The door to his ivy draped, stone house was open and the girls found him in the wine cellar selecting libations. A little over forty, tall, blue-eyed and sandy haired, their host was a good looking, well spoken, sartorially correct, Harvard educated entrepreneur who, enjoying a good deal of leisure and financial ease, devoted much of his time to just playing.

"So you're off to college, are you?" Hugo looked Susan up and down critically, then chose a bottle. "We'll take this upstairs and drink to your future academic successes."

"I'd rather drink to my future erotic excesses," Susan replied.

"I'll look forward to reading your memoirs," Hugo commented, though without much interest, as if Susan's libido bored him.

"Why don't you help inspire them?" the petite blonde teased.

"Susan, behave yourself!"

"Why should I?"

"Because if you don't, I'll spank you," he threatened.

"What did I do wrong?" Susan demanded. "I even brought you Laura."

"It's true. She dragged me here against my will," Laura said.

"Susan, you're too young to be manipulating people!" Hugo put the bottle down and seized Susan by her slender wrist.

"What are you doing? Let go!"

"Come here, you fresh brat. This is what you need!" Hugo yanked Susan over to a high backed, armless, oak chair, promptly sat down on it and effortlessly pulled the small girl over his knee. Laura stared spellbound, as Hugo locked her sister's wrist against the small of her back and began to spank Susan at once. It was not a long spanking, nor did Hugo even lift Susan's nubby tweed skirt. But it was a hard spanking; and in spite of the skirt, it had Susan kicking her shapely legs and shouting to be released in a very few minutes.

She was deliberately wearing penny loafers and white anklets. Her bare legs were shaved so silky-smooth that they gleamed even in the low light and their perfection was not lost on the practiced player. The various charms of her body and mind numbered in the dozens and he noticed new facets of her immensely attractive person and personality every time they met.

After giving the precocious Susan about 20 hard smacks, Hugo stopped, but held her firmly in place. His punishing hand rested where it had landed, on the swell of her girlish behind.

"Now, Miss Susan Ross, are you going to behave like a nice girl for a change, instead of a managing little baggage?" Hugo demanded, in a tone that made Laura's stomach flutter.

"I could, but I'd rather not!" Susan maintained, although her bottom was already smarting and radiating heat.

"Oh really? We'll see about that!" Hugo pushed her skirt up to her waist. She was wearing white eyelet panties. The hemming on her folded back half slip was tinged with pink. So was the round, dimpled bottom, which Hugo briskly bared. Laura watched without a word, melting.

Now Hugo's hand felt more severe. It now came down harder and faster. Until then Susan had not found the spanking unduly harsh. The damp crotch of her lowered briefs was exquisitely pungent with her essence. But when Hugo spanked her harder still, Susan's excitement was supplanted by very real discomfort. This was Susan's first serious spanking and she was finding it shockingly painful! Her sobs and cries rang out in rhythmic counterpoint to the sharp slaps impacting against her firm flesh.

Laura's heart was thumping when Hugo finally pushed her sister off his lap and onto the floor, where she knelt whimpering for some time, her hands clasped to her glowing bottom and her face turned away.

Hugo looked at Laura with the faintest of smiles, as much as to say, "Your turn is coming." His eyes still fixed on Laura; he brought Susan to her feet and gathered her into his arms, carefully winding one hand in her long, rippling, wheaten-gold hair.

"Are you going to behave now?" he demanded, gently pulling her head back. When Susan stubbornly shook her head no, Hugo laughed, letting go of her hair.

"Yes, you will," he told her. Then he bent Susan over a trestle table, pushed her skirt up to her waist, and deliberately took her from behind, holding Laura's gaze all the while.

William did not speak to the girls about being home late until they were tensely playing Scrabble in front of the fire after dinner, which had been a simple affair of salad, hummus, basmati rice and fresh fruit. William's vegetarian tastes were easily satisfied. The girls had shared a bottle of wine.

Laura's husband was thirty-five, with dark hair, a pleasant face, iron sculpted musculature and a wardrobe of tailored suits that displayed his superb physique to advantage. Though he possessed little finesse and even less patience, his serious demeanor, the handsome "V" shape of his torso and other equally attractive natural endowments had made him a popular favorite with any number of highly sexed women over the years. But Laura was the only one he had ever urgently longed to possess.

William had been involved with Laura exclusively since their meeting and subsequent marriage several months before. She was his first official "submissive and the only woman who interested him seriously now.

He had first played with Laura in the room where they now sat, when she'd finally come to him, after months of correspondence, which had begun when she'd answered his ad in a periodical called The New Rod Quarterly, a spanking fiction and contact magazine, published by Hugo Sands.

The magazine was available by subscription, at Marguerite Alexander's bookshop and other venues like it all over the Eastern seaboard. It was a nice little sideline for Hugo, who had searched for a New England spanking scene, found none hip enough to suit his personality and had therefore decided to create one himself. It was the net of this network of writers, artists, photographers, correspondents and personal advertisers that now and then caught shimmering prizes like Susan Ross and Laura Ross Random. Laura was a gifted illustrator who had become a constant contributor to Hugo's journal. Her erotic drawings appeared with the bi-line: Sub Rosa. Susan wrote spanking stories and drew comic strips for the magazine. Both young women had been recruited for the editorial staff by Marguerite Alexander, Laura's old roommate from Bennington, and a protégé of Hugo Sands going back five years.

As William sat watching the sisters, deep in their thoughts, picturesquely preppie in the firelight, he wondered if he really had any right to play a little scene with Susan. Ever the pragmatist, he told himself, "After all, the summer's over. What can I lose? If she resents what I propose, it'll show in her eyes and I'll drop the whole thing."

Susan, a well provided for orphan, had been living with the newlyweds since graduating from a New Hampshire prep school the previous spring. On the following day she was to begin her freshman year at the Boston Art Institute. William had long been aware that the reason Susan had been so willing to move into his house for the summer had to do with the interest in discipline which she shared with her sister, but so far he had not tested her commitment to the scene with a physical challenge.

"What were you girls doing out after dark? You know that worries me." William began, in a tone sharp enough to electrify the atmosphere.

"We stopped at Hugo's," Laura said, without looking up.

"Oh?"

"Susan insisted," Laura explained.

"I wanted to say good-bye before tomorrow," Susan volunteered. William waited. "I made Laura come with me."

"Why?"

"I just didn't like to go alone," Susan hedged. William caught the hint of a smile in her eyes to belie her grave expression. He looked at Laura and noticed her nervously twisting a lock of dark hair around her finger.

"Laura," William snapped, "didn't I tell you to stay away from

Hugo Sands?"

Laura threw down her letters and flashed her provocative sibling a look before answering her husband directly. "Susan insisted I go with her to Hugo's. It seems she and Hugo are lovers. And they wanted to share their secret with me," said the flushed brunette. William studied both sisters for a moment before commenting.

"And then what happened?"

"What makes you think anything happened? "

"Because you were very late."

Laura suddenly jumped up, upsetting the board and pieces. "It's all Susan's fault!" she declared with some pique. "You know you forced me to go," she accused her sister, who innocently straightened the board. "You explain what happened, since you're dying to!" Laura told Susan, exiting with a flounce of frustration, while adding airily, "And I hope you get what you deserve for it!"

Susan laughed, not taking her sister's irritation with her antics seriously; for until then she had only witnessed, and never experienced, one of her brother-in-law's spankings.

William said, "Susan, come here and sit next to me," patting a place on the leather couch that faced the hearth. She came to him willingly, and snuggled against him, throwing her arms about his torso and pressing her head to his chest.

"I'm going to miss you, brother-in-law," she confessed.

"Sounds like you'll be missing Hugo a lot more," William said, enfolding the small blonde in his arms.

"We're not really lovers." Susan confided, though she could still feel the warmth of the hand of her first "older man" on her bottom, and it made her press against her sister's gladiator with feverish emotion. "He spanked me," she explained. "Then he penetrated me, from behind. But he only did it to impress Laura, and steam her up."

"Steam her up, I'm sure he did. But you're the one who brought her to him, aren't you?" William gave her a shake that erased the smug grin from her face. While William was deciding whether or not he too was going to spank her, she quickly recovered her composure.

"I was just having fun."

"Dangerous and illicit fun, as I see it!"

Since William had a way of making her feel more like eight than eighteen, she meekly replied that she was sorry.

"Not as sorry as you're going to be, my little dear," he told her. "Maybe you did get a spanking from Hugo, but it wasn't nearly as hard a one as you're going to get from me!" Then he took Susan by the elbow and put her across his lap. At 5'3" and 100 pounds, Susan was easily handled. Having firmly positioned the breathless girl, he said, "Now young lady, I don't want you to keep leading your sister into temptation!"

He delivered a stinging smack. After a few dozen even harder swats of William's thickly calloused, weight trainer's palm on her already tender bottom, she eagerly promised to obey his injunction.

"I was lucky to get Laura away from Hugo in the first place," he informed her.

"Oh? I didn't realize that!" Susan lied, trying to wriggle out of spanking reach but being pulled back into position every time she did and smacked all the more firmly.

"Hell, yes," he explained, pausing to let her catch her breath, with his hands folded on the small of her back. "She had started drawing for him but hadn't met him yet when I answered her ad. Hugo went on one of his extended trips to Europe and I had the opportunity of meeting her before he did. By the time he got back, she was pretty much mine. All's fair in love and war, but technically he seems to think I stole the jump on him and even though we're married, he's still after her."

"Well, why don't you let him have her once or twice? Might get it out of both their systems," Susan suggested blithely.

"Let me express how I feel about that idea," said William proceeding with the spanking until the girl restrained across his corded quadriceps began to kick and sob.

"Mercy!" she cried, at last.

"Mercy you'll receive in due course, but I never want to hear about you maneuvering Laura over to Hugo's again!" He delivered six more full bodied and resounding swats.

"All right, young lady, go to bed," William told the girl, who knelt on the floor in a crumple of disheveled clothes and tawny hair, clasping her glowing bottom, for the second time that night. "And think about what you got from me tonight the next time you're tempted to pull strings and make things happen," he added.

The modern reader may wonder why an intelligent, on her way to being very well educated and spirited young woman like Susan Ross was ready to tolerate and even relish this type of treatment from the several older men of her acquaintance which have just been introduced. But her affinity for such esoteric diversions had not been born overnight. Susan's deep and abiding interest in discipline dated from the nursery, for reasons she'd formed theories on, but still did not completely understand. The simple fact was that Susan Ross had always been fascinated by spanking. She knew this was not a secret to share with just anyone. She knew that it was naughty and loved it all the more for that. Even before she knew what sex was, she knew that spanking made her tummy flutter, a delirious sensation which defied definition and stamped her sexuality submissive, since before she could read or write.

By age six, she was searching for spankings in books and finding them. She was raised by older parents, who would bring home videos of silver screen movies to watch on TV, many containing spontaneous spankings, visited upon daintily defiant leading ladies in smart suits and chiffon gowns by handsome, commanding leading men in romantic settings, concluding with avowals of love, classic embraces and wedding bells. By age twelve she'd begun writing stories and drawing cartoons about spanking, creating a private universe of mythically dominant males and correspondingly idealized, willful but ultimately compliant young ladies who together engaged in a never ending battle of the sexes perpetually concluding with a series of over the knee surrenders.

Her real life role models could hardly have been considered romantic, which may have contributed, in part, to her compulsion to escape into her own fantasy world whenever possible. Susan's father, already in his middle forties when she was born, was a bossy, bad tempered, incessantly critical, often generous and occasionally affectionate tyrant, who had inherited the family glove shop, which had thrived in the same lower Manhattan location for the past forty years. Her mother, only slightly younger, was a faded dreamer, beaten down in spirit after living twenty years under the inflexible rule of a rigidly domineering male. Her sister Laura, nine years her senior, had suffered far more than she under her father's suffocating regime, due to a lack of caution and a more defiant attitude whenever she was caught breaking the numerous rules imposed upon her during her teens. A scholarship to Bennington got Laura safely out of the house before their father became too addicted slapping her for everything from impertinence to wearing mini skirts. After graduation, when Laura insisted upon moving in with her boyfriend without the benefit of a wedding ring, she was officially disowned and forbidden access to the apartment in Tudor City, Manhattan. If there was one thing their father hated more than anything else, it was the notion of his daughters being sexually accessible to men.

Thereafter, Susan would sneak out of the house to meet her sister for long walks in Central Park, afternoons at the Metropolitan Museum of Art or strolls along the boardwalk at Brighton Beach. Wherever they met, they were always sure to rendezvous miles from lower Manhattan, to insure a miniscule likelihood of running into their father together. Unlike Laura, Susan was terrified of incurring her father's considerable wrath and facing corporal punishment from this large and frightening individual. Meanwhile, alone in her room every night after her homework was done, Susan continued to write her cartoon strips, watch her old movies and compile voluminous lists of references to spankings in novels, in magazines, in vintage movies and television shows, rented from the local video shop.

She acquired her first boyfriend at age 14, a fellow student at her Manhattan prep school. That same year her mother passed away and life became even more strained at home. Susan was allowed to walk home from school with her boyfriend, to go to a movie on Saturday afternoon or to Central Park, but was never allowed out after dark, either for skating, sporting events or Broadway shows. Susan knew that if her father ever caught her so much as holding hands with her boyfriend that the relationship would be instantly and forcibly dissolved by him, and lived in a constant state of anxiety lest the rapid progress of her maturing romance ever be discovered by her controlling and violent parent.

Mistrusting the temptations of the city, Susan's father enrolled her at the New Hampshire prep school in her sophomore year. Thinking to keep her safe from the attentions of adolescent boys, he selected an all girls school, without being aware that the neighboring all boys school shared many of the same facilities and continuously promoted social interaction between the students. Susan promptly lost her virginity to the first boy who had the imagination to spank her in the woods and her father was never the wiser. Mercifully, he died the following year and Susan was left in the blissful state of being well provided for and the legal ward of only her nice older sister Laura.

After this the two became much closer, corresponding on an almost daily basis and spending all their holidays together. At the end of her senior year at prep school, Laura's friend from college, Marguerite, who also had a strong interest in the bondage and discipline arts, revealed to Laura and Susan that she had come under the patronage of a publisher of a wonderful magazine, to which the sisters both ought to be contributing. And this was how Susan and Laura together discovered Random Point and Hugo Sands, at approximately the same time.

There were two bookshops in Random Point. Marguerite Alexander's was the one worth visiting. A spiral staircase invited the browser to climb to three galleries lined with scholarly and esoteric tomes. The loftiest tier was crammed with erotica from every era and all corners of the globe. Marguerite prided her shop on offering the most complete collection of connoisseur's literature in New England.

But even more of an attraction of the shop was Marguerite herself. Certain male denizens, who had never read literature more sophisticated than Stephen King, could attest that it was worth the price of a coffee table glossy just to be able to watch her undulate up and down the spiral staircase in a tight mohair skirt and a snug sweater.

A lustrous mane of light red hair gorgeously offset Marguerite's flawless bisque complexion. She was 30 years of age, wasp-waisted, provocatively tall, interestingly educated and completely uninhibited. She looked especially tantalizing when she kept her glasses on, for they gave her a shy expression, which was piquant in contrast to her showgirl silhouette.

Marguerite was Hugo's favorite submissive. He had brought her out 5 years before and she was still realizing her potential under his management. Some of her exercises involved her playing the dominant role over others. Handsome tokens were always tendered to Marguerite after such efforts. Thus, for the good of her bank account, Hugo had turned her out.

Marguerite also published B&D stories in Hugo Sands' journal, writing under the pseudonym "Alma". Laura Random, whom Marguerite had first met at Bennington, always illustrated her fiction.

Marguerite Alexander was late in arriving at Hugo's that evening, but thought she had a very good excuse. There was New Talent in town.

It was raining and she'd walked the two miles from her shop to Hugo's house, to revel in the inconvenience, while mulling over what had happened at the stop just before closing time.

The couple came in at 5:30. They were strangers to Random Point and the man was very attractive. Marguerite noted that he was possibly 6'3", broad shouldered, fair complected, blue eyed and about her own age. He was dressed in a suit of gray Donegal tweed, the cut of which she could not help but openly admire.

A young woman whom Marguerite found instantly disagreeable accompanied the excitingly tall and nattily dressed young man. The companion was content to remain on the lower level, perusing works by politically correct female authors, whereas the interesting gentleman immediately noticed the plan of the shop, which clearly stated one could find erotica on the third level. He ascended to the loft at once and there remained engrossed until his woman finally sought him out just before 6:00.

Marguerite, who had been covertly watching him all the while he browsed alone in the gallery, now was able to observe them in conversation from her excellent vantage point below.

They were standing together in front of the stacks that held all of Marguerite's favorite books. He had never stirred from these stacks all the while he was above. Now Marguerite could hear the girl pronouncing judgment.

"All these books share the same vile theme!" the girl loudly declared: "Women being Abused by Men!" Then she flung aside in disgust the offensive volume she had rudely dislodged from her friend's large, capable hand to shallowly skim. Marguerite later went up to the gallery to search for the book the girl had thrown down. It was on the floor and the cover had become soiled. Marguerite lamented the ruin of the copy of the novel Frank and I.

"Oh, how I'd like to fix that one," mused Marguerite, as the unpleasant young woman began to descend the gallery stairs. An instant later, the resounding thump, thump, thump of the young woman's bottom sliding down the steps, after a freakish slip, gratified Marguerite.

The tall man rushed down to the landing to help his friend to her feet, but the girl was cranky and pushed him away.

"Oh, leave me alone. I'm all right. She must wax those steps! I should sue Reebok. Who ever heard of skidding with cleated shoes on? Come on, Michael, let's get out of here."

"I'll meet you downstairs. I'm going back for a book I wanted," he told her, going back upstairs before waiting for a reply. Marguerite observed this conspicuous absence of gallantry and was amused.

The girl continued downstairs by herself, but stopped at the counter to rate Marguerite for the slippery steps. The redhead could not apologize enough, and even pressed the volume of feminist poetry the girl had been fondling a few minutes before upon the sore fall victim, as a gift.

"Please take it. It will make me feel so much better!" Marguerite insisted, unable to resist peeking up at the loft in the midst of wrapping the thin volume in tissue and handing it to the girl. He was back in the spanking novels again!

"Well, all right. Thanks. I guess it's fair compensation for a black and blue butt," the girl said, rubbing the seat of her sweat pants gingerly. For an instant then, she seemed quite likeable, but quickly ruined this impression by suddenly demanding, "Why do you stock so many books that promote violence against women?"

Marguerite replied, "It isn't violence, it's merely C.P.. Ask your companion to explain." The girl followed the redhead's upward gaze to the gallery where her escort was still browsing.

"C.P.?" The girl was becoming annoyed. "What's that?"

"Ask him," Marguerite reiterated, smiling with evil satisfaction at her customer's innocence. "I'm sure he'd be only too happy to demonstrate the rudiments of corporal punishment to you."

The girl now sensed that she was being toyed with. There was something in the lush-lipped, ripe-bosomed, expensive smelling woman that was at once offensive and alarming to the Boston social worker.

"Michael, I'll be outside!" she announced, as he joined them at the counter. She let the door slam behind her, not bothering to disguise the irritation she felt for this stranger who apparently knew her man's likes and dislikes so intimately.

Michael handed a copy of O Wicked Country to her along with some cash.

"I think you'll find this oddly compelling," she said.

"I'll be back," said Michael, pocketing the book and the change.

"I'll be here."

Marguerite perched upon a low, 3-legged stool, in front of the open hearth in Hugo Sands' kitchen, to dry her rain-soaked hair. She was wearing only Hugo's flannel robe, with her splendid body naked under it.

"You still haven't told me why you were late," Hugo said, handing her a glass of wine.

"A man came in today, just before closing..." Marguerite sipped from the glass, set it down on the floor beside her, then commenced combing out her wildly tangled hair. Hugo waited, but Marguerite drifted.

"And?" he prompted.

"And nothing. I just want him. I walked over here in the rain, because I wanted to luxuriate in fantasies about my new lover."

"You're confident. Who is this paragon anyway?"

"His name is Michael. He's even taller than you. And much younger."

"Thanks!"

"He was up in the loft the whole time. He read one of our favorite books from cover to cover, then bought it."

"Haven't you left something out, Marguerite?"

"Yes, he was dressed in a handsome tweed suit. The drape was magnificent."

"Aren't you forgetting something else, Marguerite?" Hugo interrupted, impatiently.

"Something more important than the cut of this man's suit?" Marguerite pondered deeply.

"Wasn't our natty out-of-towner accompanied by a pretty girl in an ugly jogging suit?"

"Yes, how did you know?"

"Detective Flagg has just joined our local police force. Jane Elliot is a caseworker in Boston. They're engaged but their wedding isn't set to take place until spring, when she intends to quit her job and relocate to Random Point."

"How do you know all of this?" Marguerite demanded, a stab of jealousy piercing her heart.

"They were in the shop today. He bought a mahogany four-poster...for their love nest."

"How horrifying," she cried.

"Don't worry," Hugo told her. "You've got until spring. And we know what Jane is like. It's hardly even a challenge for you. Now, if you only had until next weekend to get him to call off the wedding, that would be a challenge worthy of you."

"They aren't suited to each other," Marguerite pointed out.

"I agree, but that does not alter the fact that you were late for our appointment. You know how I feel about tardiness, Marguerite. It shows a want of feeling and a lack of respect. Doesn't it?"

"Yes," she answered meekly, putting her hands in her lap and waiting for him to pronounce sentence.

Circling her he said, "Marguerite was naughty to keep Hugo

waiting."

"I just wanted to go for a walk in the rain!" Petulance replaced docility as the disagreeable information about the new talent's approaching nuptials began to twist her heart into knots.

"Marguerite, do you remember what happened the last time you used that particular tone of voice with me?" Hugo knelt beside her on the highly polished parquet floor and handed her glasses to her. "Put your glasses on, darling."

Marguerite put her glasses on. Then he told her to stand up and she obeyed. Hugo untied and relieved her of the robe.

"Now go up to the bedroom and put your garter belt, hose and boots back on. Then come back to me." Hugo turned her around and gave her a slap on her lush, womanly bottom that made her gasp. "Go on, don't keep me waiting!"

When Marguerite came back downstairs, still naked except for the articles Hugo had named, her milky white skin was suffused with an all-over blush and the rose-colored nipples that capped her full, firm breasts stood to attention.

Hugo was sitting on the stool she'd vacated, with a large cookbook open across his lap and a wooden spatula casually tucked in the crook of one arm. He affected characteristic indifference at her spectacular entrance.

"Now, my dear," he began, scarcely looking up; "you and I, but mostly you, are going to be baking a cherry pie. Put that apron on. Come here and I'll tie your bow."

Marguerite slipped the starched white linen bib apron over her head, then went to Hugo and obediently turned her bare bottom toward him. First he tied the apron strings into a bow that tightly cinched her slender waist and emphasized the contrasting swell of her hips and buttocks. Then he reached for the length of silver chain and leather ankle cuffs he'd stowed beneath the stool. He made her stand with her feet about 12" apart, fastened the cuffs around the ankles of her high heeled, bisque leather, lacing ankle boots.

"There," he said, straightening up; "That should make the cooking lesson more piquant." He turned her about between his hands, approving the addition of the restraints to her ensemble.

"I'll trip and stumble," Marguerite fretted, taking a baby step.

"You'd better not be too clumsy, or you'll get this!" Hugo warned, giving her a sharp swat on her bare bottom, framed by the crisp, ruffled apron and bow, with the flat wooden spoon.

"Ouch!"

"Hurts, doesn't it?"

"Yes!"

"There's lots more where that came from if you don't prove a competent apprentice baker. Now let's see what we'll need to start with." He read aloud, "3 cups drained, pitted, tart red cherries; 1/2 cup cherry juice; 3 1/2 tbs. all purpose flour; 2 tbs. butter; and for the pinch of salt we'll substitute 2 of Marguerite's tears. Step 1 says: prepare and set aside pastry for 2-crust pie. Did you get that, Marguerite?"

"Uh... how many cups cherries?" Marguerite hadn't realized she was supposed to be memorizing the ingredients as he read them off.

"You weren't paying attention?"

"I was but you read too fast!"

"Bend over the table and grip the opposite edge," Hugo told her sternly.

"But you didn't say I had to memorize —"

"Don't make me tell you twice."

Marguerite walked in small steps to the large trestle table that dominated the kitchen.

"May I take my glasses off?" she asked, before bending over. Hugo nodded and she put them down, then bent over and grasped the opposite edge of the table with her hands. She kept her legs straight and together, as she'd been taught. Hugo stepped up behind her and gave her one hard whack across each cheek with the flat of the spoon. Then he stood her up, so they could start again.

Two hours and one shapely pink, well-paddled bottom later, the kitchen was powdered in flour, and the cherry pie stood cooling on a rack. Then, still locked into her anklets, Marguerite was firmly marched up to bed.

The following morning dawned cloudy and raw. William, Laura

and Susan were having breakfast in the dining room when the bell rang. William looked up from his paper annoyed, while Laura and her sister exchanged puzzled glances. When Laura went to the door she was surprised to confront Hugo and Marguerite.

"I hope we're still in time to see Susan off," said Marguerite, handing a ribbon wrapped pink box to Laura. "I baked this for her. Myself!"

"How sweet of you both," Laura said, without meeting Hugo's eyes. "Come in and have some coffee with us. What kind of pie is it?"

"Cherry," Hugo told Laura; "Just like your lewd little sister wasn't."

"Did you expect her to save it for you?" Laura returned scornfully.

"Not at all. I knew she was a little slut the minute I met her. William up?" Hugo followed Laura confidently through the house, pulling Marguerite along behind him by the hand.

William was far from overjoyed to see his competitive neighbor settle in so cozily between his charming sister-in-law and lovely wife; however, he grunted at Hugo, let his eyes linger on Marguerite a moment, for she was well worth lingering over, sleepy-eyed and tawny in her fur; then reburied himself in the Wall Street Journal. He had no flair for small talk and disliked the gossipy, girlish hilarity which tended to ensue when two or more women who hadn't seen each other in over twelve hours happened to converge.

Delighted at the surprise appearance of Hugo and Marguerite, Susan served the sweet, flaky pie. She knew better than to offer William any. Even so, he came out from behind the paper to volunteer the information that they were all about to consume mass quantities of "white death."

When Hugo asked Susan how she was getting to Boston, it was revealed that Laura would be driving her, and staying with her for a few days. William had found Susan loft space in Back Bay and Laura was going to help her furnish it.

"You know," Hugo said, "I was going up to Boston today myself. There's an auction I want to attend."

"Really, Hugo?" Susan was instantly aglow. "Won't you consider driving in with us, then? We've got plenty of room."

"I was going to offer to drive you girls in myself," Hugo said. "I plan to be in town for several days."

"If those are your intentions anyway," William said from behind the paper, "then you can take Susan and settle her in. I'd rather not have to do without Laura."

Susan looked at Hugo. If he was piqued at missing the opportunity of getting the two girls alone in the city with him, he didn't show it.

"Fine," Hugo said, giving Susan's knee a sharp squeeze under the table that sent a rush through her stomach. "I'll drive little Susan in myself." Susan put her hand into his under the table, her heart pounding fiercely with joy. But she remained outwardly poised and let it shine from her eyes.

William lowered his paper briefly to note his wife's reaction to his change in her plans. Marguerite also scrutinized her friend. Laura ate her pie without looking at any of them, her face a mask that disclosed no emotion.

Hugo whispered something in Susan's ear that made her laugh. This annoyed William and Hugo was content.

Feeling that a new theme might be timely, Marguerite said, "I have a story ready for you to illustrate, Laura." Laura pounced on the distraction, becoming animated at once.

"Maybe I'll come with you and get the copy right after breakfast," said Laura, "Since I'm not going to Boston with Susan after all."

"Your story will have to wait, Marguerite," William said, putting his paper down and standing up. "I need Laura to do some ad sketches for me this morning." He put his jacket on. "Laura, I've left the photos I want you to work from in the studio. Get them done before two. I need them for a presentation. Okay?"

"Yes," Laura said, with lowered eyes, but blushing fiercely at being spoken to in this manner before the others.

William was an architect who also owned Random Point's largest construction firm. Because of her rendering abilities, William sometimes gave Laura the onerous assignment of sketching properties being offered by the company for sale, for trade publications and Sunday supplements throughout New England. It was a task that Laura equated with punishment.

Missing the trip to Boston didn't disturb her. She was happy for Susan's sake, for she knew how much her sister admired their elegant guest. It wasn't even having to do William's boring real estate drafting that Laura found so distressing. It was that William had humiliated her by issuing these commands in front of the others.

Having charged the atmosphere with tension, William kissed Susan good-bye, warned her to be good, excused himself politely to Marguerite and exited, ignoring Hugo.

Laura walked him to the door, as was her custom. He took her in his arms in the foyer.

"You're pouting. I don't like that," he said, but kissed her red mouth anyway. Her lips were trembling and when he let her go she tried to hide her face. He turned her around. Her eyes were wet.

"What's this?" he demanded. She shook her head and tried to push him away, wondering why he so seldom stepped out of the fantasy. Yet, all of her senses were athrill, to see how he would respond to the physical rebuff.

"I hope you're not throwing a tantrum, Laura. Look at me!" He gave her a shake that opened her eyes. "I have no intention of letting you run around Boston with Hugo all week. Now get those drawings to me by two."

Laura flashed her husband such a mutinous look then, that he was compelled to set his briefcase down, tuck his stubborn wife under one arm, and give her a hard half dozen smacks over the seat of her skirt.

"There," he said getting her back on her feet. "Now you've got a reason to pout."

She stood rubbing her bottom resentfully.

William put on his fedora, picked up his briefcase and went out the door. However, half way to his car he turned around to give her a wink. Laura still felt indignant but liked the way he looked in the fedora and reluctantly returned a small smile.

William was pleased when Laura arrived with the sketches at 1:00. He'd gone to lunch with a client and returned to find her patiently seated on one of the leather sofas in the reception area, in her raincoat and hat, with her portfolio tucked under her arm, like a school girl arriving early for her piano lesson.

On the way into his office, William introduced Laura to his new secretary, Damaris Perez, a petite New Yorker, who'd graduated with honors from the best business college in Boston. With black hair and a patrician complexion, Damaris displayed her charming figure in a smart suit with a peplum jacket, nipped waist, straight skirt and 4" heels. She had a sensuous mouth, wore her long hair in a French roll and painted her fingernails dark red.

"Like her?" Williams asked, once they were alone. She nodded. "I thought you'd admire her taste," he went on. "Though any girl who wears her skirts that tight and short, clearly deserves to be spanked. Don't you think?"

"That depends on the girl," Laura replied.

"Have you brought the sketches?"

Laura presented her work for her husband to approve.

"You're a good girl," he told her. "And since you've been so agreeable today, you may have a reward."

"A reward?" Her response was wary. This was an unusual word on his lips.

"Yes. I've decided that I'm going to let you play with Hugo after all. You'd like that, wouldn't you? Don't bother answering, I know you."

"But this morning you said —"

"I changed my mind."

Laura wondered if this had something to do with the new secretary, who appeared the perfect size and shape to fit across her husband's knee.

"You have my permission to go crazy on Halloween. But just on Halloween," William told her.

Chapter Two

Random Point

When Damaris Perez put her phone down, William Random appeared at her shoulder, impatient for her words. "Well?"

"He'll be right over," his new secretary replied, loudly clicking her gum. William scrutinized the girl with irritation through his first pair of glasses, which were heavy and uncomfortable.

"All right Damaris," he said. "Send Detective Flagg in as soon as he arrives."

"'Kay," she replied, with a snap of her gum, starting to dial the phone.

"Hang up, young lady, "William told her suddenly. "Sit up straight when I'm talking to you and get rid of the gum."

"Did I do something wrong?" she was mystified but obeyed both commands.

"Yes. You came to work today. These new glasses need adjusting and they're making me cranky."

"Are they magnifying my faults?"

"They're allowing me to see that your comportment leaves a lot to be desired."

"I'm sorry. What can I do?" Damaris wasn't taking this seriously and gave him a saucy smile.

"You can start by buttoning that jacket properly. You should also be wearing a shirt under it."

"It's too tight."

"Of course it is, you're wearing it."

Damaris sobered, her dark eyes glittering. Her pert bosom heaved as she fumbled with the chunky buttons of her glove-tight princess cut jacket. Her long red nails slowed her down.

William adjusted his glasses, folded his arms and began to lecture her sternly. But she only saw his body without hearing his words. She had been distracted by it all day.

William strode up and down while reminding her of the many privileges she enjoyed as his secretary. Her salary, car and apartment were mentioned in turn. Damaris covered her fluttering heart with her tiny hands.

Almost certain she was going to be fired; her full red lower lip began to quiver. But William was expanding on his theme and did not notice. "It isn't your work I'm complaining about," he went on. "It's the way you look and act, the way you flirt with my clients and fraternize with my employees. Oh yes - I've actually seen you out in back, behind the warehouse, getting high with the boys. You behave more like a shipping clerk than an executive secretary."

"So," she ventured timidly, "am I on probation?"

"Is that what you'd suggest? I was thinking more in terms of a good spanking."

"What did you say?" asked Damaris deliberately, unconsciously clutching her stomach, where she'd felt a sharp stab, then a rush.

"I said that you deserve a good spanking. And if that detective weren't due any second you'd get one right now. All right, make your phone call. But remember what I said." William advised, then disappeared into his office.

Detective Flagg arrived in due course and remained closeted in William's office for a half hour. Damaris was standing at the window, staring out at the rain falling softly on the woods that surrounded the building when the two men emerged.

"Don't forget to call me," William urged Michael Flagg, who was in no hurry to be ushered out. Damaris leaning on the windowsill, with her curvaceous bottom, so prettily outlined by a tight merino skirt, had captured his entire attention.

She quickly straightened up as the men walked through the office, and remained at attention until the detective was gone.

"Having your wife followed?" Damaris teased.

"You'd better not be so fresh or you'll get that spanking yet," William warned, but turned his back on her too quickly to notice her shudder.

The next afternoon it was raining again. It was a slow day and the phones had hardly rung. At around three, Damaris wandered into William's office without an official reason. He was reading through some tiresome correspondence he'd already postponed far too long.

Although he hardly noticed her enter, William couldn't fail to acknowledge her presence when Damaris boldly perched her pert bottom on his desk, and began to swing her daintily shod foot. He stared at her with wonder, her nerve rendering him temporarily speechless.

Damaris smiled, batted her lashes, then blew an enormous pink bubble at him with the huge wad of gum in her mouth. William threw his pen down and leaned back in his chair.

"Young lady, didn't you hear a thing I told you yesterday?"

"Boss, are you a pervert?" she asked ingenuously.

"What sort of question is that? And does this look like a chair?" He thumped the desktop.

"Three times yesterday you mentioned spanking me," she reminded him. William pushed his correspondence aside. Suddenly she had his full attention.

"There's nothing perverse about that," William told her. "That's what you do with a brat."

"Do you ever spank your wife, boss?"

"I assume you have a good reason for asking?"

"Just prurient."

"Yes, I spank Laura."

"Often?"

"Yes."

"How does she feel about that?"

"You two go out to lunch together. Ask her," William replied carelessly.

Damaris wiggled off the desk and took a stroll around the room. His gaze followed her taut little bottom with a connoisseur's savor.

Her waist seemed impossibly small, perhaps 22" around. He watched her promenade awhile. Then he rose and locked the door.

"To answer your original question, Damaris, yes, I am a pervert. And your questions seem to indicate that you are one as well."

He pulled a chair into the center of the room, then stepped up to her and took her by the arm. "Come over here,' he said, pulling her to the chair, sitting down and putting her briskly across his lap.

"No! Don't!" she cried, fully breathless yet feebly trying to resist. This seemed necessary. She had her pride. But as she only weighed 100 pounds to his muscular 165, she was tucked neatly under one hand and easily held fast. Damaris squirmed in vain.

"Right," he said; "This won't take long." And he smoothed down the seat of her pencil skirt, pausing momentarily to admire her shapely legs, glamorously hosed in seamed stockings and shod excitingly in spike-heeled pumps.

While holding her firmly in place by her impossibly small waist, he administered no more than a dozen resounding smacks to the well-rounded seat of her skirt. But each spank was a shock to her system that left a penetrating sting in its wake.

The spanking was over almost before it began, and she was set back on her feet. To Damaris, it had been a teaser, like a spanking in an old film that you catch by accident at 2 am

"Boss, that hurt!" she told him, because this was a normal thing to say. To keep acting normal seemed crucial to her.

Similar thoughts were flashing through William's brain. Which was why he had kept her first spanking so short. If he kept it light and flirty, she mightn't be scared off. "Spankings hurt," he told her, while watching her rub her buttocks with both hands.

"No," she replied, "that huge boner sticking into my ribs was what hurt."

"Are you still being fresh?" He pulled her down to sit on his lap, locking his arms around her waist.

"In my culture," lied Damaris, "when a man smacks a woman on the bottom, it's as good as a proposition." She nuzzled his ear as she purred this, grinding her freshly warmed seat into his corded thighs.

"Mine too," William said, boosting her off his lap with a swat. "Go lock the outer door," he told her.

Michael Flagg had been asked to detect the security leak at Random Construction. Damaris was the prime suspect. But William needed proof before acting. It was his contention that she had been selling information to his largest competitor, Price Enterprises. William hadn't gotten near a property in almost a month; just about the length of time that Damaris had been his secretary.

It was quiet on the Cape at that time of year, with the rowdy summer crowd long gone. So Michael Flagg had plenty of time to devote to solving the sordid little corporate mystery revolving around the seductive secretary. Autumn had taken hold fully in the village and tracking Damaris to and from her coke dealer made for a delightful drive through leafy, dappled lane and pumpkin patches. He'd found her motive for selling her company out. No salary is ever large enough to support a coke habit. Now he only had to spot her making one exchange.

There was to be a land auction on Friday. Damaris typed and sealed the bids herself on Thursday night, not forgetting to make a photo copy for herself.

That evening Michael followed Damaris straight from work to The Serpentine Lounge, where she began to drink, while awaiting the arrival of her contact. Michael sat in his car outside until Randall Price himself strode into the bar. This was the arrogant young owner of the company to which Damaris had been selling information.

Michael slipped into the club just in time to observe them swap envelopes the instant Price slid into the booth beside her. His went straight into a breast pocket - it was thin. Hers immediately vanished into her large handbag. It was thick. Randall Price ordered a cocktail, but left well before it arrived. He hadn't much to say to Damaris after picking up what he'd come for. Soon after this Damaris paid her bill and also left.

The wind was whipping leaves around the street when Damaris came out. She was half drunk on cocktails. The sky was filled with clouds. Soon it would rain. Damaris turned her collar up and started to walk towards her car, feeling lonely and sad. She hated the things she'd been doing. She never had an ounce of coke all to herself before. She resolved to quit using for good when it was gone. Nor would she ever deal with the officious Price again. It wasn't a bad resolution, but it could not dispel the guilt that now oppressed her.

Damaris felt utterly wretched when she thought about her boss. The pleasure she'd enjoyed with him lately had been intense. But it always ended all too soon; and then he went home to his wife. A strong man to lean on was missing.

Hearing steps behind her in the street, she turned. He was tall and seemed familiar. And he had left The Serpentine to follow her. Something was wrong.

Up until this moment she had liked the new arrangement of trading information for cocaine instead of cash. Serial numbers on bills worried her, for she could imagine stranger things than being set up by Randy Price. Particularly after she had ceased to be of use to him.

"Just a minute, Miss Perez," said the man, closing the distance between them in a couple of strides. With a sinking feeling she remembered him as the police detective who had visited the office a few weeks before.

"We need to talk," he said.

"We do?"

"Yes, and you know why. Come on, we'll go in there." He took her arm and steered her towards Basil's Coffee Shop. Lightening flashed and thunder rumbled as they entered. Then rain began coming down hard. He led her to a booth by the window. Damaris asked for coffee.

"You ought to eat something, you're getting thinner every time I see you," he commented.

Damaris excused herself to go to the bathroom. But when she reached for her purse Michael stopped her.

"Leave that," he said firmly. Evidence had a way of disappearing in bathrooms.

"Can I just get my lipstick?"

"Sure."

Damaris reached into the enormous handbag with an unerring hand

and pulled her lipstick out, then disappeared. Clearly, the stash she had just acquired was about to be seized. She was now more depressed than before. She reached into the pocket of her well-cut suit jacket for the tiny brown glass bindle containing all her remaining cocaine. With a sigh she spilled it out on the porcelain tank top and used her little straw to snort it up in two very long lines.

While she was blotting her lipstick in the mirror, the drug hit her brain with a blast. "Maybe I can book," she thought, suddenly wired, "Except there's no window in here to climb out of. Do I really have to deal with this?"

She rejoined Michael, who was giving the girl an order. Coffee had been served. Damaris slid into the booth in her tight skirt and reached a cigarette out of her bag.

"How long do you think you can keep your good looks when you treat your body like a toxic waste dump?" the detective demanded.

"I should quit smoking," she agreed.

"Not just smoking, young lady. You drive up the Cliff Road to your dealer every other day. I've been keeping tabs on you."

"Oh," Damaris said, taken aback, but unable to prevent herself from sniffing once or twice. She drank her coffee, smoked and waited for Michael to speak.

"You've played your little game with Randall Price for the last time tonight. I saw what went down between you just now and that's all the proof your boss needs to nail you."

"So he's suspected me all along?" Damaris suddenly did not feel well. Her heart was pounding frighteningly, and not just from the drug.

"Of course. Who else?"

"When are you telling him?"

"Right away."

"Couldn't you wait until I get out of town?"

"Get out of town - you'll be lucky not to get arrested tonight."

"Arrested?"

"If William Random chooses to press charges against you I'll have to take you in and book you. Naturally, bail could be arranged."

"I can't be arrested! I don't have anyone to bail me out."

"That's a shame."

"Please don't arrest me!"

"If it were up to me, I wouldn't arrest you. I'd spank you. Hard."

Damaris stared at him.

"But it's up to your boss," Michael continued. "If it wasn't for him I could try to forget about what I found in your purse."

"You took it, huh?"

"What do you think?"

"Oh god - what am I going to do?"

"Stop taking drugs."

"I don't have much choice now. You have my drugs and I just lost my job."

"Cheer up. I might decide to rehabilitate you personally," he said, because she seemed so sad and sweet. And in spite of the things she had done, the girl appealed to him.

When Damaris realized she was being flirted with, her black depression lifted somewhat. This tall, good-looking cop was here to save her, to protect her from everything bad.

"You don't want to arrest me, do you?"

"I want to reform you. I can see myself giving you the guidance that's been missing in your life."

Damaris confessed, "I've been living in a company apartment, driving a company car and spending every penny I earned. I don't even have enough cash for a bus ticket back to New York. God - everything I had, my boss gave me. And I did this to him."

"Bad girl."

The waitress arrived with soups and sandwiches.

"I'm not really hungry," said Damaris.

"Eat something anyway," Michael advised, "Just to show me that you can be good."

Damaris smiled her beautiful smile for the first time that night and lifted a spoonful of soup to her lips.

Michael had often wondered what it might be like to have a girl that one could scold and boss around. Jane had always been the perfect adult, self-reliant, sensible, responsible, and mature. Even Marguerite, who was far from sensible, radiated independence and power. But this little waif was different. And she aroused the nesting instinct in him as no woman had done before.

"All right," Michael said, after watching her toy with her sandwich; "I'll see if I can make him not press charges. I'll go now." He pulled out some bills for the check.

"What about me?"

"You can go home for now."

"I can't go back to that apartment. He won't want me there."

"Then you can stay at my place until I get back. All right?"

"Yes," Damaris agreed and her anxiety began to wane.

The cold rain was still washing the streets at ten, when Damaris looked out the bay window of Michael's second floor sitting room, chain-smoking while watching for his car. When it appeared she went to the mirror to paint her mouth dark red.

"You can relax," Michael told her as soon as he walked in. "Random says he won't press charges as long as you don't get in touch with Price again."

"That's right, now those bids that I sold Randy are no good. But Randy doesn't know it yet."

"You haven't called Price, then?"

"No. I didn't even think of doing that."

"Then it looks like you're off the hook."

"Until tomorrow when Randy gets stung at the auction and concludes that I double crossed him."

"I wouldn't worry about that."

"That's because you won't be the one going to Emergency with two broken arms."

"Don't be silly."

"He's very powerful and I think, vindictive."

"I'll have a talk with him and make sure he knows I have enough evidence to implicate him in two felonies. That ought to keep him in check."

"Did my boss say anything about me?" she hesitantly asked.

"Lot's of things. I wouldn't expect a Valentine this year."

"What about my things?"

"He wants the keys to the car and apartment back, of course. I'll help you get your stuff tomorrow."

Damaris picked up the drink she'd been nursing.

"I got into your whiskey. I hope you don't mind."

"I think it's time you sobered up."

"I know you do."

"Are you getting smart with me? Already?"

"Sorry. Bad habit."

"You have a lot of those."

"So, I'm really not getting arrested?"

"I don't think so."

"When will you know?"

"When I make up my mind."

"When will that be?"

"I'll let you know," he promised, deciding he would also have a drink.

"We were having an affair," she blurted out, because she'd gotten into his whiskey.

"What's that, sweetheart?"

"Me and my boss. But it wasn't an ordinary one. At least, not from my point of view. In fact, it was the most exciting purely sexual affair I've ever had."

"Do I get to hear the sordid details?"

"Do you want to?"

"Sure. I might be able to pick up some pointers."

"You don't need any pointers," she told him, turning her head to hide a shy smile.

When Michael decided she should spend the night, Damaris did not protest. He put her in the back bedroom, thinking, "I can't rush this." This room contained the four-poster bed he had bought with his upcoming marriage in mind. It was spread with a blue counterpane. She admired the bed.

"Jane and I picked it out together."

"Who's Jane?"

"My ex-fiancée."

"When did you break up?"

"About a month ago."

"That recently? What was she like?"

"Wholesome, healthy, athletic and politically committed."

"Doesn't sound like she and I have much in common," Damaris observed.

"And she never wears shoes like that," Michael said with a glance at her gleaming black high heels.

"You like the way I dress?"

"It's an art form."

"But, your fiancée was pretty, huh?"

"You're pretty," he said, in a way that made her face grow warm. She nervously fumbled with her lighter. He sat down on the bed beside her and lit the cigarette for her.

"We've got to break you of this habit too," he told her. Then he said goodnight and left her alone.

A little while later, Michael was reading in bed, when Damaris appeared at his door, wrapped in a cashmere robe that belonged to Marguerite.

"If the bottom half matches the top I'm not leaving this room," she remarked of Flagg's torso.

"Come over here, young lady," he said, patting the bed. Damaris came to him.

"I hope the girl this robe belongs to won't mind if I borrow it."

"I'm sure she would."

"Maybe I should take it off."

"By all means, do."

"Well... just don't tell her." Damaris enjoyed being teased.

"She'd smell your perfume on it anyway."

"This doesn't look like the sort of robe your ex-fiancée would own."

"It isn't,' he replied, wondering how the robe ever stretched to fit Marguerite.

"Listen, what's your name?" Damaris asked.

"Michael."

"Well, Michael, the reason I came in here was to ask you, do you think that it would work for us in bed?"

"It's always worked for me before," Michael said, indicating a sizeable erection under the cover.

"I see what you mean," she laughed. "That size always works."

"We can test that theory after you've had your spanking," he said, pulling her face down across his lap. "And don't bother arguing. You know you've got one coming after all the wicked mischief you've been up to."

But Damaris didn't argue. She had been stunned into silence. He then began to spank her in a slow and measured manner. And much harder than William had spanked her, right from the start. He paused for a beat or two between smacks and alternated cheeks, though his palm was almost broad enough to cover both at once. After about 10 stingers, the girl began to wriggle and whimper. His hand was very heavy. She counted 20, 30, 40 smacks. He went on and it stung more and more.

"Take it," he told her.

After his metronome arm had descended about 100 times, Damaris started squirming in earnest, and whimpering much louder than before. And though he hadn't even lifted the cashmere robe yet, she put up one tiny hand to shield her bottom.

"No you don't," he told her, pinning her wrist to her side. "Starting to feel it, huh?" He then raised the skirt of the robe to her waist to reveal her ravishingly well-rounded cheeks, now tinged a dusky rose. "I'm just getting started," he told her, pausing with his arm locked on her waist. "And you've got such a lot to answer for. Like disloyalty." He gave her a resounding smack that made her cry out. "Dishonesty," Michael continued, administering another spank; "Deceitfulness... Be still!" he warned, for her squirming was annoying him. "I'm not through with you," he told her, speaking sharply for the first time. "You've done some reprehensible things lately, haven't you?"

"Yes," she admitted, sobbing aloud and hiding her face.

"Did you think you could get off Scott free?"

"I didn't think about it."

"That's your problem, you don't think. But apparently you do feel." And he proved this by applying an additional volley of hard smacks, so that she was kicking and sobbing aloud by the time he let her up.

"Tears of shame, young lady?"

"I'm contemptible!" she sobbed, burying her face in her hands.

"Stop that," Michael said, pulling her hands away from her face and taking her in his arms.

"I hate myself!" she cried.

"But I like you," he said, holding her tighter. "Now let's find out if it'll work."

On Saturday morning William told Laura he'd be driving into Boston to visit his tailor and wouldn't be back until late that night.

"Poor Damaris," Laura said as her husband got into the convertible.

"Don't start that again."

"She was my friend..."

"Was is the operative word."

"I'm sure she's flat broke. If you throw her out of her place, where will she go? What will she do?"

"She's lucky she's not in jail. Laura - the girl stabbed me in the back."

"I just can't stand to think of her stranded."

"She isn't stranded. Michael Flagg has a crush on her. Didn't you pick up on that when he was over last night?"

Laura blinked in surprise.

"I have a feeling," William said, starting the engine, "that Damaris is going to be Flagg's headache from now on."

William drove off down the lane as Laura remembered Flagg telling them that he was going to let Damaris dry out at his place for a couple of days.

She resolved to go and see her there at once. She would bring some money and help her friend in any way she could. William would not have to know. She even knew where Michael Flagg lived, as Marguerite had shown her one day.

Laura rode her bike into the village. Michael lived in an Edwardian triple-decker, just a few blocks from Marguerite Alexander's bookshop on Shadow Lane. She locked her bike outside and went straight up to the second floor flat. Damaris answered her knock. "Who's there?"

"Laura."

Still in Marguerite's cashmere robe, Damaris opened the door.

"Come in. What are you doing here? Do you have any cigarettes?"

"No."

"Damn."

"Are you all right?"

"I'm okay."

"I was just wondering."

"Is that why you came by?"

"Actually, I brought you some cash. I figured you'd be pretty strapped." Laura handed Damaris two hundred dollars in fifties. Damaris took it, in a daze, then shook her head and thrust the bills back into her friend's hand.

"No. I couldn't. But thanks. You're really sweet. You can't believe how sorry I am about everything."

"How long will you be here?" Laura asked, walking about Flagg's sitting room.

"Permanently, I hope," Damaris confided.

"You like Michael Flagg?" Laura was once more surprised by the concept of Flagg and Damaris.

"Don't you like tall, handsome men with big dicks?"

"How big is it?" Laura could not resist asking. Damaris framed seven and a half to eight inches between her hands.

"That big," she said. "Just like homeboy."

The next moment, Damaris reeled at her own indiscretion. Being straight was a dangerous thing. "Homeboy" was a nickname Damaris had for William and well did Laura know it.

"What?" Laura stared at her.

"I mean, just like I'm sure Homey must be." Damaris amended hastily.

"You're sure all right!" Laura charged, understanding now why William had shown a minimum of compassion for his secretary. "You've been with William!"

Damaris didn't answer, but could not look Laura in the eye.

"You were sleeping with him and you still sold him out? That's unforgivable!"

Damaris agreed and hung her head.

"Not that he didn't have it coming," Laura said. "The treacherous reptile!"

Tears pricked the backs of Laura's eyes. William had been having an affair and she had never suspected it. When she thought of the way she had worshipped him, of the way he ran her life, she felt dizzy with mortification.

"Well, good-bye," said Laura. "And thank you for opening my eyes." Then she left. She noticed she was trembling when she got back on her bike.

Laura peddled slowly up to Marguerite Alexander's bookshop. It was a blustery, overcast afternoon. A melancholy autumn afternoon, Laura thought. For her brand new husband had broken her heart. "So he was going to let me play with Hugo on Halloween! How extraordinarily generous of him!"

Laura stopped to unburden herself to Marguerite. Her russet-haired friend, who was unpacking a carton of shiny new volumes, was not inclined to take William's office affair seriously. But Laura felt betrayed.

"And I've been the perfect submissive!" she protested to Marguerite.

"Wrong," Marguerite corrected. "If you were the perfect submissive you wouldn't question your dominant's motives in taking a mistress."

"Is that the way it works?"

"That's the way it works."

"Well, I don't care."

"Then you're not the perfect submissive."

"I'm William's wife. That entitles me to feel jealous, wounded and furious off when I find out he's cheating on me," Laura maintained.

"If I were you, I'd bite the bullet," Marguerite advised. "You've got everything you want and you're a spoiled brat. You don't even have to work."

"I don't mind working," Laura said. "It was William who decided to keep me in his dollhouse."

"You're really upset, aren't you? Don't worry, you aren't going to lose your hunk to that little minx," Marguerite assured her.

"I know. She's shacked up with your hunk now," said Laura, and reported what she knew about the budding romance between Damaris and Michael Flagg. It was as though somebody had pulled the world out from under Marguerite. To lose her lover to a woman half her size, was grossly humiliating.

"I think I'll take a short vacation," said Marguerite, immediately putting the closed sign in the window. She had to get out of town.

"Where were you thinking of going?"

"New York."

"I'll go with you."

"Really?"

"Why not?"

"You're not afraid of William?"

"Not anymore."

"You just think you're not."

"Just let me know when you're ready to leave," Laura said. "I'm definitely going to New York with you."

When William returned from Boston late that evening, he found Laura in their bedroom packing a valise.

Upon ignoring William's greeting, avoiding his embrace and pulling off her wedding band to cast it at his feet, Laura announced that she was going away.

"What does this mean?" he said, mystified, bending to pick up the ring.

"It means that I renounce my marriage vows," she declared snapping shut her little suitcase.

William digested this for a moment. "Any particular reason? Or do you just feel like a change of pace?"

"Yes, there's a particular reason," Laura took a cherry red dress from her closet. "I hate you!"

William watched her hold the dress up to her slender body in the mirror.

"What happened between this morning and now?"

Laura went behind a lacquered screen.

"You've been fucking Damaris!" Laura charged with vehemence, exchanging her grey skirt and white cotton blouse for the red dress. There was such a long silence then that Laura thought William had gone from the room.

"That would be like him," she fumed savagely, "Not to even give me the satisfaction of calling him a swine!"

But when Laura emerged from behind the screen in the clinging jersey, she saw that he was simply leaning against the mantelpiece, thinking. Finally he spoke. "What you said was true, but it's over now and it never had anything to do with us."

"Really!" Laura laughed. "You suave snake. You've humiliated me for the last time."

Then she changed her shoes for higher heels.

"You're over-reacting," he told her. She had picked up her valise.

"Excuse me, I have to catch a ten o'clock train."

"A train to where?" he moved out of her path, but followed her downstairs.

"New York." She paused at the hall closet to remove her raincoat. "Good-bye!"

When the door slammed behind her William finally understood that their honeymoon was over.

A few minutes later, William sat at the kitchen table ruminating over a bowl of cereal, unable to decide whether to feel flattered or irritated by Laura's jealousy. He looked up at the kitchen clock. It was already 9:30. Laura's leaving town would interrupt his whole routine. It was bad enough he had to find a new secretary. Now this had to happen as well. William decided that he was irritated. Where did she get off, carrying on like Doris Day? He had a mind to give the spoiled brat a good thrashing, right on the station platform, before dragging her home.

Of course William did not for a moment seriously consider going after Laura. He had never chased after a woman before and wasn't about to begin. Loss of dignity wasn't the issue; he was just too busy. It would be nice to be able to go rushing off to New York whenever one felt like it, William reflected, a few minutes later, while lacing his running shoes. He himself had to work, and exercise. When he went for his run he could think without being distracted. The girl would either come back or she wouldn't. He would wait and see.

Laura didn't look for William at the station, though she did begin to miss him as she and Marguerite were boarding the train. However, she wasn't allowed to brood on this for long, for Marguerite was pawing her with excitement.

"Laura - did you see who got on the train down the platform? Randy Price!"

"You know him?" Laura knew the name, but had never met the man.

"I should say so - although it's been about 3 years since we played. Laura, Randy Price is a multi-millionaire. Let's go and pick him up in the club car. What a stroke of luck. He'll be mad about you. We'll get him to pay for our trip to New York!"

Chapter Three

Jane Eliot

The incident took place just before noon at the antiques shop. Hugo's new assistant, Jane, did not expect her boss in until after lunch. As usual, business was slow. Jane even had time to practice walking up and down the aisles in the dainty high-heeled pumps Hugo had given her. He had given her other handsome items to wear while she was working in the shop. A silk dress, a wool suit and a string of pearls enhanced her wardrobe considerably and caused her to regard her own reflection in a new and interesting way.

It occurred to Jane that she might reasonably protest being asked to dress in an objectifying manner, but she'd never worn high heels or form sculpting dresses before, and she decided that she enjoyed doing so. She'd practiced classic feminist values since high school and knew she had nothing further to prove in this regard. What possible harm could it do to look sexy for a change?

Bored with the chapter on colonial sideboards that Hugo had marked for her to read, and not expecting any customers to tinkle the bell until at least 12:15, Jane wandered into the cedar-scented room marked: Special Collection, which Hugo had told Jane she was not to disturb.

Hugo specifically did not want Jane in this room because it contained folios, books and drawings of an erotic nature. And he knew how she viewed such material.

The room into which Jane now slipped, was furnished with a table and chairs and was comfortably lit for book gazing. She had not examined the contents of this room before. When she did, she recoiled at what she found. For even in the less offensive novels, Jane recognized a preoccupation with the notion of feminine submission.

On discovering this treasure trove of handsomely bound erotica, Jane was uncomfortable and confused. She had signed petitions against pornography. Now she found herself employed by a man who sold it and she didn't know how to react. Because in the few weeks Hugo Sands had employed her, she had already become attracted to her first poised older man.

The books in his collection celebrated sexism. Yet, upon reading a particularly sensual passage, Jane became aroused. However, this was easily explained. Since being jilted the previous month, she had been without a lover. And this was much on her mind.

When Hugo came in at 12:30, somewhat earlier than expected, he seemed very surprised to find Jane reading a volume of Sweet Gwendolyn, with a deeply creased brow.

"You're not supposed to be in here," he chided her.

"Hugo, what are you doing with all of these perverse books?"

"The stock in this room is of interest to collectors like everything else in the shop," he explained. Hugo took the volume out of her hands, snapped it shut and put it away. "And you shouldn't be touching these books without putting white cotton gloves on first," he chided.

"I'd like to know how you can justify pandering to the sadomasochistic tastes of these collectors!" Jane demanded.

"I'm sure you would, but you've got a customer waiting," Hugo said, hustling her out the door and switching off the light behind them. "He's been waiting ten minutes," he added. "He made a point of telling me so."

These comments worked to instantly remind Jane of her position, and she calmly went out front to attend to the needs of the shop.

The customer Hugo had spoken of proved a happy distraction, as he immediately purchased, without haggling, an oval mirror for his wife's boudoir, at the cost of fifteen hundred dollars.

Hugo came out after the customer had gone. "Good girl," he said. "Now you're doing your job."

It was only Jane's second respectable sale since beginning work and she was thrilled. But after she had asked Hugo as many questions as occurred to her about the origins of the mirror she had just sold, she remembered what they'd been talking about before.

"So why do you have all those books?" she attacked the old subject with fresh energy.

"My Special Collection?"

"Yes, that collection of exploitive, woman-oppressing smut."

"Jane, you're a Philistine."

"What?" Jane sputtered.

"You're so ignorant I can barely hold a conversation with you," Hugo informed her, before strolling back to his office. This silenced Jane momentarily and at one she left for lunch. When she returned at two, he was still in his office. As there were no customers in the shop, she went back to confront him again.

"Excuse me," she said, walking into his office, where he sat at his typewriter, adrift in correspondence. "Could we continue our discussion from before? It's been bothering me."

Hugo sighed, leaned back and motioned to a chair. "All right, Jane. Sit down." He turned off his typewriter and lit a cigarette. "Now what's on your mind?"

"Why do you sell pornography?"

"Jane, I'll answer you honestly. Erotica - collecting, selling, even publishing, is my real interest. Not antiques. Now, your purpose in my life - the reason I hired you, is to work in my antiques business. That's why you should be spending your free time reading the books I give you - on furniture, not the books I don't give you, on sex. Understand?"

Once again, he'd deflated her carefully formed arguments. "Now please go back out front, Jane. I just heard a customer."

Jane was speechless and frustrated when she hurried out front. The customer turned out to be just a browser who quickly left. So Jane went back to Hugo's office again.

"Are you back? Again? Well, as long as you're here, you can make me some coffee."

Jane had never been asked by Hugo to do this before. "Everything you'll need is in the lounge," he said, pointing to the door to the adjoining room.

But now, thoroughly distracted from his letters, Hugo got up and followed her, admiring the shape of her beautiful bottom under the smooth electric blue silk dress.

"Tell me something, Jane," he said, watching her busy herself at the long chrome range. "Did that ex-boyfriend of yours ever spank you?"

"Spank me? Of course not."

"Amazing," Hugo observed, for Michael Flagg had been on his mailing list from the start.

"What is?"

"That he could resist the impulse for so long," Hugo said, going back into his office again.

A few minutes later, Jane came in with the coffee tray. Although she was being terribly annoying that day, Hugo was finding it hard to keep his eyes off her stunning body and long legs.

"As a matter of fact," Jane admitted, "Michael threatened to spank me on a number of occasions, but never did." She smiled, but the recollection also brought her color up.

"Did he! And yet it never came to pass. Why not?"

"I don't think he ever seriously intended to spank me."

"No. Of course not." Hugo tasted the coffee.

"Saying that was just his way of letting me know that he thought I'd gone too far," Jane explained. "How is the coffee?" she added anxiously.

"Horrible. I'll have to teach you how to brew coffee."

"You shouldn't drink so much coffee," Jane said. "And you shouldn't smoke."

"And you shouldn't lecture your employer," Hugo said; "If you wish to continue to not be spanked."

After Jane turned on her stiletto heel and strutted out of his office, Hugo sat for a few minutes wondering again how Michael Flagg could have ever resisted paddling that pert behind for two days, no less two years. He himself had only been around Jane on a regular basis for two weeks, but even so far, the day did not go by when he did not imagine the pleasure of putting the opinionated little activist over his knee.

It was when Jane began to expound on her philosophy and interests that the urge to upend and correct her was strongest in Hugo. Today he'd fought the urge valiantly, but did not know how much longer he could continue to do so, especially if she thought she was going to lecture him each time she got bored.

Chapter Four

Return To Random Point

October was vivid, the air cracking fresh, the skies above Manhattan gorgeously blue for days. Laura and Marguerite did not check into the Bennington Club, as originally planned, but stayed at The Plaza at the expense of Randy Price instead. Marguerite went shopping every day and lunched with a variety of interesting men in the scene.

Laura passed her days in an orgy of bittersweet remembrance, revisiting the various places in and around the city where William had disciplined and made love to her the previous spring.

If Laura's days were moody rambles under leaf dappled skies and looming gothic spires, her nights were spent in a contrastingly high tech and blindingly glossy atmosphere, as Marguerite shepherded her through all the hottest bars and clubs in Manhattan. If Laura's goal in coming to New York was to even the score, Marguerite helped her achieve it beyond her most decadent fantasies, arranging for a number of highly paid sessions, between a series of gentlemanly dominants, Laura and herself. "Playing" in the scene with jaded executives and lust-starved dreamers, had for years kept Marguerite in the luxuries of life, but receiving "allowance" for submitting to or administering corporal punishment was entirely new to Laura and extremely empowering.

Occasionally, the session Marguerite arranged would include an act of sex, with Laura as the object. The fact that Laura would allow any number of liberties to be taken with her charming body insured her universal popularity with players of every stamp and Marguerite felt fully justified in asking enormous allowances from some of her

44

wealthiest admirers, in exchange for the rarified thrill of taking Laura, while Marguerite either assisted or observed.

Laura saw nothing immoral in making a few thousand dollars while evening the score with her husband. She was, in fact, beginning to feel like a very clever and independent girl.

The more men she allowed Marguerite to introduce her to, the better she felt about the whole William - Damaris situation. Once Laura realized that she'd been had by eight different men, since last seeing her husband, William's one short-lived affair with his secretary virtually ceased to disturb her.

Hugo Sands was certain that Marguerite and Laura would return from their antics in Manhattan for his party, an annual event for which he had this year rented a mansion called The Cliff House.

He was still vaguely irritated with his favorite pet, Marguerite, for departing from town so abruptly, without even bothering to ask whether her absence would be convenient at this time. He was particularly irked at her for not calling to let him know where she had gone until three days in New York had elapsed.

However, he understood the redhead's motives well enough and couldn't help but feel a thrill of excitement when she described how perverse their Laura could be.

Hugo threw a good party, with a full bar, amply furnished buffet tables and continuous atonal music. Everyone important in Random Point showed up. The remainder of the guests were divided equally between Hugo's associates in the antiques business and his numerous colorful and bizarre connections in the B&D scene. It made for a compatible mix. There were even crossovers. Why shouldn't a collector of rare manuscripts also collect antique Hermes riding crops?

Marguerite and Laura sauntered in through the front door at ten, confidently leather clad and glamorously sleek. The milling throng of revelers crowding the foyer and staircase swallowed them up almost at once. Most of the women who came from the New England B&D scene wore leather, glove-tight latex or shiny PVC. Mixed in with these glamorous creatures was a traditional selection of vampires, mummies, ghouls, witches and sorcerers. There was also a small avant garde fringe who arrived dressed as five pieces of sushi, a couple that came as a plug and socket and several Easter Island statues.

"I see Marguerite's gotten Laura into her first pair of 5" heels," Hugo remarked to William Random, who stood beside him on the gallery above the choked hall and staircase. William made a splendid barbarian in a leather torso harness that displayed his impressive muscularity dramatically. Studded gauntlets garnished his forearms and lacing sandals latticed his massive calves. His full leather facemask might have been as menacing as its designer had intended if it were not for the horn rimmed eyeglasses, which he'd strapped on over it.

"Do you think Laura will recognize me?" William queried his companion, leaning his granite abdomen against the railing.

"Considering you have no clothes on, I wouldn't be surprised!" replied Hugo patiently, wondering if it would really be possible to remain William Random's friend while actively pursuing his wife.

Hugo, who considered fancy dress appropriate for everyone but himself, wore his usual well-tailored evening clothes. Like William's, his gaze followed the forms of Marguerite and Laura, wriggling through the crowd in the foyer. "Your wife looks even cockier than Marguerite tonight," Hugo observed at the moment eye contact was fixed between themselves and the girls. But Laura's mien of careless defiance melted at the sight of her husband.

"Marguerite, let's go up!" Laura touched an elbow-gloved hand to her friend's white shoulder.

"Ouch!" Marguerite cried suddenly. Looking back over one bare shoulder she saw she had been struck upon the right cheek of her large, luscious bottom with a toy arrow, which adhered to the surface it had struck, by means of a suction cup tip. She yanked it from her leather-clad rear end as she raked the press of guests surrounding her with a glare.

"Did you see that?" Hugo laughed.

"That was priceless," William agreed, of the minor assault on the haughty Marguerite.

"No it wasn't, look over there," Hugo pointed to the doorway of the cloakroom, where a tall, ruddy blonde with a thick ponytail, dressed as Robin Hood, stood laughing behind her hand.

"Who's she?" William asked, admiring the robust good looks of the flaxen haired imp, who even now was reloading her bow from the quiver of arrows slung across her back.

"That's Marnie Price, Randy's little sister."

"Why haven't I noticed her before? She looks like a real New England girl." William said with approval.

"Drinks like one too."

"Doesn't seem to impair her aim though."

"You'd have to be legally blind to miss that target," Hugo remarked ungallantly.

His companion agreed, while still admiring the voluptuous posterior of Marguerite, who now gave it a brief rub, after breaking the arrow in half with a toss of her glorious mane.

As the girls filtered up through the crowd on the stairs, the roar of a Harley skidding to a stop outside let everybody know that Randy Price had arrived.

Price enjoyed making an entrance. He was twenty-eight, tall, lean and swaggering. He wore a black bomber jacket, ripped tee shirt and black jeans. From his left ear an inverted cross dangled and his skull had been completely shaved, the first sight of which caused not only Laura and Marguerite, but also every other woman who recognized Randy to gasp.

The manipulative C.E.O. of Price Enterprises was William Random's most serious competitor. He was a Harvard business school drop out, but this had not stopped him from pulling his family's floundering land development company out of the red several years before and building it into a corporation with wide holdings all over New England and enormous liquid assets.

With his uncanny business acumen and total lack of ethics, Randy's deals seldom blew up in his face. The incident with Damaris Perez was not typical and he was still steaming about her trading him bogus bids for genuine drugs.

He scanned the halls and stairs impatiently, ignoring all who greeted him, but acknowledging Laura Random with a smirk. Laura turned and fled up the stairs. Her violent reaction was noted by

William, who now folded his arms belligerently, as he considered the immense annoyance Randall Price had become.

Even as William confronted the fact that Laura had cheated on him with his unscrupulous competitor, he found his wife especially appealing in the cherry red leather dress that clove to her buttocks, sleek thighs and firm bosom so enticingly.

"Why does Randall keep following Laura?" William suddenly demanded of Hugo. But Laura was with them before Hugo could answer, throwing her arms about William's neck. He embraced her without hesitation, locking his arms about her so tightly that she squealed as he lifted her off the ground and swung her around.

"Well?" he demanded. "Have you decided to come home?"

"Yes," Laura said shyly, hiding her face against his chest.

"Good!" Nothing could have been more emphatic than this pronouncement.

Laura had expected him to be stern and remote. The quality of warmth did not often emanate from William Random, but it enveloped her completely at that moment of reunion. Then Randy was upon them.

"Hi Laura! Like my haircut? Billy, how's it going? Hugo, no costume?" Randy was bubbling with abrasive energy. William's hands balled into fists as he let Laura go.

"A good haircut is no substitute for the frontal lobe job you really need," William pointed out.

Before Randy could respond, Laura asked Hugo to take her to the bar.

"Don't go, baby," Randy said, touching Laura's bare shoulder. "There's so much I want to say to you."

"Leave my wife alone," William told him.

"She's got a mouth," said Randy; "And we both know she can use it. Why doesn't she tell me herself?"

"She asked me to deliver the message, so you'd read it loud and clear," William said, stepping aggressively in front of Laura, who took the opportunity to seize Hugo's hand and scurry away with the amused voyeur in tow.

"If I stay they'll come to blows," Laura explained to Hugo, who seemed reluctant to exit.

"I should have thought you'd enjoy that," Hugo remarked, allowing himself to be dragged down the stairs by his pretty companion. "Marguerite would be selling tickets."

"Gee, she's pretty," Randy sighed, to taunt William.

"Randall, let's go outside," William suggested.

"When the chicks are in here? Listen, we'll do lunch, okay? Later." Randy had spotted Damaris Perez and the next instant he was gone.

"Believe it, asshole," William muttered, as he too caught a glimpse of his ex-secretary, encased in a PVC jumper that glittered like black ink, clinging crustacean-like to Michael Flagg's impressive arm.

"I'm glad you've left your husband," Hugo said, when Laura had had her first drink. "That means we can finally play."

For the first time since he'd known her, Laura looked Hugo boldly in the eye. "I haven't left my husband. But yes, we can finally play."

"In that case, come with me. I have everything arranged," Hugo said, and took her by the hand. He led Laura up to the attic, where he knew there was a private little room. Earlier that day he had fitted it out with a padded leather bench and a mirror opposite. It was here that he'd intended to take her.

"Nervous?" he asked her, leading her in.

"Not at all," she lied, tossing back her silky brown hair.

"Yes you are. Come here and sit next to me," he told her, pulling her down on the bench. "And tell me why you've been so naughty lately. It really isn't like you."

"Hugo, I didn't come with you to be treated like a child," she protested.

But Hugo hadn't waited patiently for eighteen months to treat her like an adult. "If by that you mean I'm not supposed to spank you, you should know better, Laura."

"But why?" she cried, pulling off the domino that had covered her eyes.

"Because," he said, putting his arm around her shoulder and drawing her to him, "that's what I'm into."

"But I don't want you to!"

"Look, there are all sorts of spankings. Some of them hurt a lot and some hardly hurt at all. I happen to be an expert in administering what are called erotic spankings. Now if I give you my word that I'll only spank you in a way that will arouse you without making you kick, scream or cry, will you trust me enough to submit?"

The concept was a new one on Laura, but she liked the way Hugo's arms felt about her, the way he smelled and the comforting firmness of his chest to lean upon. "Okay," she told him.

"That's a good girl," said Hugo. "Now stand up. Right here," he pointed at the floor in front of him. Laura obeyed after some slight hesitation. He raised her arms, which she held stiffly at her sides until one hand rested on each of his shoulders. Then, using both hands, he pushed the hobbling skirt of her expensive leather dress up, from the backs of her knees to her waist. It slid very slowly upward, and as he pushed, his fingertips caressed the backs of her thighs and the curves of her buttocks, which were finally revealed, after considerable effort. The skirt, with its leather laces going up the back, was exceedingly tight.

Finally the dress was pushed up to her waist and Hugo confronted a ravishing black satin garter belt, with silk-satin panties to match, the suspenders holding up black nylon stockings, with seams up the back. He dropped his hands to trace her stocking seams, from ankle to thigh top and back, with a whispery touch. Laura shivered, not prepared for tenderness.

"All right," he said, "Come here," and pulled her down across his lap. Her sharp little intake of breath as he did was enough to let him know that nothing had changed with the doe-eyed brunette; she was as susceptible as ever to the position in which she'd been placed.

She kept her legs straight and together, with the toes of her shoes on the floor.

"You mustn't be tense," he told her, running his palm, for the first time, across the jutting oval contours of her bottom, through the clinging satin of her panties. Even in the low light of the little attic room, the expanse of exposed thigh she displayed above her stocking tops gleamed as white as starlight. He could not remember ever touching anything so smooth or so soft as the insides of Laura's thighs. She shivered at his light caresses, not knowing what would come next, but felt herself relaxing more each moment that she lay across his lap. With one hand on her waist, he drew her closer. With the other, he continued to stoke her shapely buttocks and thighs.

"Do you ever pretend when you play?"

"You mean, assume a role?"

"It's fun to do once in a while."

"I never met anyone who wanted to pretend."

"Sometimes I like to pretend. With the right person and at the right moment."

"Yes," Laura said, "I think it might be fun to pretend that I'm five or six years old."

"That's perverse but I can go there," said Hugo.

"I wouldn't admit this to everyone, but sometimes I fantasize I'm just small." she went on.

"That's sweet," he told her, bringing his palm to rest on the rise of one firm cheek. Suddenly the party seemed very far away. It was so quiet in the attic that Laura could hear his watch tick. "You're the little girl who lives down Shadow Lane," he continued. He paused without moving his hand, to let the notion germinate. Then he went on speaking in a hypnotic tone of voice.

"Most of the time you're a good little girl. But today you were naughty. You brought your cat into the shop. You had a ball of yarn tucked in your apron pocket. You took it out and trailed it on the floor. The kitty saw the bright blue string and leaped on it. You laughed and dragged the sting away. Again it jumped and pounced. You ran behind a corner with the string whipping after you fast. Faster and faster you ran. You became so excited while playing that you completely forgot my rule about running in the shop. At last you were totally breathless. You'd run until your little legs felt weak. No wonder you lost your balance and knocked over the lamp."

At this pronouncement Laura, completely caught up in the story, gasped in guilty astonishment.

"Yes, it's very sad. You broke the frosted glass shade of the lamp.

It was one of those fluted monstrosities with flowers, fruit and birds worked in relief. No one with taste would have bought it, but I'd have sold it for a profit all the same. So naturally your naughtiness has made me very cross."

Hardly conscious of what she was doing, Laura ground against his lap. Her heart was fairly pounding and the power of suggestion had planted a lump in her throat.

"After you heard the lamp crash to the ground and you saw the kitty scamper away, you knew you were in trouble. So you came up here to hide. But the blue ball of yarn left a trail plain as day, and I followed it. I found you crouched behind a dusty old trunk, pulled you straight out and gave you a shake!"

Laura actually sobbed aloud.

"I gave you a very stern scolding. And two big tears rolled down your face. That's because you knew that you deserved a spanking. And that was what you were going to get!"

"No! Please!" she whimpered, putting her hand back to shield her upturned bottom.

"Don't you dare, young lady," he told her, pinning her wrist to her side. "You've been a very naughty little girl!" He raised his hand and began the spanking, over her black satin panties. But each spank was no more than a sharp, little slap, the sort that one would give a child of five. He alternated cheeks and skipped two beats between each swat, to draw out this quaint punishment. When he'd given her precisely fifty of these baby smacks, he stopped to tug her pretty panties down.

He'd been spanking her so lightly, her bottom was barely pink, and yet it felt quite warm beneath his hand. Again he commenced the spanking, a fraction more sharply this time, but pausing as long between smacks.

To Laura, all this was so poignant that she felt she might really cry. She was overwhelmed by Hugo's affection. In a strange way, being spanked softly and slowly like this was much more humiliating than being spanked rapidly and hard. Because without the distraction of genuine pain to make the experience inescapably immediate and real, the childishly light little paddling ignited a lush and voluptuous shame, hitherto confined to savored threats and fantasies.

She had no way of knowing just how long he spanked her like that. She only knew that it went on for a very long time, but she still didn't want it to stop. Hugo also wanted to continue with their charming make-believe game, but the wet spot she was leaving on his trouser leg was already huge and his cock was threatening to explode.

"Now, I know my little girl has learned her lesson," he told Laura, setting her on her feet; "but here's nothing like driving the point home. Step out of those panties."

When Laura had stumblingly done this, slightly dizzy from the excitement, and still unused to 5" high heels, he stood up and placed her face down on the bench, legs together, with her dress still hiked up to her waist.

She heard him yank his zipper down then felt Hugo straddle her. He parted her thighs with his hand just before guiding his cock in. She rejoiced as she felt there was more than enough of Hugo to fill her in this or any other position. Some instinct told him Laura was a grinder, and that she'd cum while humping the bench. In any case, he liked the warm feel of her spanked bottom under his groin.

As a rule, she was not highly orgasmic. But in this case she came within two dozen thrusts.

When she climaxed with William, it was always by accident. It happened only two times out of ten. Possibly this was because her husband never gave her a half hour of relentless foreplay first.

As her spasms subsided Laura felt she understood Hugo's genius for the first time. When he was ready to burst in a moment or two and could not prolong his pleasure even for a second longer Hugo pulled out of her snug sheath and ejaculated all over her bottom. For Laura this was the perfect ending.

Leaning up on her elbows, Laura ruefully looked over her shoulder and rubbed the thick puddles of cream in circles with the heel of her hand, until they disappeared into her skin.

"Now you're a good girl again," Hugo said, zipping up his trousers.

"And you are a good man," said Laura. "Maybe even the best."

After returning Laura to the bar Hugo had little desire to remain at his own party, which now seemed to him one giant distraction. He now knew he wanted Laura more than ever. Two to three times a week sounded right. But would this be possible without jeopardizing her brilliant marriage?

Hugo knew that Laura would not be revolving these thoughts over in her beautiful head for a week or so. But sooner or later she would remember the chemistry of their encounter and seek to repeat the experience. They'd start meeting whenever they could. The more they saw each other, the greater their need for each other would grow. Finally the night would come when she would want to stay with him until the following morning, regardless of consequences. And how was William going to take that?

While traversing the teeming corridor between the bar and ballroom, a possible solution to Hugo's potential problem appeared. Radiant, sexy Marguerite came toward him now, in sections, with her flame colored hair on her shoulders and her glorious curves packed into a smart leather dress.

Marguerite owed him a favor. Not only had she rushed off to New York without even saying good-bye, but between her airs, pretensions and recent infatuation with Michael Flagg, she'd been a less than perfect submissive that Autumn. She embraced him, pressing her smooth cheek to his face. He breathed in her perfume.

"Are you angry with me?" she broke the embrace.

Hugo crossed his arms and replied, "What do you think?"

"Oh Hugo, you don't know what it's been like! Have you ever been rejected for someone half your height?"

"It must be very humiliating," he was sympathetic.

"It's perfectly hideous!"

"Doesn't Michael Flagg know that there are better ways of humiliating you?" said Hugo, leading Marguerite towards the ballroom at the end of the hall.

Without noticing Hugo and Marguerite, Michael Flagg had preceded them into the rotunda, escorting both Damaris Perez and a beautiful young dominatrix from New York named Isabel Bruno.

"You see!" said Marguerite to Hugo before they went in. "I can't take a step without being reminded of my improbable defeat! I can't go in there now!" she turned from the door.

"All right, but don't go home yet. I may need you later," Hugo advised her as she hastened away.

Hugo caught up with Michael, Damaris and Isabel Bruno, who were standing on the edge of the strobe-lit ballroom, arguing.

Michael had come as The Spirit and was wearing a zoot suit and spats. A domino masked his eyes. Isabel, a leggy beauty in her middle twenties, with ink-black hair and a slender torso, was as graceful as a lily in a black strapless gown with a bell shaped skirt of sequined chiffon. It was a dress to kill for, and Damaris wanted to. For Isabel looked like fairy queen. While she, Damaris, in her polyvinyl mini dress, looked like a B&D club girl.

"Every dominant goes submissive occasionally," Isabel insisted, as Hugo joined them, coming up behind her and locking his arms around her small waist.

"Isabel, what did I tell you about spreading subversive theories?" He gave her a smack that was barely felt through her crinoline petticoat and billowing skirt. Isabel turned her head for a kiss, grinding back against him and deliberately tightening his hold on her waist.

"Hugo, I love your party. Thank you for inviting me!" Isabel told him after nibbling on his ear long enough to give him a fresh erection. He let go of Isabel and shook hands with Flagg. Michael introduced him to Damaris. Hugo also shook her pretty little hand. He had heard about Damaris Perez, but this was the first time they had met.

It was interesting to Hugo that this diminutive girl had taken both Laura's and Marguerite's men. Tonight she seemed so shy. She clung to Michael Flagg like a small, sleek, black kitten.

"I want to whip Michael. I think we'd both enjoy it," Isabel explained to Hugo.

"Excuse me, honey, but you don't look like you could whip cream!" Damaris declared, the kitten extending her sharp, little claws.

"You should teach your wife some circumspection," Isabel remarked. "Or let me."

"In your dreams, pipsqueak!" Damaris cried.

"I'm taller than you," Isabel told Damaris. Then she was suddenly distracted when a missile struck her beautiful back.

"Maybe so, but I'm not pretending to be a dominant!" Damaris returned.

"What the hell..." Isabel's gloved hand went back to pull the rubber tipped arrow free, "Some coward shot me in the back!" she cried indignantly.

Hugo excused himself and strode off in pursuit of Marnie Price, who was romping through the house. After darting around the rotunda, Marnie led Hugo out and back down the hall to the bar, where the buffet tables attracted her attention. Hugo stole up behind her as the tall tomboy began to pile her plate with roast beef, potatoes, pickles and bread.

"I've seen you make seven direct hits so far, and all of your victims have been female," Hugo said.

"Oh, Hi Mr. Sands," said Marnie; "Really? I hadn't even noticed." She began to eat with a good appetite.

"Are you hostile towards women - or just afraid of irritating men?"

"I'm not afraid of irritating anyone!" Marnie asserted between gulps. Together they strolled over to the bar. "I'll prove it too," vowed Marnie, after swallowing a tumbler full of ale. "From now on I'm only going after guys!"

"Great. Why don't you start with that one over there?" Hugo pointed at William Random, who was leaning morosely on the bar, nursing a Perrier and glowering at Randy Price, who was attempting to flirt with Jane Eliot at the other end of the room, in front of a large blazing hearth.

"That muscular guy with the glasses over his mask? You want me to nail him?"

"Yes. Nail him," Hugo advised.

"Consider it done," Marnie assured him, abandoning her plate and mug to put a good amount of distance between herself and her target before drawing a bead on William.

Hugo strode off, satisfied that Marnie Price would receive justice before much more time had elapsed.

Marnie launched her arrow at William while he was in the midst of tearing off the mask, which had become suffocating and was starting to make him dizzy. While he didn't see his assailant, he felt her dart smack into his rib cage and this did not amuse him.

By the time William got the mask off and his glasses back on Marnie had sped away. He decided to pursue her and an epic chase began. It was a large house with attics, wings and numerous stairwells, dozens of rooms, garages, gardens, tennis courts and grounds. Marnie did not expect to be chased through more than a couple of rooms, but William was determined to run her to ground no matter how many times she scampered up the stairs and down the stairs in her efforts to evade him. She was in athletic shape. But William was a runner and this was fine sport! By the time Marnie began to get winded, William was just warming up. If it weren't for the masses of guests lining the stairwells and halls, he would have caught her long before. Meanwhile, he was having a great time, and looked forward to an even better one he turned her over his knee.

Upon momentarily losing sight of Marnie Price, still fleeing his relentless pursuit, William crossed paths with Damaris Perez. She was in the picture gallery, admiring a portrait of a 19th century lady in striking velvet gown, when he came running through.

When he stopped short at the sight of her, Damaris pulled back, all but plastering herself against the wall.

"Well! Look who's here!" breathed William. "Don't worry, I'm not going to hit you."

"Oh William, I can't tell you how sorry I am for what I did. And after you were so good to me ..."

"What a touching speech!" said a voice behind William, then Randy Price stepped into view. "But I was also good to you," he told Damaris menacingly; "And how did you repay me?"

Instinctively choosing the lesser of two evils, Damaris shrunk closer to William.

"I'll tell you how, you little cunt, you set me up!" Randy snarled.

"Don't talk to her like that," said William, putting Damaris to one side.

"Stay out of this," Randy told William.

"I don't want to stay out of it."

"You'd better make restitution, Chiquita," Price warned Damaris.

"I will!" she promised feverishly.

"Shut up," William told her. "You'll do no such thing. And you," he said to Randy, "had better let the whole incident rest. You ought to be grateful I'm not taking you to court."

"I love going to court," Randy returned without missing a beat. "And as for you," he looked at Damaris, "You owe me a grand. If you can't raise the cash, don't worry. I'll take it in trade."

"Randall, you fucking maggot, leave Damaris alone." William did not like Randy Price to the degree that veins were beginning to pop in his head.

"I'll be expecting to hear from you, Chiquita." Randy had already begun walking away. "You can't find the cash, you come to my office. Don't forget."

Marguerite wandered through the strobe-lit ballroom in a preoccupied daze.

"Marguerite!" A deep, familiar, dulcet toned male voice startled her back to reality, as the tall, broad-shouldered form of Michael Flagg blocked her path. She aborted the embrace he attempted, swiftly brushing his face with her cheek, then pulling back at once.

"Michael, your costume is perfect. The Spirit, right?" Her heart seemed to twist when he touched her, but she flashed him a charming smile.

"I like your costume too."

"Thank you." Marguerite scanned the room for topics of frivolous conversation.

"I left messages on your machine last week. How come you never called me back?"

"I've been out of town. Just got back this evening." she explained.

"I need to talk to you," he said.

"Sure Michael. Anytime. Stop by the shop," she said casually.

"I'll do that."

"Look at that Isabel Bruno," she said. "That young Viking is her foot-slave. What a physique! Isn't it astonishing the people who turn out to be submissive?"

"I've met that girl," said Michael. "She's interesting."

"She happens to be a world class Mistress," Marguerite pointed out.

"I suspect she's no more dominant than you."

This cool remark made Marguerite wonder why she was being so nice to this insulting man. "Well, you are the detective," she observed, with a faint smile, before excusing herself and rushing away. She had no heart to be nasty to him, no matter what he'd said. Besides there was a lump in her throat.

"What an incredible asshole!" Jane Eliot cried, taking refuge in the powder room from the oppressive attentions of a half drunk Randy Price.

The two girls in front of the mirror looked up. Laura leaned against the vanity console, smoking a cigarette. Marguerite paused in brushing her hair with a silver-backed brush.

"I'll bet it's someone we know," the redhead said to Laura.

"Which asshole was it?" Laura asked the attractive brunette.

"I don't know the idiot's name, but he's got to be the most chauvinistic male I've ever met!" Jane disclosed, sinking into an elegant armchair.

"Oh, you must have met my husband," Laura said, exhaling streams of blue smoke through her nose.

"Aren't you Hugo Sands' new assistant?" asked Marguerite, suddenly recognizing the ex-social worker in the sophisticated beauty who now lounged before them in a black beaded cocktail dress that clove adorningly to her curves. Hugo had rented her jewels for the night and her legs looked superb in her sheer hose and heels.

"Yes, I am," said Jane, trying to place Marguerite.

"I'm Marguerite. We've met before. You came into my shop with Michael Flagg. Remember?"

Jane did. Because that was the night he had broken their engagement. Jane even recalled thinking at the time that the witchy redhead both of them had words with in the bookshop had been some sort of catalyst to Michael's ending their relationship so abruptly that day.

"Yes. I remember," said Jane, not meeting Marguerite's eyes.

"You looked very different then," said Marguerite. Jane self-consciously fingered the gems at her smooth, milky throat.

"I know," said Jane. "I'm in a different phase now."

"Yes," thought Marguerite, "the Vargas gatefold phase."

"Hugo wants me to project a certain image to his clientele," Jane explained.

"Don't worry, you are," commented Laura, admiring the chic cocktail dress.

"Oh excuse me," said Marguerite, "This is my friend Laura Random. Laura, Jane Eliot."

"Nice to meet you," Jane said politely to Laura. Then she turned to Marguerite again. "How did you know my name?"

"Hugo told me."

"Oh," said Jane, relieved to hear it hadn't been Michael.

"How do you like working for Hugo?" Laura asked, rolling a joint.

"I'm enjoying working for Hugo very much."

"You aren't finding him to be a hard boss?" Laura asked. Marguerite gave her friend a look, which Laura ignored.

"Not at all," Jane replied. "He's really amazingly patient, considering how ignorant I am." At this remark Laura and Marguerite again exchanged looks. "Hugo's making her feel humble already!" they thought simultaneously.

Marguerite offered Jane some champagne, which the sleek brunette accepted as they spoke. "To tell you the truth," added Jane, who was not used to drinking, "I'm beginning to develop quite a crush on my boss."

"We'll never tell," promised Laura.

"Thanks," Jane replied, smiling shyly, and making both of them like her at once.

"By the way," said Marguerite, "that is a striking dress."

"Yes," Laura agreed. "I love the way it clings. Did Hugo choose that dress?"

Jane blushed. "He did, actually."

"Stand up and turn around," commanded Marguerite. "We want to see how it drapes in back." To their amusement, she obeyed at once.

During the instant Jane's back was turned, both women appraised the classic proportions of her waist, legs and buttocks. Marguerite drew the shape of an inverted heart in the air, in imitation of Jane's perfect bottom, which swelled so firmly underneath the shiny beaded skirt. Laura nodded at the outline in agreement. Hugo had unearthed another gem.

"It's a brilliant dress," Marguerite concluded, when Jane turned to face them again. "And you're a dreamboat in it."

"You're very kind," murmured Jane.

"Has Michael seen you since the, uh, transformation?" Marguerite asked.

"You know Michael well, don't you?" Jane put out her empty glass for a refill.

"I wouldn't say that." Marguerite replied.

"Are you two seeing each other?" Jane asked, as though it meant nothing to her.

"No," Marguerite reported truthfully. "We went out together a few times. That's all."

"Is he here tonight?" Jane asked.

"Yes."

"No, he hasn't seen me since I became Hugo's protégée," Jane said coyly; "nor do I care to see him." She gulped almost a full glass of champagne at once.

"Did you used to date Detective Flagg?" Laura asked, smoking.

"We were engaged," Jane said. "Then he broke it off. Because of her," she added, pointing at Marguerite. Jane was becoming drunk. "No offense,' she said to Marguerite. "I just remembered that five hours before it happened we were in your bookshop. That seemed more than coincidental."

"Do you wish you had him back?" asked Laura.

"I'd never give a man a second chance to hurt me," said Jane emphatically, presenting her empty glass for another refill.

"Really? I'm just the opposite," said Laura. Jane stared at the other brunette.

"Don't pay any attention to Laura," explained Marguerite. "She's not very bright."

"So, you think that Michael would be surprised to see me like this?" Jane asked Marguerite, after putting down her glass in mid-air.

"I think he'd be astonished," replied the redhead, catching Jane's empty glass before it hit the floor.

"Well frankly I couldn't care less," asserted Jane.

"Is that so?" Laura doubted Jane's avowal.

"To me, he's just a well endowed form of pond scum."

"Jane, is this just bravado, or are you really off Michael?" asked Marguerite.

"I wouldn't give him the time of day," Jane declared.

At that point the door opened and Damaris Perez walked in. She stopped short on seeing Laura, not knowing how to behave. Finally she made a nervous greeting, then found a place in front of the mirror to fix her lipstick.

"Oh hi!" said Laura." We were just talking about you!" She offered Damaris the joint.

"About me? Thanks," she accepted the offering. "I haven't been stoned in a while."

"No, I wouldn't think Michael would let you." Laura said.

"Oh," said Jane, with interest, "Are you the one who's going with Michael now?"

Marguerite began to brush her hair again. Damaris looked from Jane to Laura.

"This is Jane Eliot," Laura explained. "And my friend Marguerite Alexander. J and M, this is Damaris Perez."

Damaris did not consider either of the women strangers. Jane she'd hear about from Michael, while she recognized Marguerite's scent as the same one that lingered about the cashmere robe she'd found in Michael's closet. Not many women wore Joy. She was certain that the robe belonged to this one.

"Actually, Michael and I are married." She extended her hand to show Laura a modest gold wedding band.

"When?" Laura cried, seizing the tiny hand.

"2 days ago," said Damaris, devastating Marguerite and confounding Jane.

Jane was completely drunk when she went stumbling out of the powder room to look for Michael, leaving Laura and Damaris behind in a heavy haze of smoke. The news had amazed but not hurt Jane, and she was fairly sure that she wished to congratulate Michael. Damaris was pretty cnough to have made Jane ill with jealousy, a few weeks ago. But as the serious brunette's affections were currently fixed on another, how could she feel any real pain at the bizarrely unexpected announcement of her ex-fiancé's hasty nuptials?

Meanwhile, Damaris could see that Laura had forgiven her. She also noticed, shortly after her announcement, the gorgeous redhead's fine green eyes fill up with tears. Then Marguerite excused herself and hurried from the room.

"There went your husband's two ex-girlfriends," Laura observed "Now tell me absolutely everything!"

Jane found Michael in the bar, where he had been for some time.

"Well! If it isn't the man whose name is on everyone's lips!" she declared, stepping up to the bar beside him.

"Jane?" Michael was stunned by her appearance.

"Champagne please," Jane told the bartender. "I understand congratulations are in order, Michael."

"Uh, yes, I ..."

"I know, I met your wife. She's adorable."

"You met ...?"

"Just now, in the powder room. Along with the woman who owns the bookshop. I must say, she didn't take the news of your marriage well," Jane reported. "I took it worlds better."

"Damn it. I wanted to tell her myself," Michael swore. "Well, never mind that. Tell me what's happened to you?"

"What do you mean, happened to me?" Jane drained her glass of champagne as soon as it was served and for a moment slightly swayed.

"I've never seen you wear heels, or such a sexy dress, or even lipstick, come to think of it." He lifted one of her manicured hands. "Red fingernails too! I thought you despised all that stuff."

"I thought I despised you, but instead I just feel numb," said Jane dramatically. "Another please," she added to the waiter.

"That's probably because you're so drunk."

"I am not drunk."

"Yes you are."

The waiter brought a new glass to Jane, but Michael took it out of her hand.

"What are you doing?"

"Sweetheart, you've had enough. Do you want to become violently ill? How many of these have you had?"

"Waiter, another drink please," Jane sweetly asked, adding, "Some goon took that last one."

Michael sighed. He watched her down yet another glass of champagne.

"You're going to regret this tomorrow," he warned.

"Butt out, Copper!" Jane told him, and tossing her hair over one creamy shoulder, began to march away. The high heels gave her a cute, sexy walk, especially in the tightly skirted dress. And he could not recall ever having seen her toss her hair that way before. She'd taken her precious time about it, but Jane had finally turned into a siren. Someone had transformed his dull and dedicated Jane into a pin-up girl and she was apparently beginning to realize the mayhem she might be capable of inflicting on mankind.

"Ha!" said Michael aloud. He had a good mind to go after the little minx and repay her for two tiresome years of consciousness-raising with two minutes of skirt raising.

Somehow it had never seemed appropriate to spank Jane. Until tonight. Even at her most irritatingly self-righteous, she had always been a sensible and responsible adult. But there was nothing adult about the cute little pout she threw him over one beautiful, bare shoulder before melting into the crowd.

Long after she had gone, the erection she'd given him lingered.

Marguerite was about to leave. But Hugo intercepted her as she strode through the picture gallery. "I've been looking for you, come with me," he took her by the hand to drag her after him.

"Hugo, I have to go home," she said, stopping him before he could pull her out of the room.

"Home? Why? What's the matter?" He scrutinized her face. After having broken down once already in the powder room, Marguerite thought she was under control. But when he lifted her chin and made her look at him, fresh tears began to well in her eyes. "Baby, what's wrong? Come over here and sit down." He led her to an upholstered bench. "Now tell me what's upset you."

"Michael's married," she sobbed, accepting Hugo's handkerchief to mop her wet eyes.

"No kidding!" said Hugo, taking her hand.

"Oh Hugo, I wanted him so badly," she confessed.

"Don't worry, you'll have him again. Haven't you been reading the statistics? One out of two marriages ends in divorce you know. Now, if anyone could break up a happy home, it's you, Marguerite."

"Don't try to cheer me up," she said with a sniffle.

"Listen, sweetheart, I've got something to take your mind off all this. That's why I was looking for you. Who do you think just showed up? Anthony Newton!"

"Anthony Newton?" Marguerite looked blank.

"Anthony Newton. The composer. You must have heard the name He's written hit shows for the last fifteen years. He's got one on Broadway right now."

"Oh. That Anthony Newton," said Marguerite without interest.

"He happens to be a collector. He's been one of my best customer's for years. He's owns a huge collection of vintage instruments."

"Really? That's nice," she replied dully, her eyes glazing again.

"Yes, it's very nice," Hugo agreed, "because I have a hundred and seventy-five thousand dollar piano in the music room which I fully intend to sell Anthony Newton tonight, and you're going to help me."

"Me?"

"Yes, you're going to play piano and sing for us right now."

"What?"

"To help me sell the piano."

"Sing? And Play? Before a professional? Haven't I been humiliated enough tonight?"

"Marguerite," said Hugo sternly, "You can play. I've heard you.

And there's plenty of sheet music there. All familiar to you."

"Oh god!" Marguerite cried with anguish.

"It's true your keyboard style is somewhat halting but with that ravishing cleavage, nobody's going to notice."

"Please Hugo, don't make me do this."

"Now as to the program - I'd suggest Rodgers and Hart."

"Hugo, please, I'm really not up to this."

"Marguerite, you're not going to let me down," he declared. "I just don't ask you to do that many things for me."

"No. It's impossible!" she stood up.

"Help me sell the concert grand and I'll give you a 10% commission on what I realize."

Marguerite sat back down. But momentarily she rose again.

"No. I can't. Honestly, Hugo, I'm too upset to sing. You see... my heart's been broken."

"Oh brother."

"It's true!"

"Are you deliberately trying to irritate me, Marguerite? I offer you a chance to be the focus of attention, which you love, meet a Broadway luminary and go home with seventeen grand and all you can do is whimper!"

"Wouldn't it be seventeen five?"

Hugo saw he had finally caught her interest. "Marguerite, Anthony Newton's in the scene."

"Oh really? What's his orientation?"

"I don't think I'm going to tell you. You ought to be able to figure out whether a man is dominant or submissive by now. I will say this, though, he isn't a switch."

"I'll bet he's submissive," said Marguerite. "These high powered types usually are."

"That's a popular myth, but either way, I think I'll let him watch me spank you."

Marguerite sprang up, as though to run away, but Hugo caught her by the wrists and pulled her back down. "That's right, Marguerite, since you've refused to entertain my precious guest, I'll have to. I'll probably use your birthday as a pretext."

"My birthday isn't till December."

"So what? I still owe you one from last year. And thirty is a nice, round number. The more I think of it, I almost prefer this solution. You've had a good one coming for awhile."

"Hugo, please don't do this to me!" she put her hands together in supplication.

"Think of it Marguerite, being spanked in front of all those people who must be in the music room right now, along with Anthony Newton. Normally, in such a situation I wouldn't raise your skirt, but trying to spank you through that leather one would be pointless."

Marguerite thought, "What if Michael comes in?" That she could never survive.

"I'll sing and play piano," she said firmly.

"Are you sure?" Hugo tried not to smile.

Marguerite jumped up and took his hand. "Come on, let's get this over with."

As Marguerite and Hugo approached the music room, lush swells of piano music cascaded out the opened French doors.

"Sounds like Anthony's already discovered the piano," Hugo told her. "You're saved, Marguerite."

They entered the large, balconied room, where several dozen guests had already entrenched themselves. A few were still sober.

Their celebrity guest motioned them over to the piano. He stood up to shake Hugo's hand and Marguerite thought, "He's elegant, but not terribly tall. I wish I hadn't worn such high heels."

"Hugo, I've got to have this piano," Newton murmured. "Do you think the owner will sell it?"

"Couldn't you have waited five minutes to say that? You owe me seventeen thousand five dollars," thought Marguerite.

"Anthony, this is my protégée, Marguerite. She's a novelist."

Anthony shook Marguerite's hand. "Have I read anything you've written?" asked the composer from New York. Marguerite was thinking, "He really very good looking."

"She writes under the name Alma for me," said Hugo. "And I imagine you've read just about everything she's written."

"Really!" Newton gazed at Marguerite with profound admiration. "I'm one of your biggest fans."

"How nice," she replied, forgetting to add that she was also one of his.

"So, Marguerite, sit down here next to me and tell me all your fantasies," said Newton, patting the piano bench beside him.

"I told her if she didn't sing for my guests I'd have to spank her in front of them," reported Hugo, to Marguerite's chagrin.

"Really! We can't let that happen, can we, Marguerite?"

"No," declared Marguerite, "Absolutely not!" She thought, "He must be submissive."

Anthony Newton accompanied her, as Marguerite sang for Hugo's guests. Damaris and Michael, attracted to the sound of Marguerite's lovely contralto voice, were drawn through the double doors.

"La Marguerita is feeling better," Damaris thought. She longed to scrutinize Michael, as he watched Marguerite, but was too proud to do this. "Of course they were in love," thought Damaris, "She's so tall!" The sight of Marguerite, so perfect and poised, made Damaris fret. How could he prefer her to this goddess? Ultimately the redhead would get him back.

Meanwhile, Michael's thoughts were quite the opposite. Now that he observed what a leather clad, celebrity seeking, cleavage exposing prima donna Marguerite truly was, he felt almost relieved to have escaped a more entangled relationship with the paradoxical young woman, who at this moment appeared to be a good deal more dominant than she was ever submissive. Fortunately, Marguerite could not read minds, because the tenor of Michael's alcohol muddled thoughts would have thoroughly twisted the knife.

William was finally able to pounce on Marnie Price in The Rose Parlor.

"Got you!" William snatched her by the wrist and dragged her over to a Victorian settee, whereupon he sat down and yanked her across his lap. "Now you're going to get it!" he promised, deftly unstrapping the quiver on her back, which still contained two arrows, and tossed it aside, while restraining Marnie with his other hand.

And Marnie was not a girl to be easily restrained. From the moment he touched her she'd resisted with all of her considerable strength. Now that she was pinned across his knees, she struggled heroically to free herself from his leaden grip. "Give up," he told her. "You can't get away from me." Her full but extremely firm buttocks, so snugly encased in the nubby green tights, were ideally formed for corporal discipline. He raised his arm to give them the attention they deserved.

But this was not a spanking that was meant to occur. Before he could bring his palm crashing down even once on her beautiful bottom, the gods intervened for Marnie, in the form of her brother, who all but began to foam at the mouth when he passed the open doorway and observed what William Random was about to do.

"Get your hands off my sister!" Randy barked, charging into the room. William pushed Marnie off his lap so that she fell to the rug with a thud. Then William got to his feet.

Marnie saw what happened next in a blur. Undeniably, Randy threw the first punch. That was very like her brother, especially when he'd had a few drinks. But anyone could see that it was not a fair fight. This Neanderthal who had tried to spank her was obviously an athlete, while her brother was a dissipated punk.

Randy had initiated hundreds of fistfights in his life; most resulting in him being knocked down. This had not deterred him from making a career out of baiting people to the point of violence. This was not the first time Marnie had seen Randy knocked out, but usually he regained consciousness in a couple of seconds. Marnie checked her brother out then looked up at William.

"He's never been out cold for this long. We should call an ambulance."

William looked at Randy, to make sure he wasn't faking. He hadn't hit him very hard.

"He must have hit his head on the floor," William said, punching 911 on the nearest phone dial.

Randy Price awoke seconds later and Marnie had William cancel the distress call. An awestruck Laura let her husband take her home; and Marguerite enchanted the composer from New York, who began to fall in love with Random Point.

Chapter Five

Warmest Wishes

Michael Flagg didn't know it was Marguerite Alexander's birthday that day in Christmas week, when he visited her shop in search of books to help him get his brand new wife off drugs.

There was more than the usual amount of browsers that afternoon, due to the post holiday sale. Assisting Marguerite at the cash register was her best friend, Laura Random, a soft brunette whose composed demeanor concealed a much more tempestuous personality than that of her showier, red-haired friend.

Once Laura spotted the attractive young detective, who had engaged in a passionate affair with Marguerite back in the Autumn, Laura could not take Michael aside quickly enough to let him know that she would very much enjoy watching him give Marguerite the thirty-one swats which were her due.

Marguerite, who was chatting with a customer before an enormous Swedish stove, did not fail to notice, with a spasm of profound infatuation, that Michael was in her shop again, that Laura was talking to him in a disturbingly conspiratorial manner, that they were looking at her, and that Michael had started to smile.

"I dare you," Laura challenged, her demure facade dropping away.

"You little brat!" Michael accused. "You're the one who needs the spanking!"

Laura blushed and cried, "But it isn't my birthday!"

"So what? I missed your last one, didn't I?"

"But what about Marguerite?" Laura pressed him.

"She'd hate a public spanking," he maintained.

"Why do you say that? I've known Marguerite since college. She's into it."

"Giving, maybe."

"Who told you that?" Laura demanded.

"She did."

"You must not be much of a detective if you can't figure out when a simple girl like Marguerite is lying," Laura declared, in a way that made Michael Flagg again consider spanking her instead of Marguerite.

"I think it would be much more amusing if you were to volunteer to take Marguerite's birthday spanking for her. Don't you?" Michael took Laura out from behind the counter and across the room to Marguerite. When he wished her a happy birthday and kissed her face she almost purred.

"Your friend is quite an instigator," Michael reported to Marguerite, catching Laura's wrist in a hard grip as she tried to inch away.

"That doesn't surprise me," replied Marguerite tartly. "Ever since she lost her angel wings she's been a holy terror."

"How did that happen?" Michael kept a tight grip on Laura, who was still attempting to bolt.

"She cheated on her husband and got away with it - - so now she thinks she can get away with anything."

"Let her get away with it, did he? Now that surprises me," Michael observed.

"My husband doesn't feel threatened by any man!" Laura returned with positive arrogance.

"H'm, I suppose that's one way of looking at it," reflected Michael. (But if he ever caught Damaris fooling around...!)

"Don't tell us you're expecting your wife to be faithful to you, Michael!" Laura baited him, for she was feeling contrary that day.

"And why shouldn't I expect exactly that?"

"Well, we know she didn't scruple to sleep with her boss, who was also another woman's husband," the brunette riposted, referring to her own history with Michael's bride.

"I assure you that Damaris has been totally reformed and now holds the sacred marriage vows in the highest esteem," reported Flagg.

Laura chuckled.

"What was Laura attempting to instigate?" Marguerite asked.

"I was only teasing," said Laura, still trying to wrench her arm away.

"She wanted to watch me birthday spank you," said Michael. "Right here in the shop."

"Oh, did she?" Marguerite was clearly not amused.

"I told her she ought to be the one getting spanked, as a special entertainment for your birthday," Michael reported to Marguerite, and in so saying, took a seat on one of the low wooden stools which flanked the old fashioned stove, and turned Laura over his knee.

Marguerite, who noticed several customers pause with books held in midair to watch this extraordinary event, casually announced to the dozen or so people in immediate earshot, that Laura Random was about to receive a traditional birthday from Random Point's own Detective Flagg. Everyone beamed at such cuteness and stopped to watch.

"Shall we have Mrs. Random count, or do you want to count?" Michael asked Marguerite, pausing, with his large, heavy palm resting squarely on the luscious curve of Laura's pert right bottom cheek, snugly encased in a wool flannel skirt.

"I'll count," said Marguerite, folding her arms and leaning back against a counter.

Michael's hand descended with a swift report, drawing a shocked gasp from Laura upon impact.

Marguerite said, "One."

"It's fitting that you take your best friend's spanking," Michael told Laura, vigorously bringing his palm down again.

Marguerite said, "Two!"

"Because," Michael continued, "you are obviously the naughtier girl."

Now Michael administered ten medium hard smacks to alternate cheeks, and these were duly counted aloud by Marguerite, who was becoming transfixed by the spectacle of her traitorous friend being chastised like an irritating child by her ex-lover. Marguerite thought,

"Better you than me," yet it almost pained her to watch another woman being held, handled and thoroughly controlled by the man she still wanted more violently than any other. Was she jealous or thrilled as she watched that uncompromising hand come down?

After the 12th smack fell smartly upon Laura's perfectly rounded, though slim, shapely bottom, Michael commented, "She isn't even feeling this," and began to raise her skirt.

"Michael, no!" cried Laura, shocked, trying to fight him and hold down her skirt. He ended by pinning both skirt and wrist to the small of her back with one hand. This procedure revealed the lower half of a silk crepe teddy, in a spotted print of crimson, orange and gold, trimmed with crimson Calais lace. Except for Marguerite, no one watching had ever beheld such a lavish undergarment before, and a couple of low whistles went around the room. The teddy, which displayed virtually the entire lower half of Laura's perfect bottom in this position, was also off-set by a black satin garter belt, the suspenders of which were attached to sheer, black, seamed stockings. The picture of the pin-up was completed by a pair of 4" stacked, ankle strap heels.

Observing this scene, wide eyed and athrill, a happy prep school boy standing closest to the action, was not the only male to suddenly find himself with tented trousers in Marguerite's overheated bookshop. Even those who weren't into spanking, as most people in this world are not, couldn't fail to be charmed by the lascivious yet elegant sight of Laura's half bare, lightly pinkened backside bouncing under Michael Flagg's huge, paddling hand.

"Marguerite, don't let him do this to me!" cried Laura, still struggling to break free.

"I believe we were at 12," Marguerite told Michael coolly.

"Right," said Michael, tightening his grip on Laura's waist and spanking her again, but more slowly, and harder. Each time Michael's palm came down, the force of the swat caused Laura to kick up her slender legs high in the air. However, she'd decided she wasn't going to give any of these horrible people the satisfaction of hearing her cry! At any rate, she thought, this couldn't last much longer. He now was at twenty. Eleven more to go, or twelve at most.

Laura would just have to get through this as she survived every other ordeal as a submissive, like a good sport. It didn't really bother her to have a roomful of strangers watch her get a spanking. She knew how sweet and interesting her charms must appear to every man who had bothered to stand still and watch. Possibly some of the Random Point matrons were enjoying the performance as well. What bothered her was being treated so summarily by Michael Flagg, who'd laid hands on her just as though he had the right to!

"Oh, Michael," said Marguerite, "do give Laura something interesting marks to show William tonight!"

Michael stayed his hand looked at Marguerite questioningly.

"Do you suppose he'll be amused to learn that his wife provoked a public spanking?" Marguerite murmured, with a flash of spite. She still couldn't believe that Laura had attempted to goad Michael into turning her, Marguerite, over his knee, in her own shop! For that piece of insolence from her dearest girlfriend, Marguerite could not seem to get enough satisfaction.

"Michael, don't you dare mark me!" Laura cried, horrified by the idea of having to explain any of this to William, and forgetting all about good sportsmanship.

But Michael had no intention of placing the smallest mark on Laura's flawless bottom and was shocked at the unapologetic manipulativeness operating in both the bosom friends. The problem with Marguerite and Laura was that they were a couple of jaded brats. Michael was heartily glad that his own little beauty, with all of her faults, was nowhere near as diabolical as this scheming pair.

"I think Laura's had enough," Michael said, letting the brunette up. "Now it's your turn," he told Marguerite, taking her by the arm and leading her back to her office.

Setting herself to rights, Laura realized that she had no choice but to return to her duties at the cash register. But at least she'd escaped being marked. What a relief! Now William would never have to know about the mischief she'd gotten up to today.

She was certain Michael Flagg could have marked her with ease, leaving an imprint that might have lasted for days with a couple of emphatic smacks. The current pinkness would fade long before the evening. It was probably already no more than a blush. Laura delighted in Michael's gallantry in not giving into Marguerite's evil demands.

Many times in the weeks to come, Laura would relive various aspects of her experience that day. The shop, spectators and even Marguerite, would melt away in retrospect, leaving behind only the actual sensation of being held down across those tree trunk thighs and firmly spanked by the superb Michael Flagg.

Meanwhile, Michael shut the door to Marguerite's office, while the bookshop owner retreated behind her desk.

"That was a very irresponsible request you just made about me marking Laura," Michael told her.

"I notice you didn't do it," Marguerite replied crossly. She never seemed to get her own way!

"Come here, you," he said, crossing to her and taking her in his arms. "You're not getting spanked, but you are getting something for your birthday!" he promised. Then he bent her over her own desk, pulled up her skirt and unzipped his trousers.

"You stop!" cried Marguerite. "How dare you? You may not!" She was outraged, had he obeyed her just then, she never would have forgiven him. "You... you wolf!" she accused as he pulled her black silk panties down to her creamy white thighs.

"I'm sorry, but you brought this on yourself," he sighed. When he took her by the waist and drove into her to the hilt, she was very glad that she had. "Why, you naughty girl," he said. "You're rather wet! I believe you enjoyed watching me spank your girl friend."

As he had begun to thrust into her slow, hard and deep with all 7.5" of his cock (measured topside), Marguerite could only whimper in response. If only he did this a little more often, not just on her birthday, Marguerite might be able to forgive him for marrying someone else.

Michael gave Marguerite the rest of the spanking that Laura had escaped, while he was driving into her, and Marguerite adored it. A resounding smack could be highly stimulating, when one was in the proper mood and the one giving it was charming.

Twenty minutes later, when Michael walked back out into the shop, of the people who had witnessed Laura's spanking, only the adolescent boy remained milling around the area in front of Marguerite's new stove, unwilling or unable to remove his eyes from the girl who was now so calmly ringing up sales.

As Michael passed her counter he leveled a stern glance at Laura and told her to behave. The rueful smile with which she responded to this injunction let him know that she was not upset with him. And the seductive look she flashed him from beneath her long lashes as he went out the door with the tinkling bell was easily understood as an invitation to punish her again whenever he liked.

He'd never bought the book on conquering addiction for Damaris, but that was probably just as well. How many girls could he reasonably hope to correct in one day?

Chapter Six

The Honeymoon Is Over

"Don't you want to quit smoking?" Michael Flagg demanded of Damaris, on the first day he began working nights.

His pretty, black-haired wife of one season paled and crushed out her cigarette. "I don't know if I can," she protested, but quailed when he narrowed his eyes.

"You can," he insisted, rising from the table, after one of her excellent suppers.

"I'm too nervous," she maintained, watching him strap on his shoulder holster and insert his service revolver.

"Damaris, get a grip on yourself," he suggested without sympathy.

"But what if I can't?"

Michael said put on his jacket, saying, "You'll get a good strapping if I catch you backsliding." He pocketed her Luckys. "Understand me, young lady?"

Damaris flushed and bit her lip, but meekly replied, "Yes."

"Yeah, I'll bet," he said before going out the door.

As adorably submissive as she was, Damaris had no more impulse to obey her husband's edicts than any modern, non-submissive married woman might, and probably less, since her multiple vices still exerted more influence over her than her conscience. She would naturally continue doing just as she pleased, though perhaps a bit more slyly than before.

Several nights later, at the off-color hour of two a.m. Damaris finished her shift inputting copy at the local type house and arrived home mere moments before her husband unexpectedly walked in.

Halfway through his own shift, he had taken a break to stop home, mainly to make sure that his wife had returned from her evening job without mishap.

Unfortunately for Damaris, Michael had already filed two reports that night on accidents caused by individuals driving while under the influence. Therefore when he smelled the telltale odor of marijuana on Damaris, it was enough to make him lose his temper.

"So! This is how you keep your word," he charged, while unbuckling his belt. "Well let me demonstrate how I keep mine!"

"Hey wait!" she protested, backing away. "You said stop smoking cigarettes!"

"Come over here!" he took her by the elbow. "You're getting a licking!" Then he bent her over the back of the tufted leather sofa in their sitting room.

Damaris had never received a strapping and was shocked to feel him folding back her skirt and pulling down her panties before beginning. His fashionably slim leather belt snapped across her smooth, pale bottom fifteen times. Each stroke stung and penetrated deeply. He was harsh and made her cry.

He pinned her to the sofa with one hand in the small of her back, pushing up her skirt while firmly holding her in place. The other hand wielded the strap, hard enough to make her sob each time it smartly cracked against her pearly flesh.

"You'd better start thinking of this as your own personal rehab clinic. You'd be in one now if I'd arrested you like I should have that night I caught you with all that coke," he told her, as she buried her face in her hands and her thin shoulders shook. "It's really greatly similar. You get to do all the humbling chores you can stand, but instead of tedious group therapy sessions, you get corporal punishment. No compulsory drug testing and no enforced surrender to a power any higher than myself. Haven't you got the best of all possible worlds?" But Damaris was sobbing too violently to respond.

Michael neither soothed nor caressed her after finally letting her go, but instead coolly put on his topcoat and left to complete his shift without a backward glance. He was extremely disappointed with

Damaris.

Meanwhile Damaris tried to decide whether the show of force to which she'd just been treated qualified as discipline, wife beating or police brutality. Had he comforted her after the strapping, which had left her bottom violently striped, there would have been no question in her passionate, fiercely devoted mind. But his indifference left her feeling dejected, betrayed and a little afraid. She wondered, as she wept, how far he might go in his efforts to make her conform. Damaris considered strapping a form of tenement discipline, insultingly unsuitable to her tender self. What next? The cane viciously applied in the manner of an English corporal punishment video? "Whipping in" with the birch as described in the novels of Dedeaux?

At dawn she was shocked to discover her bottom latticed with smears of black and blue. As often as he'd spanked her with his heavy hand, Flagg had never marked her, nor had anyone else. She had no way of knowing how long the marks might last and their appearance depressed her. Then he didn't call. This hurt Damaris very much.

She knew his schedule. His shift would end at seven, after which he would go work out at the gym before coming home for the day. Their large, handsome apartment was already immaculate, but Damaris cleaned for hours while she waited for her husband to get home. She was aching for a smoke now, but for once, she didn't dare.

That morning it was blustery and raining; still she showered, changed her clothes and went out. Had it been a normal day she would have gone to the bakery for fresh bread or rolls for Michael's breakfast. As it was, she didn't know where to go. Rather than wander around aimlessly she decided to go back to the type house and work a half shift, but she couldn't concentrate on her word processing tasks and after an hour she claimed a headache and left. Several minutes after Damaris walked out of the typing bureau, her husband called for her.

Damaris drove her little car out to the beach, which was completely deserted in the wind, cold and rain. She got out of the car and walked. As he'd never think of looking for her here, she smoked with abandon. The churning of the choppy slate-grey sea soon lifted her spirits and Damaris began to feel better. She decided to visit Laura, who lived in the cul-de-sac at the end of Shadow Lane.

Twenty minutes later she was pulling up her skirt and lowering her black wool tights to show Laura the purple marks Michael's belt had left upon her perfect bottom.

"He did that to me just for smoking a joint!" Damaris complained, setting her clothes to rights.

"That must have really stung!" Laura said with feeling.

"Did William ever use his belt on you?"

"Not like that," replied Laura, trying to imagine how it might have felt to be punished so severely by Michael Flagg. "But it's your own fault for getting caught," Laura observed. "You're going to have to learn how to cover your tracks. If William found out every time I did something he doesn't approve of, I'd be permanently marked. Learn how to sneak!"

Laura extracted a cigarette from Damaris' pack and enjoyed an illicit smoke with her husband's ex-secretary.

"It must be easy to get things by William. He's so self-absorbed. But Michael isn't that way. His whole new hobby is catching me at things. And he is a detective."

"So what? He's only a man, which means he can be deceived."

However, when William walked into the room where the two girls were drinking coffee a few minutes later, he flashed Laura such a disapproving glance and slapped his Wall Street Journal against his thigh so emphatically that her cockiness was instantly vaporized.

"Get over here," he told Laura from the doorway, while giving Damaris a cool nod. As soon as Laura emerged into the hall William flung down his paper and dragged his wife into the kitchen.

"What do you think, you can do whatever you like now?" William demanded, pulling a straight-backed chair into the middle of the floor and taking Laura straight across his lap. "Didn't I tell you to stay away from that …that traitor?!" Smack! "Was I talking to myself?" Smack! Smack! Smack! The palm of his hand came down hard on Laura's bottom through her wool challis skirt. Each spank made her kick up her legs, which were shod in dainty little Victorian boots that laced tightly to the ankle. "This is my house," William told her. "See that you don't forget it again!"

William pushed the bell-shaped paisley skirt up to her waist to finish spanking Laura on the seat of her cranberry silk-satin briefs. He did not need to lower these luxurious underpinnings to make his displeasure felt.

"Tell me what she's doing here," William demanded of Laura, who'd been gasping between wallops, "If it's a good enough reason I'll postpone the rest of this until later and return you to your guest."

"Damaris was upset —" Laura began to explain, twisting around on his lap to fix him with her most appealing doe-eyed gaze.

"Talk fast, I'm getting bored," William said, pushing her head back down and tightening his grip on her slender waist before delivering a brisk, measured volley of half a dozen smacks.

"I'll tell you if you'll let me!" Laura twisted again and put back her hand to protect her satin-wrapped oval cheeks. "Michael gave her a terrible strapping! And she's never been marked before. She didn't know what to think!" Laura blurted out dramatically.

"Ha!" William snorted. "The both of you girls should be permanently marked!"

Laura was relieved to be set back on her feet. She meekly followed William back into the sitting room, giving her bottom a rub through her skirt.

"I'm intrigued," William said to Damaris, who was blushing with embarrassment at what she had just over-heard. "Let me see the damage." He folded his arms and waited.

"Go on, Damaris," Laura urged, "Show William. He'll tell you whether Michael went too far." William gave Laura a look, as much to say that such a thing was hardly possible.

Damaris pulled her skirt up and lowered her tights a second time that morning.

"Very sexy," William commented, without hesitation. Then he added, for the sake of her dignity, "Looks like you took a pretty good strapping, young lady." Damaris dropped her skirt again but her blush was slow to fade.

"He'd never used a strap on her before," Laura helpfully put in, by way of explaining the emergency nature of the visit and hence her decision to override his rule against fraternizing with an employee he'd had to dismiss as a result of criminal conduct.

"Let's hope it's the beginning of a trend," said William. "I can't think of a more deserving recipient." And yet he was becoming tired of staying angry with his excitingly submissive ex-secretary, who seemed so ideally suited to be his wife's companion and cherished friend.

"So...you don't think what he gave me was so bad?" Damaris asked William, hesitantly, even while knowing he'd be bound to take her husband's side

"Whatever it was you did, you got off easy," William said. "And you ought to be glad you've got a man who cares enough about you to accept the Herculean labor of correcting your faults."

"I would be glad if I did think he cared, but I know he doesn't like me now at all!" Damaris said, then she let it spill out all at once in a flurry of sobs, how he had simply walked out after punishing her - how he'd been a block of ice!

As Damaris dissolved into a bundle of tears, Laura said, "You see!"

"Now look here, Damaris, you're all wrong about Michael," William said.

"He only married me because he felt sorry for me," Damaris whimpered. "He hates me for being weak. I'm a grave disappointment to him," Damaris was careful to articulate between sobs. "He really loves that redhead, Marguerite."

"All men love Marguerite," Laura said. "That doesn't mean a thing. After all, he married you."

"So you don't think Michael cares for you!" William took Damaris by the hand. "Come with me, young lady. I want to show you something!" They went into William's study, where he selected a blue print from a long, flat wooden drawer and spread it out on his drawing board. "I don't ordinarily discuss my clients' projects until they are under construction, but I don't think this particular client will mind my doing so, especially since it directly concerns you."

Damaris gazed at the blueprints, mystified.

"These are the plans to your new house," said William.

"Michael's having you build a house for him?"

"For you, silly. Look, it's even going to have a cozy little dungeon for your punishments."

Damaris was overwhelmed.

"See here? It's even got a nursery," William said.

"Shut up!" Damaris cried, coloring.

"It's for you," William replied. "For when you need that sort of therapy. It's the first house I've ever designed for a client in the scene and it's going to be really special."

Damaris was touched, thanked William and hastened to her car.

"Don't forget to act surprised when he tells you," William warned.

When Damaris got home she found that her husband had fallen asleep, fully dressed on the four-poster in the little back room with the window on the woods. He awoke at the sound of her footfall.

"Come over here, you brat. Where have you been?" He wrapped his arms around her when she came to him, making her sit in his lap. He seemed very glad to see her and kiss her full red lips. "I was beginning to wonder if you'd left me," he told her, reluctant to break the embrace. She shook her head but couldn't speak. She was embarrassed. "Did you think about leaving me?"

"No!" Damaris lied.

"Let me see your bottom."

Damaris shook her head again and tried to resist, but he easily turned her over on his lap, pulled up her skirt and rolled down her tights to reveal her firm, round, thoroughly marked bare behind. He stroked and kissed the punished flesh.

"Poor baby," Michael said softly, and Damaris knew this was much of an apology as she was going to get. He righted her once more on his lap and crushed her to his chest.

"You feel sorry for me?" she asked.

"Not nearly as sorry as you feel for yourself," he replied.

"I can see that you're not at all sorry for thrashing me!" she accused, looking into his cool, pale eyes with her enormous, glittering black ones. As she began to complain of her whipping, she felt something throb under her. "Oh, The Beast!" Damaris thought; "He's getting turned on!

"I'm as sorry for given you a licking as you are for disobeying me."

"It's true, I'm only sorry I got caught," Damaris declared, with some spirit.

"That's why I'm not sorry I thrashed you."

"I'm afraid of you now!" she exclaimed, resentfully, which made him throb again.

"You'd better be afraid of me," he told her sternly. Instantly, a blush suffused her cheeks and Damaris hid her face between his shoulder and throat. Flagg's raging erection sent an urgent message to his brain, but he decided to ignore it for the moment and continued to cuddle her.

Michael told her, "The odds are against you. You're genuinely naughty and I genuinely like to spank you hard. Even if you tried to be good, you'd slip up constantly. So any way you look at it, you're in for many trips to the woodshed in the years to come."

"We don't have a woodshed," Damaris murmured, enjoying the feel of his tightening arms.

"Don't you worry, we will," Flagg promised.

Chapter Seven

Irresistible Force

It was a foggy afternoon in mid-winter and Susan Ross, 18, was peddling a bike around Random Point in her usual self-absorbed daze, when she cut off a very large, vintage silver sedan that had the right of way.

As the Bentley screeched to a halt to avoid steam-rolling her, the driver rolled his window down and screamed: "WAKE UP!!!"

Continuing to coast across the cobbled intersection, the small blonde craned her head around to scrutinize the savage pilot of this impressive vehicle, a gentleman roughly twice her age, of an appealing, clean-shaven, suited demeanor. His sharp, dark eyes held her blue ones in a fascinating gaze that proved her immediate downfall. There had been a thaw that morning, but ice still glazed the streets in spots. Susan skidded onto a glassy patch, the front wheel went out under her, down went her bike and Susan followed immediately thereafter, spilling off to one side and landing on her right hip and the heel of her right hand.

The expensively tailored gentleman was out of his car in a heartbeat. "Are you okay?" he cried, helping her back up to her to her feet, which were very dainty ones, in tiny, lacing ankle boots. Susan Ross wore a cream wool sweater and blue tartan skirt. Nubby cream tights snugly wrapped her shapely little legs; a white blouse with a Peter Pan collar underlined her rosy, heart shaped face and a blue beret adorned her tawny head.

He sat her on the hood of his awe-inspiring car, and began boldly kneading her voluptuous calves through her thick woolen tights, ostensibly feeling for broken bones.

"Is anything twisted or sprained? What were you thinking of, running that light?"

His fingers were deft and extremely strong. He was agile and faintly redolent of some classically masculine scent. He continued to question her reason while examining her. "Do you always ride so recklessly? Don't you realize you might have been killed? I have a good mind to turn you over my knee for almost giving me cardiac arrest!"

Susan had fallen on her hip, but she saw no reason to confess this when his squeezing her legs felt so delightful.

"...And you've ruined your pretty skirt!" he concluded his harangue, which had combined elements of concern, irritation and frank interest.

"How come you have a car like this? Are you a V.I.P.?" she demanded.

"Anthony Newton," he said, extending his hand, fairly confident that this would mean something to her. He'd been famous for a long time.

"You're Anthony Newton?" Susan colored up and dropped his hand. Her pulse, which was only beginning to slow down after the spanking threat, began to race again.

"You have heard of me! I'm relieved."

"You're the man Hugo said I was to visit this evening. You just bought the Cliff House, right?"

"Hugo Sands was sending you to see me?" Newton was puzzled and pulled an appointment notebook from an inner jacket pocket. He flicked through the pages rapidly then looked up at Susan with something approaching enchantment. "Are you Susan Ross, the Art Student from Boston who is, and I quote: submissive and decidedly anal?"

"Who said that?" Susan cried, trying to look into the notebook and blushing even more deeply.

"This is too good to be true!" pronounced Newton gleefully. "Sands told me about you in detail, of course, but I didn't believe a word. Now here you are exactly as foretold! A life-sized baby doll for me to play with!" He seized his new toy her around her tiny waist, lifted her up off the hood, then set her back down, as can easily be done with a hundred and five pound girl.

"You're not to believe a thing Hugo said!" Susan protested, scarlet now. "He was kidding you."

"If that's the case then why were you coming to me at six o'clock?" Newton snapped.

"Hugo probably thought I'd enjoy meeting a famous ..." Susan squirmed, as she couldn't remember exactly what Newton was famous for and finished lamely, "...celebrity!"

"Don't fib," Newton chided; "You know you only heard my name for the first time when Hugo gave you your — dare I say — first assignment?"

"I don't know what you mean by assignment," Susan became flustered, jumped off the car and made for the fallen bike.

"You will. Just be at my house at the appointed hour and all will be revealed."

"I'll think about it," Susan said airily, righting the bike and mounting the seat.

"Don't make me come and find you!" Newton threatened with relish as she cutely peddled down the lane without looking over her shoulder this time.

"Just as long as you weren't rude to him..." Laura Random said to her younger sister as she drove her up the road to the Cliff House on that rainy December evening.

"I wasn't rude to him. Maybe a little fresh..." Susan fretted.

"That sounds like you," Laura observed.

"I'm getting this terrible feeling that it's going to be like with Hugo, where he plays with me once, I fall madly in love and he loses interest right away."

"I don't think Hugo has lost interest in you. He did arrange tonight's meeting after all," Laura pointed out.

"Right, to palm me off on some other devastatingly attractive older man who may also get bored with me after one night! Damn it Laura, these older men have ruined me for boys my own age. They just know so much more."

"We're here," said Laura, pulling up in front of the imposing main entrance of the twenty-five--room house. "Better run in. You don't want to annoy him by being late."

The next thing Susan knew she was standing in front of the Cliff House alone. Before she had a chance to knock the door swung open and Newton greeted her.

"Hello. I saw you drive up. Was that your ravishing sister with you? You should have brought her in! I'm certainly going to spank you for that!" he told her pleasantly, and actually took her over to the staircase that wound grandly up to the second floor, used the third step as a bench, sat down and hauled the little pony tailed blonde right across his lap. Then he briskly proceeded to dust off the seat of her slim cut pegged jeans with the palm of his hand.

"Oh! Ow! Stop! You can't!" Susan cried, kicking her miniature feet, which were shod in shiny black penny loafers and white sox.

"How sweet of you to dress like this," he said, running his hand across the snug seat of her jeans. "And I love the ponytail," Newton added. Her bottom was beautifully rounded and firm. And her reactions were a joy to him. A tap had her kicking her legs. "But why didn't you ask your sister in?" he demanded, spanking her ten or twelve times sharply.

"I didn't think I was supposed to," she replied.

"Next time please remember that you're supposed to," he said, letting her up with a final few smacks.

Susan was amazed at how long the feeling, the actual sting of those twenty or so sharp smacks remained with her. She fancied she could feel them a full fifteen minutes later, though they hadn't seemed particularly hard.

When he pushed her off his lap her legs felt weak. She was dizzy with excitement. He saw everything in her face and kissed her passionately on the mouth. Then he took her by the hand and dragged her after him. "Come with me, young lady," he said with determination. "The only proper place for our first formal interview is the library!"

Newton's impulsiveness confused her, however she allowed him to pull her along, a waifish figure in her little black cotton turtleneck, snug chinos and childish white sox, noticing none of the house's elegant features as she went.

In the oak-paneled library, classic bastion of the upscale disciplinarian, Newton made her sit in an enormous leather arm chair, which dwarfed her, while he paced the floor and lectured her on traffic safety and visiting strange men in their homes without a chaperone. Susan couldn't concentrate on what he was saying. Somewhere between the staircase and the study she had fallen in love.

"There's no question in my mind that you need a really sound spanking, little miss!" Newton said happily, dropping down to kneel before her so that they were eye to eye. She was too embarrassed to look at him, and hide her face against his chest.

"What are you thinking?" Newton coaxed gently.

Susan whimpered, "You have a hard hand!"

"If it's too hard just say mercy," said Newton, lifting her off the chair and taking her place on it, then putting her back over his knee. Tightening his grip on her waist he began to spank her over her jeans, his palm first falling on the right side of her bottom, then the left, as though he were in no great hurry. "Relax, little girl," he advised her; "You know I'm not going to hurt you."

Susan's tiny clitoris began to ache with longing. She couldn't help but whimper while he spanked her. For although the smacks were by no means severe, the way he held her, firmly and close up against his trim torso, made her feel like a very small child.

"Get up!" he told her suddenly. "And get those jeans down." She hesitantly obeyed. "Those are awfully grown-up panties for a little girl like you!" Newton remarked of her sheer black bikinis. He pulled her back down across his lap and spanked her on the seat of her nylon panties. "This is for wearing provocative lingerie," he told her. Then his hand fell many times, taking Susan's breath away.

"That's better," he reported at length. "Pink and black go together. Now let's have these down!" And he rolled her panties down with such infinite slowness that she thought she would swoon with embarrassment.

"Getting used to being over my knee, Susan?"

"No!" Susan replied, in spite of her enthrallment.

"Well you'd better get used to it because there's still the matter of you cutting me off in the village today to be dealt with. I certainly intend to punish you for that!"

Newton was now inclined to lingeringly stroke her small, plump cheeks, which were pink from his hand.

"It's been so long since I've spanked a natural blonde, I'd forgotten how quickly they color up!" Anthony commented. "But this bruise on your poor, little hip! Tsk, tsk!" he lamented, lightly tracing the outline of a sizeable hematoma on her upper left hip from where she had fallen on the cobblestones. Susan's hand went back to cover the offending mark.

"I know it's horrid!" she cried, adding, "I shouldn't have come!"

"Move your hand," Newton said.

"No, I won't have you looking at it!" she insisted, simultaneously attempting to cover the bruise and wriggle off his lap.

"Where do you think you're going? You stay put!" he instructed, capturing her slim wrist and pinning it to the small of her back while administering a half dozen stinging swats to either side of her bottom. Susan cried out with surprise as each successive spank fell, as these smacks were sharp!

"Ouch! Ow! Oh!" Susan intoned, as she jerked about on his lap in her efforts to avoid his punishing hand.

"Settle down, young lady," Newton warned. "You've got a sound spanking coming for scaring the life out of me this afternoon!"

His stern tone stilled her kicking legs momentarily. He took the opportunity to pull her jeans off completely, as they had been bunched around her ankles and inhibiting a full range of movement. He also pulled her panties completely off, so that her shapely lower half was bare from her waist to her bobby sox.

"That's right," Newton continued, "You calm down and behave. I think you're beginning to realize that I'm serious now."

"I didn't mean to cut you off!" Susan twisted her torso around to cast him a look that was the picture of contrition.

Newton pushed her head back down, saying, "It's a bit late for apologies now. You're getting spanked!" With that he raised his arm and brought it down hard and fast sixty or seventy times. Susan kicked her legs so high she almost kicked him in the head several times. Finally he solved this annoying problem by locking one of his legs over the backs of her knees.

"Please stop!" she whimpered desperately, terrified of being locked in place across his lap.

"Not until I'm positive that you will never run a light again."

"I swear I won't!" Susan cried desperately.

"Very well then, how many more will you take to prove that you're sincere?"

"More?"

"More."

"Um...one?"

"I'm afraid that isn't good enough," Newton said with a sigh. "I don't think you're taking this seriously."

"Oh dear! I mean — one dozen more!" Susan quickly amended.

"One dozen more it is then. And since you've decided to take responsibility for your actions I'll tell you right now that you only have to worry about the last one."

"Oh!" He was really awful, thought Susan, bracing for a heavy assault. But instead of spanking her terribly hard, he took his leg off the backs of her knees and let go of her wrist. Then he renewed his firm hold on her slim waist, bent to plant a kiss on the back of her neck, just behind one pink shell ear, and gave her a slow eleven finishing smacks, which were hard enough to sting, but not to make her kick or squirm. When the last smack fell it was only the lightest of pats, yet the threat of a hard one to finish had kept her tense and panting for the entire dozen.

Susan began to rub her bottom and complain the instant he put her off his lap. "You said you weren't going to hurt me!" she charged, snatching her panties off the carpet and snapping them back on in a blink. For a long, drowsy moment Newton seemed content to lounge in the large leather chair with his fingers lazily laced behind his head while he watched her scamper to retrieve her far flung penny loafers and jeans. Then he suddenly sprung to his feet with a surge of frenetic energy.

"Where are my manners? Here you are, my guest, and I haven't even offered you refreshments! Come with me." He grabbed her by the hand and she trotted after him to the kitchen.

"I find it amazing that you're taking all of this so calmly, young lady," Anthony observed, watching her devour meat sandwiches; "Don't you realize that meeting me could change your entire life?"

"I don't need my entire life changed, I just need a boyfriend," she replied pragmatically.

"Why stop there? How about adding my initial to your monogram?"

"Ha ha," laughed Susan.

"What's the matter, don't you believe in marriage?"

"Sure, I guess so," Susan thoughtfully replied. "But I'm a free spirit."

"I've been married five times myself," he confessed proudly; "And I'm on excellent terms with all my ex-wives."

"How come you keep getting divorced?"

"Chronic unfaithfulness."

"On your part?"

"Exactly."

"Why?"

"Because none of my wives were into spanking and I consequently spent a large portion of my time in the company of professional submissives. This proved unacceptable to my wives."

"How did you manage to avoid scandals?"

"Large cash settlements or alimony checks to follow until the end of time."

"What do you do with these professional submissives you mentioned?"

"Everything I did and am going to do with you," he explained, pouring her a cup of tea.

"My sister does professional sessions sometimes. Maybe you'd like to play with her instead of me," Susan suggested casually.

"I would like to play with her, but not instead of you," Newton firmly replied; "I see that like most would-be submissives you're already trying to run things!"

"I'm finished. Thank you," she pushed her plate and cup away and neatly wiped her mouth with a napkin like a well-behaved child.

"Ready to let me subject you to one or more of those embarrassing ordeals I was told you were interested in experiencing? I have all the equipment necessary to humiliate a naughty little girl."

Color flooded Susan's face, he was gratified to note, but she nodded and allowed him to pull her upstairs by the hand.

"You didn't think I'd forget what Hugo said about you being anal oriented, did you?" he teased.

"What are you going to do to me?"

"Everything you want and need."

Shadow Lane Volume 2

Return to Random Point

The Romance of Discipline,
Spanking, Sex, B&D and Anal Eroticism
in a Small New England Village

Contents

Chapter One

New Talent

Jane Eliot was an appealingly soft spoken young woman, and physically much to Hugo Sands' taste, yet even after watching her trim bottom wiggle around his shop for five months, he still was not tempted to seduce her.

The first time she bluntly suggested they sleep together, he felt flattered. He had even wanted to want her, but her lingering political correctness posed an obstacle he could see no way around. Ivy League bred, sophisticated, fair and rational, Hugo of course considered himself a fully evolved male whose properly raised consciousness gleamingly reflected the stringent feminist ideals of the 1970's. However, his sexuality, as he most often chose to express it, presented a direct contradiction to his politics, unless viewed through the eyes of a fellow devotee of the dominant/submissive subculture.

But Jane's comprehension of the masculine psyche was not keen, especially with regard to the more advanced examples of the sex. Her intelligence was quick but not penetrating. And it would never have occurred to her that a male she desired might possess a more complex and textured sexuality than her own. So that when he refused her overture, Jane was simply shocked.

"Are you offended by the notion of a sexually aggressive woman?" she demanded, cornering him in the galley, which connected to the lounge, in the rear of the large wooden building that housed his antiques shop.

"First of all, you're not sexually aggressive," Hugo informed her dryly. "You barely even know how to flirt."

Jane felt humiliated, because this was perfectly true.

Never the less, she argued, "A self realized woman is always direct."

"Jane, you know that your convictions clash with my proclivities," he countered cryptically.

"People can change," Jane protested weakly, not exactly sure of what he meant but willing to venture into uncharted territory.

"Do you think you're really ready to give yourself to me?"

"I'm ready to have sex with you."

"That's not the same thing," he replied and left her to wait on a customer whose arrival in the shop was heralded by the tinkle of the bells attached to the front door.

Growing lonelier for sexual companionship with every passing day, she approached him several more times about taking their relationship to a more intimate level. The more sincere her longing for him grew, the more bashful and self-conscious her forays into his editing offices became. Finally, this new and alluring shyness began to penetrate Hugo's defenses. However, he felt bound to speculate that she still wasn't ready for him.

"When will I be ready?" Jane demanded, one afternoon, as they were arranging the table for the cocktail party he was giving that evening to show some choice new acquisitions to a number of wealthy local collectors.

"Jane, this is not the time to discuss this. We have a lot of details to take care of before Mrs. Granville Reagle and her friends arrive."

Jane knew better than to argue with him, but brooded the entire afternoon while neatening up the stock. By and by the sun went down and Hugo's fur swathed matrons began to arrive. Unused to working after hours, Jane forgot she was on duty and drank two Greyhounds in rapid succession. Then she walked straight up to Hugo, interrupting his conversation with Mrs. Duncan Blandings, to pull him into his office and brazenly confront him with her cravings yet again. Emboldened by the spirits, to which she was unaccustomed, Jane gave voice to her frustration and confusion.

"Why are you being so elusive? I'm beginning to think that you're gay!"

"Jane, what the hell are you're doing? I have 20 customers out there and no one's on the floor. You're supposed to be working, remember? I was seriously interesting Mrs. Duncan Blandings in the rosewood writing desk. Are you mad to interrupt me like this?"

"I'm sorry!" she responded insincerely.

"Are you drunk?" he asked, lifting her chin and scrutinizing her eyes.

"No!"

"Yes, you are drunk! Well, I'll deal with you later!"

With that, Hugo strode back into the shop.

But when he got there, Mrs. Blandings had departed, along with Mrs. Granville Regal. This development peeved Hugo no end. It was uncanny the way Jane picked that particular moment to pester him. When Jane reemerged he gave her a look that froze her. She looked around and noticed that the best clients had left. "This is not good," she thought, sobering up. And then, she wrote no sales.

Hugo, on the other hand, could always move something, and was mollified when he managed to persuade William Random to buy a black lacquer art deco mirror for his wife. There were also some less significant sales. These events lessened Hugo's pique to a degree, but when the last patron had finally departed, he locked the door purposefully, and not just to count up the sales.

Jane's heart was fluttering when Hugo crossed the floor to seize her by her wrist and drag her back into his office. "Come with me, young lady!"

"Oh, Hugo, I'm so sorry about ruining your pitch!" she exclaimed.

"Not as sorry as you're going to be!" he promised, pulling her into his office and tossing her onto a tufted, brass riveted, chestnut brown leather sofa. "Sit down," he told her, then went behind his imposing desk, sat in his chair, irritably lit a cigarette and glared at Jane through the blue haze it emitted. Presently he spoke coldly.

"I'd just like to know what you were thinking to interrupt a discussion between me and my most valuable client to air your sexual frustrations?"

"I...wasn't thinking," Jane replied weakly.

"Do you think that was businesslike?"

"No," Jane meekly answered. "And I'm terribly sorry. I feel

horrible."

"I'm not impressed. And furthermore," he added, crushing out his cigarette, "I would like you to give me one good reason why I shouldn't put you over my knee and spank some common sense into you. And I do mean right now!"

Jane, who had never been quite so much in the wrong before, did not know what to say in her own defense. If only she herself had not behaved in such a highly objectionable manner! But as she thought of why she'd pulled him off the floor, she blushed with shame.

"Well, can you think of a single good reason why I shouldn't paddle you?" he demanded, coming to sit beside her. "Haven't you been childish?"

"Yes," Jane admitted, feeling her face grow warm as she unconsciously shifted away from him on the leather couch.

"Haven't you been completely thoughtless and totally unprofessional in your comportment?"

"Yes, Hugo," Jane agreed, staring down at the shiny hardwood floor. She'd begun to twist her hands in her lap.

"Why do I go to the expense of throwing parties and teas?"

"To sell," Jane replied, feeling quite as guilty as he wished her to feel.

"And who subverted my best efforts to do just that tonight?"

"...me," Jane almost sobbed with remorse.

"Jane, you're getting a spanking!" he told her, pulling her across his lap with one firm yank. She was lithe, slim and easily adjusted. That day she had on two-piece tweed dress with stacked, high-heeled pumps. He applied his palm as firmly as he knew how to the seat of her a-line skirt for two to three minutes without saying a word.

Jane made a number of protesting sounds, none of which could have been termed an actual word. Resigned to accepting the spanking, she soon mused, "This isn't so bad." Apart from the embarrassment of being held fast in this childish position, she couldn't say that it felt other than vaguely stimulating. This was the first physical contact they had ever had and in a strange way, it felt sexy.

"Are you learning a lesson?" he demanded, tightening his grip on her waist while smoothing her skirt down over her firm, oval buttocks.

"Yes," Jane choked on being spoken to like this, and yet she knew that she alone was to blame.

"You know, Jane, you've behaved like an impatient little girl," declared Hugo, just before lifting her skirt to expose her athletic legs and buttocks, snugly encased in a pair of sheer, seamed, black tinted tights, with a textured panty woven into the seat. When he stroked her through her designer pantyhose she shuddered. He noticed that she made no move to free herself. "However," he observed, "You're taking this very well. I may have to forgive you."

"I hope you do," she said, venturing a look over one shoulder.

"Sure. It could happen. But first you have to be thoroughly punished."

Jane bit her lip.

"Tearful supplications will get you nowhere," he informed her, gently pushing her head down and taking hold of her waist once more. "Jane, do you remember how much money I spent on the refreshments for tonight? You filed the receipt from the package store."

"It was about a hundred and eighty dollars," Jane replied, with trepidation. She was suddenly feeling very vulnerable.

"Then why don't I give you about a hundred and eighty smacks? That way I'll be able to feel I've gotten my money's worth."

"Oh!" cried Jane, as the spanking commenced, a bit sharper than before. In fact, the smacks grew somewhat harder with each short volley of five or six, until each one that fell began to impart a real sting.

"I hope you realize you're getting off lightly," Hugo informed her as she whimpered and squirmed across his lap to try to avoid getting smacked on the same spot too many times. "Better learn to get used to this," he advised. "If you stay on as my assistant after tonight's performance, it's going to be on my terms. That means you'll be getting spanked whenever you annoy me; figure on an average of once a day."

Hugo went on spanking her while waiting for the protest that didn't come. One thing he had to admit, and it surprised him, was that Jane seemed fully and cheerfully capable of taking a damn good spanking.

"Are we up to 180 yet?" he suddenly asked.

"That was 187," she replied, timidly, looking over her shoulder at him again.

"Counting, were you?" he pushed her head down again. Then he rolled down her pantyhose and exposed her radiant, rose-tinted cheeks. He rubbed her bottom in circles with the palm of his hand. She relaxed across his knees, making no move to escape.

Now he began to smack her bare skin.

"Are you ever going to behave so immaturely during work hours again, Jane?"

"No, Hugo. I mean, that is, I'll try not to!"

"What do you mean, try? Is that the best you can do?"

"It's just that I've been so distracted lately."

"You mean you've been restless, don't you?"

A few more smacks prompted her embarrassed reply.

"Yes, I've been restless!"

"Lie still," Hugo ordered, inserting one finger into her narrow, throbbing vagina, only to pull it out wet with her fluids. "Look at that!" he held his hand in front of her face. "Who would have thought you'd get turned on from a spanking?" He resumed masturbating her quite slowly. "You of all people."

She protested, "It's just because of you!"

"Really?" he affected surprise.

"It's not that I approve of what you're into..." she insisted, "but you're magnetic. I can't stop thinking about you."

"Really, Jane, I think you've said enough!" he pretended to be scandalized. "After all, you're my employee."

"Don't tease me, Hugo," she complained weakly.

Hugo noticed an interesting reaction after he inserted his middle finger into her bottom instead of her pussy. Jane had been purring, now she began to moan, nor did she pull away, as many women might have done.

"Did your ex-fiancé ever penetrate you like this?" Hugo asked.

Jane took such a long time to answer that he withdrew his finger from her snug anal ring to smack her hard.

"Answer the question, young lady," he snapped. "Did Michael

Flagg ever sodomize you?"

"He did," admitted Jane.

Hugo carefully reinserted his finger into her bottom. "That's so interesting," he told her.

"Does make a difference?"

"It's one of my favorite things to do to a lady."

"Please do it with me! I want it so badly with you. I think about it every night."

"I should force you to climax like this first, then sodomize you."

"I could never come like this!" Jane protested.

"Want to bet?" Hugo withdrew his finger again to spank her six or seven times. "You doubt my ability to give you an orgasm?" More smacks. Jane twisted on his lap and tried to cover herself with her hand. He caught it and pinned her wrist to her waist. "Lie still!" he ordered. "It's your sexual frustration that's been causing all the problems around here, so let me relieve you of it."

Once Jane realized she wasn't going anywhere until Hugo got her off it didn't take long, particularly as he continued to methodically switch back and forth between spanking and masturbating her bottom with equal firmness. The way she responded simply to being held in place indicated to Hugo a potential for engaging in a variety of bondage and discipline adventures with his new protégé. And her reaction to the careful anal stimulation left no doubt that she could be taught to associate and enjoy spanking with the anal orgasms she obviously craved. There was obviously a whole world of untapped response in Jane and she was inviting him to explore it without restraint.

After that distinctive shudder which Hugo knew so well, he ceased his rude attentions to her bottom and assisted her in putting her clothes to rights then sat her on his lap the right way up. She seemed content to be held and breathed a heartfelt sigh.

"I spanked you," Hugo said.

"Yes," Jane replied.

"Gonna quit?"

"No."

"Gonna sue me?"

"No."

"You did have it coming."

"That statement is one that I would normally associate with sexist swine, but somehow I don't care."

"You don't feel compromised?"

"No."

"I'll certainly spank you again," he warned.

"It's okay, I'm up for it," Jane admitted, feeling soft and relaxed.

"You need it," Hugo told her.

Jane felt a fresh flutter as his tightened his arms around her waist. He'd called it punishment, but that was not what it had felt like for her.

Tonight he'd take her home with him for the first time. Possibly he would give her another spanking before bedtime, if only to bring back that adorable blush and confusion to her face. Then he'd take her upstairs and slowly sodomize her, as requested. He imagined she'd fall asleep softly. It was pleasant prospect to contemplate Jane's being his, so long as she continued to behave as beautifully as she'd done tonight.

Of course, he'd have to quit smoking, thought Hugo crossly. One couldn't dominate a morally superior woman. This would make him cranky and she would suffer for it, but if she introduced a note of wholesomeness into his life and he injected a dose of perversity into hers, then it wasn't a bad exchange.

Chapter Two

Susan and Sherman

Susan Ross had been attempting to seduce Sherman Cooper, the modest, well bred and seemingly conservative young lawyer who was administering her late father's estate, for over a year. Cooper lived in the Majestic Apartments on West 72nd Street, over looking Central Park. It was an overcast afternoon in April when the doorman called up to announce Susan's arrival there.

The tall, fair, bespectacled attorney was never completely comfortable dealing with the charming little person to whom he opened his door several minutes later. He acknowledged that encounters with the precocious eighteen year old always left him restless and the moment he saw her tossing her luxuriant pony tail and smiling up at him he realized that his resolve not touch her was about to be tested again.

The petite, well proportioned blonde was dressed in a short, pleated, black and yellow plaid skirt, a black v-neck vest, a white blouse with a short open collar, white woolen anklets and black penny loafers. In addition, the fragrance of carnations wafted from.

"Susan. What are you doing here?"

"I know our appointment was for Monday at your office, but I just couldn't wait. May I come in?" She spoke without faltering and seemed confident.

"If you promise to behave yourself," he said doubtfully, ushering her into the green sitting room, where he'd been having tea. Susan studied him as she followed; admiring his slimness in his well cut khaki trousers and plain white cotton shirt. There was a degree of sobriety in Cooper's demeanor that beguiled her.

"What fun would that be?" Susan murmured.

Vaguely disconcerted, he invited her to sit down and took a seat in a leather wing chair opposite her.

"Did you read my letter?" she came to the point as soon as she was settled.

"I read your letter," Sherman replied.

"So? Will you okay the transfer?"

"Look... would you like a cup of tea?"

"Oh, yes! It's a bit chilly out and I've been riding through the park on my bike," Susan admitted. At that moment thunder struck and it started to rain. Susan rushed to one of the windows. The expensive new bike, which Anthony had given her, was chained to a post on the street seven floors below. She fretted momentarily about leaving it out in the rain while Sherman disappeared to get her tea. On his return he also brought a tin of cookies. He had Susan sit opposite him on the bottle green leather love seat.

"Susan, I'm not sure your father would have approved of you leaving a perfectly respectable art school to come and live in New York."

"My father didn't approve of anything, you know that," Susan replied with irritation.

"Susan, I'm not sold on the notion of you moving to New York," said Sherman, pushing the tin of cookies across the coffee table to her. "Although you have been accepted at an exceptional school, there's the matter of your residence to be considered."

"I've been invited to live with a friend of the family."

"Mr. Anthony Newton?"

"That's right."

"You say he's a friend of the family, but I rather suspect he's your particular friend, and not a very wholesome one at that."

"How can you say such a thing?" Susan jumped to her feet. "He's a Broadway luminary!"

"A man twice your age, who's been married five times... are you telling me that his interest in you is purely avuncular?" Sherman did not bestir himself, but kept to his chair in a dignified manner while she began to pace.

"No, but why should it be?" she demanded. "After all, I'm an adult. I can see whoever I like."

"So what you're really telling me is that Newton is your main reason for wanting to continue your studies in New York City."

"Mr. Newton has an entire apartment in his house that he's willing to set aside for me," Susan pointed out.

"It seems to me, Susan, that if you did transfer to school in New York, it might be more prudent for you live in a dorm. It would be more wholesome for you to live with girls your own age rather than with an older man."

"Sherman, as far as I understand it, you're authorized to administer my funds, not to coordinate my love life," Susan replied firmly. "Anyway, what do you know about wholesomeness? Everyone knows that all lawyers are kinky."

Sherman couldn't help but smile at this confident observation.

"I can see that you admire my ankle sox," she added mis-chievously as he involuntarily focused his gaze on her smoothly shaved, bare legs.

"They are cute," he conceded.

Susan came to him and knelt beside his chair, leaning her arms on his thigh and looking up at him. "Sherman, think of it," she flirted, "if I were in New York, you could offer me the guidance a wayward orphan needs, even take me in hand when necessary. Doesn't that idea appeal to you?"

"Actually, it does," he replied.

"And then, I could take you in hand," she said, allowing her small hand to creep up to his trouser zipper.

"Susan, stop that!" Sherman told her, putting his hand off his lap. "It's very rude!"

"Why?"

"Do you want me to put you over my knee?"

Susan laughed at him, jumped to her feet and wandered over to the window again. "Look, Sherman, it's really coming down. Can I stay here until the rain stops?"

"I suppose so," he said, his heart beginning to pound. Although he didn't normally smoke, he now fumbled a cigarette out of an enameled box on the table. Susan grabbed the matching lighter and lit it for him.

"Thanks," he muttered.

"I didn't know you smoked, Shermy," she commented.

"Don't call me that," he snapped.

"You wouldn't have anything good to smoke, would you?"

"No! Now let's get back to this business of you moving to New York. I suppose that your life will be over if the firm refuses to approve the transfer?"

"One way or other I am coming to New York," Susan firmly declared.

"Oh?" Sherman bristled, "And what is that supposed to mean?"

"It means that if I have to give up my inheritance in order to do what I want then I will."

"Really? And how would you manage after that brilliant move? Barnard isn't exactly a budget school."

"My sister's husband will pay my tuition," Susan opined decisively.

"Is that so? Well, why don't I get him on the phone right now and ask him about that?" Sherman went to the phone on a desk across the room.

"No!" Susan cried.

"No? Why not?"

"I... haven't exactly asked him yet, but I'm certain he'd agree."

"As I said, we can ask him now," Sherman told her, accessing Susan's brother in law's number in his rolodex and dialing it.

"I'd rather ask him myself, if you don't mind," she insisted, at his elbow instantly.

"But I do mind," he told her, pretending that he heard a phone ringing in Random Point. "And I don't mind telling you that I've met your brother in law and I don't think he's going to go for it." Susan paced in front of the desk as Sherman quickly told William that he had just been nominated Susan's benefactor.

"... What's that you say, Mr. Random? You have no intention of paying Susan's tuition this year?... Oh, I agree... She's very naughty!... You suggest I do what?... Well, I can't say the thought hadn't occurred to me... " It was at this juncture that Susan noticed Sherman holding one finger down on the phone. "All right," continued Sherman gravely, "I'll keep you posted. Good-bye."

Susan intuitively backed away from Sherman as he came around the desk.

"What? What did he suggest?"

"He suggested I give you a good spanking! Come over here!" Sherman caught Susan's slender wrist and pulled her over to the love seat she'd vacated in a couple of strides.

"Stop!" Susan tried to pull away. "I saw you holding that button down, you didn't even talk to William!"

"And now I'm going to hold you down," Sherman promised.

"No, Sherman, No!" she cried as he sat down and put her over his knee.

"I'm going to spank you!" he told her, holding her in place with one hand on her waist while the other one flipped up her pleated wool skirt. Snugly encased in sheer, white, nylon panties, Susan's peachy creamy bottom gleamed silken smooth through the mesh. After ten hard smacks the color of her fair skin deepened to pink.

"Stop!" she insisted, simultaneously attempting to cover her bottom with her small white hands and kick him in the head with her tiny feet.

"You're the one who suggested I take you in hand!" Sherman said, pushing her feet back down, pinning both her wrists to her back and continuing to smack her bottom sharply through her panties.

"Ow!" protested Susan. "I didn't mean literally!" She craned her head around to fix him with a beseeching gaze. "At least, not so soon!"

"But it was a good suggestion," he observed, pushing her head back down, then pausing to pull her panties down to the backs of her knees.

"Ooooh! I didn't say you could do that!!!" Susan squealed, trying to wrench herself off his lap as her bottom was bared.

"How fast you color up!" Sherman noticed, giving her a few light, admiring pats before continuing with a volley of stinging smacks. Alternating from side to side, he delivered perhaps 30 hard swats to each cheek before stopping to survey his work.

Susan wailed, "Let me go! You're mean! You're hurting me!"

"You deserve a painful punishment for even thinking about

throwing over your inheritance!" More smacks. "And don't you think it's a bit selfish of you to plan on free loading off your brother in law?" More smacks. "Now, young lady, I would like to think that you're beginning to feel a little sorry for behaving like a thoughtless, (Smack!) forward, (Smack!) arrogant, (Smack!) brat!" Smack! Smack! Smack!

"Why should I be sorry? You're the one who's going to be sorry!" she threatened, trying once more to separate his head from his shoulders with her dangerous elfin feet.

"Don't you dare try to kick me," he warned her sternly. "Put your feet down. Right now. Or I'll take my belt off and continue with it instead of my hand."

"Sherman, couldn't we talk now?" Susan tried a new tack.

"All right, what's on your mind?" Sherman paused, clasping her left wrist in his right hand and resting his forearms on the small of her back.

"Sherman, did you know you have a large erection?" Susan asked, gazing back at him again. She immediately observed a deep flush spread from his throat to his brow. He pushed her off his lap and jumped up to his feet.

"My god, you're fresh!" he charged, completely flustered.

"Gee, Sherman, you have a really big one, don't you?" Susan remarked, pulling up her panties while keeping her eyes riveted on the crotch of Cooper's pleated poplin trousers, which tented around an impressive hard-on. "Did spanking me do that to you?" she queried innocently.

"I have no idea of what you're talking about!" he demurred, putting several lengths of carpet between them as she seemed about to reach out and caress him.

"But Sherman, why fight it? I'm here, you're hard. I'm willing, you're able. Let's make love!" And before he could stop her she had crossed the room to fling herself into his arms. He found her pressed against him, her tawny head nuzzling his chest, her arms tightly hugging his waist and her limber little torso grinding ever so softly against his treacherous zipper. He looked down helplessly to meet her melting blue eyes. Her full red lips were parted in a naughty smile.

"Please?" she added, unnecessarily.

Sherman had always wanted to scoop a girl up in his arms, the way they did in old movies, but he'd never encountered one to whom such a gesture would seem appropriate before. Susan was so small and light that she was easily swept off her feet and up into the air. Once she was at eye level she wrapped her arms around his neck and pressed her pretty mouth to his throat. She purred for she had won.

He carried her into the master bedroom and sat down on the enormous white four-poster with Susan in his lap. She fastened her lips to his mouth and opened them to his invading tongue. They French kissed so long and so deeply that Sherman felt slightly dizzy when she finally pulled her mouth away. He took her down to the bed and covered her small body with the length of his long one. Then, fearing to crush her slim little frame, he moved off to one side and slid a hand up under skirt until he reached her moist panty crotch with his fingertips. He pressed his palm upon her pubic mound through the nylon panties. She stretched and sighed and turned toward him with her entire torso, to press the length of her warm small body against his lean one. Her arms went around his neck again and she clung to him. He continued to probe her through her panties, kneading her muff and palming her sex until her panties became completely soaked with her excitement. The next minute, he slipped one finger in under one of the panty legs and worked it up into her creamy slit.

"You're making my pussy ache," she whimpered, clinging to him harder and twisting her hips so as to take as much of his finger up her throbbing vagina as possible. "Don't torture me like this!" she insisted, now thrusting her well rounded bosom against his chest, then hiding her face against his chest and finally maneuvering her entire torso into the face down position, so that she lay stretched on her tummy beside him, with her pert bottom arching invitingly as he continued to probe her hot and lightly clenching little glove.

Sherman sensed that she was trying to tell him something with her body language and withdrew his finger from her pulsating sex to push her skirt up to her waist and stroke her luscious buttocks through her panties. From her faint corresponding moans of pleasure he divined that he was on the right track.

"I don't think I spanked you nearly enough," he commented, slowly pulling her silky panties down and off. On the way he also removed her tiny shoes, caressing every satiny inch of her thighs, knees and calves as he did so. When she remained face down on the bed, slightly grinding her blonde fuzzed Venus mound against the counterpane, he realized that she craved more attention to her bottom.

"Come on, back over my lap," he said, gently repositioning her across his knees. "Since you've had this spanking coming for a year, it might as well be a thorough one."

"Oh, not too hard! Please!" she cried, almost swooning with the thrill of being placed in the time honored position again.

"Not too hard," he promised, bending to kiss the back of her neck. Then, placing one hand on the small of her back, he started to spank her again, rather lightly this time, alternating smacks from cheek to cheek and pausing after every set of ten or twelve to finger her sopping wet pussy. This combination of spanking and digital penetration soon had her squirming on his lap in a frenzy of excitement. Her clitoris swelled hugely and prompted her to cry, "Oh Sherman, please, do something!"

"All right," he paused to try something new. Dividing her lightly pinkened cheeks with one hand, he slowly inserted his well-lubricated middle finger into her tiny anus. Once he'd buried it as deeply as it would go and she'd started to whimper delightfully, he resumed spanking her with his other hand.

"Oh no! No!" she cried, writhing with pleasure and shame all at once. In less that fifteen seconds he felt her tight anal ring begin to spasm wildly around his finger as she ground against his lap in a delirious climax.

When Sherman lay her back down on the bed there was a large wet spot on his trouser leg and Susan was sobbing with embarrassed emotion.

"There's nothing to be upset about," he told her, brushing some stray damp blond hair from her brow. He leaned down to kiss her on the mouth. Then he gathered her into his arms and held her tightly.

In a couple of minutes, after she had regained her composure, she began to pull off various items of apparel, the better to grind against his lean, hard body. She disposed of her skirt and her vest and began to wriggle around on the bed in just her white blouse and white ankle socks, inviting him to join her.

"Please, Sherman, let's do it!" she begged, undoing his belt for him and starting to work on his zipper.

"I'm not sure I ought to," he replied, while allowing her to pull the belt free from the loops of his trousers. "You're really too young to take advantage of like this!" he declared.

"Maybe you should punish me some more. It might put you in the mood," she suggested, handing the belt to him and assuming the all-fours position on the bed while casting him the most inviting look imaginable over her shoulder.

"The mood to take you in the bottom, I'm afraid!" Sherman warned her, coiling the belt around his hand to hide the buckle under several leather wrap arounds and ending up with a thin strap 8" in length.

"I've never had that done to me before," she murmured.

Sherman stood up beside the bed and placing one hand in the small of her back, gave her a few light, experimental licks with the end of the belt. Susan caught her breath each time the leather connected with her bare bottom. The feel of his hand pressed down on her back, the kiss of the strap, the sound of it impacting, the nearness of his hard, masculine body all combined to start the freshets of excitement coursing through her again. He inwardly rejoiced on observing her response. Clearly, domination moved her and she was obviously anal to the core.

"All right, you're going to get a good strapping, and then I'm going to sodomize you. Isn't that what you deserve?" he demanded, though in a softly caressing tone of voice.

"Yes!" she accepted the sentence with trembling anticipation, removing one palm from the bed momentarily to free her ponytail and allow her long hair to spill down her back and around her flushed face.

"Lie down," he told her, pushing her down so that she lay on her stomach. Then, placing one knee on the bed he raised his arm and began the strapping, which was slightly sharp and caused Susan to gasp with shock each time the belt struck her adorable bottom. He placed the strokes evenly, administering about two dozen across both blushing cheeks and taking care not to strike the same area twice in a row. He worked his way up and then down her bottom six times, giving her the strokes in groups of four and scoring her buttocks with light red lines which were perfectly even and precisely measured. Sherman had a very steady hand and knew how to make the lashes sting without cutting, tingle without burning, punish, but ever so lightly.

When he tossed the belt aside and went off to his dressing room in search of a good lubricant, Susan shuddered with excitement. Her bottom felt radiant. She fancied she could feel each individual stroke and relived each one of them as she breathlessly awaited his return. The strapping had been so exquisite that a shadow orgasm rippled through her while she contemplated it.

Then Sherman was back beside her, unzipping his trousers, dropping them to the floor and getting up on the bed beside her, with something very wet and sheer and sticky on his fingers.

"Don't move a muscle, young lady," he warned her, working the wetness up and down her bottom crack with one hand while shoving a pillow under her belly with the other. "I want you to relax. Completely. Understand?"

"Yes," she whispered, and groaned a little as he inserted a finger into her bottom.

"You're not nearly relaxed enough, Susan," he told her, withdrawing his finger and spreading her cheeks with both hands so that she was utterly open to his gaze. This had the effect of making her whimper and grind against the pillow in a spasm of embarrassed desire.

"No, hold still," he told her. "If you come right away you'll lose interest and tighten up."

"I can't help being excited," she protested weakly.

"You'd better help it unless you want another spanking," he warned her, placing his large, faintly throbbing cock between her buttocks and pressing the knob lightly against her anus. "Now lie perfectly still and don't move," he said.

"I'm scared, it feels so big!" she cried.

"There's nothing to be afraid of. I know what I'm doing. I've done this a hundred times before," he assured her.

"But it will hurt!"

"What did I tell you?" he paused to smack her bottom rather smartly three or four times.

"Ow! All right, I'll be good!" she promised.

"You had better be a little angel," he told her, rubbing his cock up and down her cleft, which was by now well lubricated with the sheer, sticky liquid he'd produced for this purpose. "Perfectly still, remember," he whispered, once again taking hold of both her cheeks and pulling them apart. This time he also nudged his penis through the rim of her lightly stretched anus and began to insert it into her hot, tight rectal canal a half-inch at a time.

"You know, Susan, I could play with your bottom all day and never get bored," Sherman told her, "I could spank it and finger it and plug it until you came a dozen times." Susan groaned at this as inch after bone-hard inch of his thick, seven and a half inch cock disappeared into her spread bottom. He continued to hold her cheeks well apart to ease the entry of his penis into her and this had the dual effect of embarrassing her to the point of sobs and allowing her to absorb the entire length of organ nearly painlessly.

Once he was all the way in, he let go and allowed her spanked half moons to compress around his cock.

"Now lie perfectly still and get used to it inside you. Don't move an inch unless you want the thrashing of your life!" he warned her, mainly to distract her from the frightening reality of having a large cock buried to the hilt in her bottom for the first time. Panic and fear at a moment like this could ruin everything.

"Oh!" Susan cried, wriggling ever so slightly under the exquisite impalement, flexing her bottom around his hard cock in spite of his warning to hold still and relishing the tiniest throb of his penis with her tight sheath.

"What else?" she moaned cryptically.

"What else what, sweetheart?"

"What else would like to do to my bottom?" she shyly asked. She craved the raunchy details and arched her bottom up to inspire additional verbal titillation.

Seeing that she was relaxed, ready and receptive, he began to slowly thrust, first with shallow strokes, then with deeper ones, reaming her with his steel rod, between the cheeks that he had soundly strapped.

"What else would I do? I'm so happy you asked! I'd have a special butt plug made just for you and I'd insert it in to your bottom every time I fucked your adorable little pussy, just so you'd remember what a naughty girl you are."

"Oh Sherman!" Susan cried, unable to stop herself from grinding against the pillow as he plunged ever harder and deeper into her bottom-hole, that characteristic combination of tickle and itch calling her clitoris to attention once more.

"What's more, the next time I put you over my knee for a spanking, I'm going to put a vibrator into your bottom first and turn it on. I might even buy a nice little leather paddle to paddle it in until you come," he mused.

These inflammatory threats, combined with the plunging of Sherman's penis into her pulsating nether sheath were too much for her lust-engorged clitoris. With a shudder and a groan that seemed to emanate from her very heart, she gave up a second orgasm, which caused her tiny anal ring to clench so hard and fast that he felt he in danger of having his manhood sheared off at the base.

Realizing she would be feeling too tender for further play the moment her climax had subsided, Sherman took the opportunity presented by her shudders to ejaculate ecstatically. In this manner their orgasms exploded and subsided at just about the same time and a minute or two after her sphincter had ceased to convulse, he gently pulled his penis free of it, managing to do so without causing Susan discomfort or pain.

While the rain beat on the window they climbed under the counterpane and blanket. Sherman took Susan in his arms and cuddled her until she fell asleep for a little nap on that chilly spring afternoon.

In about a half hour she awoke with a start, feeling suddenly guilty, worrying about her bike, about the time, about what Anthony would say when she confessed what had passed between Lawyer

Cooper and herself that day.

She hurriedly pulled on her clothes and dragged a comb through her tangled hair. Sherman was sad to see her go but did not press her about calling on him again. He was prepared to look upon the afternoon's delights as a gift and had no intention of making his approval of her transfer of schools from Boston to New York in any way conditional. He didn't like to let her go out in the rain, especially to ride her bike all the way back to the Village, but saw that she was determined to have her way about it. He did make her take a rain slicker and hat, which he buttoned up for her himself, as though she were his own little girl. When he kissed her good-bye in the lobby downstairs he told her that if Newton ever evicted her she could always bunk in the Majestic Apartments with him. Susan reflected on her way back to Anthony Newton's house that she might have to take Sherman up on his offer if Anthony ever discovered what she'd been up to that afternoon.

Chapter Three

Laura and Michael

Late in November, Laura Random gave a dinner for her friends. As she greeted her guests, in a golden velvet gown, she clearly had mischief in mind. Her husband had departed that morning for a month-long climbing trip in the Andes, and a month is a very long time.

Michael Flagg arrived alone. His wife, Damaris, was also out of town. He was loath to admit that she'd left him and had already been gone for a week. He knew that she'd gone to L.A. and suspected that whatever she was doing there would not be something she would tell of on a postcard. He had made her mad and she was Latin.

Marguerite Alexander, glamorous in a blue suede bustier gown, bristled at the warmth with which Laura greeted Michael. Marguerite had known for months that Laura coveted Detective Flagg and this intuition made her very cross.

Hugo Sands' companion, Jane Eliot, was similarly distressed by the affection with which Laura greeted Hugo. Hugo and Jane had been intimate for some months, but the soft manner in which Hugo embraced Laura, gave Jane a sinking feeling.

Naturally, Hugo was delighted to hear that William Random would shortly be perilously roped to a small climbing team on a windy Peruvian peak. Although it had been over a year since Hugo had made love to Laura at his Halloween party, the enigmatic brunette had never been far from his mind. With her husband out of town, Hugo's path was clear, providing Flagg didn't block his campaign.

When, toward the end of dinner, Laura casually announced that Michael's absent wife Damaris had called her from California that afternoon, the strikingly attractive law enforcement officer went red in the face the way only a Celt can.

"She working at a B&D club," Laura went on to say; "In Hollywood!"

For seven seconds no one spoke. Then Michael, who was furious at Laura for bringing up this awkward subject in company, conversationally replied, "She's just saying that to get attention."

"You think so?" Laura rejoined.

"Yes," Michael replied firmly, intimidating Laura into lowering her eyes.

"Michael, has your bride left you? Already?" Jane was jubilant, as she had not yet completely forgiven Michael Flagg for breaking their engagement the previous year.

"No!" Michael snapped. "That is, maybe."

"What's a B&D club?" Jane wanted to know.

"You don't need to know that," Michael snapped emphatically.

Marguerite frowned, resenting the paternalistic tone Michael was taking with his ex, who by all accounts, was coming along nicely these days and never lectured anyone on the pernicious influence of sadomasochistic pornography anymore. It seemed both overbearing and unenlightened for Michael to attempt to shut Jane out of their world at this late date and Marguerite suddenly felt a strong desire to tell her hero off for it.

"I need to know whatever I want to know!" Jane delighted Marguerite by replying indignantly.

"Jane, I hope you're not driving tonight because you're well over the legal limit and I might have to arrest you," Flagg informed her.

"You go to hell!" Jane advised the man she had been betrothed to for two years and tossed back the contents of her wine goblet in a couple of gulps. After an initial blue spark exchange, Michael smiled. Jane suddenly seemed very sexy.

"Just don't let me catch you on the road, young lady," he warned her, throwing down his napkin and getting to his feet. It was time to leave for his shift at the police station anyway. Jane made an obscene gesture at Flagg's retreating figure, for which Hugo slapped her hand at the table.

"Ow!" she cried. "How dare he talk to me like that!"

"Behave," Hugo told her, in spite of his amusement.

Uncomfortable about the scene, which her ill advised remarks, had given rise to, Laura walked Michael outside to his car. It was a very brisk autumn evening on the Cape and a crisp wind was blowing through the spruce and pine trees, which thickly overhung Shadow Lane.

"Laura," he said coldly, "I didn't appreciate your throwing a spotlight on my personal life tonight."

Laura blushed guiltily. Knowing that she had irritated Michael rather excited her, yet she didn't like to be thought badly of.

"I spoke without thinking," she admitted with a shiver.

"Get in the car for a minute," he told her. Laura entered from the passenger's side while he turned on both the motor and the heat. "So she called you, did she?" he asked quietly.

"She really has been working at a club," Laura said. "Shall I give you the name and the number?"

Michael scowled, "What for?"

"In case you want to call her...or go after her," Laura suggested, puzzled by his indifference.

"I'm not going after her," he replied.

"You aren't?"

"Of course not. She left of her own accord. I didn't throw her out. On the contrary, I've gone to considerable expense to build a beautiful home for that ungrateful little slut!"

"Michael, don't call her that!" Laura was shocked.

"What would you call a girl who'd rather let a succession of strangers tie her up and whip her than behave like a proper wife?"

"Oh Michael, she didn't want to leave. But she thinks you don't love her."

Michael rejoined, "Just because I nag her to improve herself?"

"It's not that," Laura said softly.

"What then?"

"The way you carry on with Marguerite."

The color rushed to Michael's face again.

"Michael," Laura went on, "Damaris wanted you know what her situation is."

"Why? Does she expect me to do something?"

"I don't know if she expects anything but I know that she would like to be rescued," Laura patiently explained.

"She'll need to be rescued from my strap if I find her making free with her favors in a B&D club!"

Laura's tummy clenched at the threat.

"Sorry if I'm skeptical," Michael continued, "but I think this jealousy bit is a red herring. My take on the situation is that Damaris has run away because she's simply bored with being straight. You see, I make her go to work without taking drugs."

"Square," Laura muttered under her breath.

"Sorry!" he replied insincerely.

"Michael, this is not about drugs."

"Anyway, rushing out to California and dragging her back home like some outraged Victorian husband just doesn't fit my personality. My wife should want to be with me. I shouldn't have to force her to be with me."

"She wants to be with you more than anything. But she smelled another woman's scent on your things and it's twisted her in knots."

Michael admitted, "When you put it like that, her running off makes more sense."

"Sure. Think of every romantic comedy from the 30's to the 60's. Stubborn girl runs off, determined boy fetches girl back home. It's a dominant/submissive tradition."

"Seems an awfully expensive and inconvenient way to get a thrill," Michael observed dryly, while glimpsing a plane reservation in his immediate future.

"Well, you know best," Laura sighed, ready to give up. She felt he was a very hard man, even more inflexible than her husband. However, when she chanced to meet his eyes she was startled by the sudden look of warmth with which he now regarded her.

"What's going on in your head, Laura?" Michael demanded; "Earlier in the evening you appeared to be giving me a signal that you yourself were available, now you want me to jump on the next plane for the coast."

Laura paused a moment then said recklessly, "Michael, you know I

121

have a crush on you." Michael was charmed. "I'd better go," said Laura, opening the car door with a pounding heart. "Will you accept my apology for bringing this up in front of the others?"

"For a forfeit," said Michael, impulsively taking her in his arms and kissing her full on the mouth. The wide bench seat of the old sedan made it possible for Flagg to fully embrace her and he crushed her slender torso to his chest throughout the long, deep kiss. Once he had her close to him he was reluctant to let her go and began to fondle her rounded bosom, dainty waist and firm thighs through the voluptuous nap of her golden gown.

Laura was thrilled but nonplussed by the force of his assault. She had thought him a tamely flirtatious scene friend, who was married to one of her girlfriends and having an affair with another of her girlfriends. It hadn't occurred to her that he might actively wish to possess her as well. She broke from the embrace and told him firmly, "I should go," and instantly slipped out the door. Michael watched her run back to the house with her long skirt lifted above her slim ankles and wondered what had gotten into him just now. And he had called Damaris a slut!

Chapter Four

Hugo and Laura

Hugo, who'd remained remarkably sober throughout the evening, was making arrangements to drive Jane and Marguerite home when Laura returned to the house with a racing pulse, flushed cheeks and tingling lips. Her over excited demeanor was duly noted by each of her departing guests with varying degrees of disapproval. That something had gone on between herself and Flagg just now was patently obvious to Marguerite, Hugo and Jane.

When Hugo stopped to let Marguerite off at her house on the edge of the village, the tall redhead invited Jane to come in for a nightcap. Hugo was pointedly excluded from the invitation. One of Marguerite's shining talents was her ability to deftly arrange complicated seductions. In this case, she knew very well that Hugo would wish to return to Laura as soon as possible. Offering herself as a distraction to Jane seemed both humane and politic to Marguerite, who was always interested in making points with her influential patron.

"Michael is right, you girls are drinking too much," Hugo observed gravely. "I think you've both had enough. I know I certainly have." The fact that these remarks were wholly out of character for Hugo, did not occur to Jane.

"I'll decide when I've had enough to drink!" Jane retorted predictably.

"Oh you will, will you?" Hugo exchanged glances with Marguerite, who was beaming at her own cleverness. "Jane, you're going to have an awful head tomorrow as it is," Hugo warned. But Jane was already getting out of the car.

"That's my business," Jane told him airily and followed

Marguerite through the picket gate into the garden. Hugo got out of the car, folded his arms and waited until Jane gave him a pert backward glance.

"Jane, you're being a bad girl. Let me take you home," Hugo coaxed her, rather gently, for him.

"No!" Jane actually stamped her foot before marching over Marguerite's threshold.

Marguerite waved to Hugo from her door, secure in the knowledge that her good deed would also keep Laura from pursuing Michael Flagg any further that night. Meanwhile, it would be interesting to study the woman Michael had almost married at that jaded hour of a full moon autumn night.

When Hugo returned to Laura's house some fifteen minutes later he found her releasing her two tabby cats into her leaf strewn back yard.

"Hugo, what are you doing back here?" she was all innocence, with soft golden light surrounding her in the doorway.

"Someone has to teach you a lesson," he told her, entering her home and locking the door behind him.

"Is that what you're really doing here?" she hooked her hands into his lapels and looked up at him so appealingly that it was hard for the besotted antique dealer to resist kissing her.

"It is," he replied, coolly disengaging her hands and retaining only one of them, to lead Laura out of the pantry, through the kitchen and down the wood paneled hall. "We're going to have a nice long talk first, you and I," Hugo told her, pulling her behind him into the room where Laura had served coffee to her guests an hour before. He deposited her on a sofa and sat down beside her.

"Cigarette?" Laura proffered a painted box deliberately.

"You know I've quit smoking," Hugo replied indignantly, though he lingered over lighting one for her.

"Hugo, was I awful tonight?" Laura's plaintive query disarmed him. The last thing Hugo expected any woman to do was admit she'd been bad.

"Well, let's see," Hugo said, "you upset Marguerite by making advances to Michael; you infuriated him by telling everyone his wife had run away; you annoyed the hell out of Jane by coming on to me; and frankly, I'm a bit put out with you myself."

"Why shouldn't I be friends with Michael?" Laura demanded; "Didn't his wife have an affair with my husband?"

"Really, Laura, that's crude for you," Hugo chided her.

"I don't care. I've always felt that Michael and I should sleep together at least once, for balance."

"Is that how you see your marriage to William, like a ledger sheet of infidelities?"

"What if I do?" she replied carelessly.

"What about Marguerite? Don't you owe her better loyalty than that? She didn't enjoy watching you come on to Flagg tonight," Hugo pointed out.

"She gets to play with him all the time." Laura returned, quite the petulant child.

"Whereas you only get to play when your husband's out of town, right?" Hugo noted with growing irritation Laura's perverse attachment to Flagg. "You're a selfish little opportunist, do you know that?"

"I just want to cut loose for a couple of days," Laura replied, resentfully; "And as for Michael being peeved at me for bringing up Damaris, well, if he'd been paying enough attention to her she never would have run away. It's appalling the way he takes her for granted."

"If he's as callous as you say, then why are you bothering to pursue him?"

"On a purely physical level he's just my type," Laura replied coolly; "Although I do have more than one type," she favored Hugo with an honest smile.

"I'm heartened by that news flash, but don't you think you might have been a bit more circumspect about broadcasting it in front of Jane? She is the jealous type, you know."

"I should think you'd know how to deal with a tantrum by now, Hugo," Laura replied smartly. "Besides, if you didn't think it was worth it, you wouldn't be here."

"You're pretty sure that you've got all the answers tonight, aren't you, young lady? You know, Laura, you're very much mistaken if you think I appreciate being kept on ice for a year then summoned to perform for you the first time your husband is well away," Hugo said, taking her cigarette away, crushing it out and in one rather suave movement, pulling her over his lap.

"I am seriously annoyed!" A flurry of sharp smacks followed this pronouncement and Laura reacted to each with a squeak of surprise.

"You've been asking for a spanking all evening," Hugo remarked, smoothing her luxurious golden velvet skirt down over her perfect oval cheeks before initiating a second volley of hard smacks. "Isn't that so, you brat?" Smack!

"It might be so," Laura responded softly, inwardly melting as her gripped her slender waist. Ten or twelve harder spanks followed.

"You've become spoiled rotten," Hugo declared, continuing to vigorously spank the seat of her skirt, which molded to her buttocks so flatteringly. She turned to look at him with her soft brown eyes and was electrified by the stern frown in his blue ones.

"You seem to think you're entitled to whatever you want," he charged, spanking her quite soundly now at a very brisk pace.

"Well, aren't I?" she dared to rejoin, attempting to stay his hand.

"You're certainly entitled to the full effect of this spanking," Hugo said, putting her hand aside, then pushing the lavish yards of velvet up to her waist to reveal a perfect bottom, gleamingly encased in ivory satin tap pants, trimmed with beige lace. Seamed stockings and a satin garter belt showcased Laura's slim legs.

"Laura, I hope you don't think I enjoy punishing you. I'd much rather spank you nicely. But someone has to set you straight," Hugo intoned, stroking her adorable bottom through the exquisite material of her panties gently for a moment, then delivering a series of a dozen, sudden, stinging smacks which took Laura's breath away.

"Yes, I thought that would get your attention," Hugo observed.

"Ow! Why so hard?" she protested, rather squeakily for her.

"So you'll realize I'm serious," Hugo told her, while lowering her pearly knickers to reveal her classically rounded bare bottom, now tinged a deep, dusky rose by the palm of his hand. "We're going to get something settled tonight, Laura," he punctuated this declaration with another ten or twelve smacks, first striking her right, then her left cheek, first reddening the outer contours of her bottom, then striking closer to the center, first slapping high up on the hips, then down low upon the silken crease which divided buttock from thigh, repeating this outer to inner, upper to lower path until he had darkened the entire surface of her ravishing bottom with the imprint of his hand.

"Hugo, please!" Laura cried.

"Please nothing, you have this coming," Hugo informed her, while continuing to thoroughly redden her bottom. "I never thought I'd have to punish you, Laura, but your behavior tonight warrants correction."

Laura fretted over this injunction in silence for several difficult minutes across Hugo's knees before bursting into sobs. It was the shame much more than the pain of the spanking that made her begin to cry, for the seductive rhythm of the smacks had begun to transport her beyond the pain and into another realm of sensation much more subtle and moving. The sense that she was being punished for having behaved dreadfully was somehow thrilling and somehow awful to Laura, especially since the punishment was being administered by Hugo Sands, whom Laura considered a discerning and elegant man.

Gradually, as the spanking progressed, the pain was replaced by pervasive warmth, which washed through her like liquid light. Now each time his palm came down upon her bare bottom, she felt impelled by its relentless impact to grind her pubic mound against his thighs. An ache of longing pierced and inflamed her. She was lubricating copiously now.

A feeling of dizzying helplessness now overwhelmed her. This sensation of acute vulnerability sprang from the position in which she had been placed and the way in which he held her there, with his hand lightly pressed upon her waist, as though he were confident that she would put up no more resistance than a blushing little girl when put across a grown man's knee.

"You can cry all you like, but you need this," he told her firmly, continuing to spank her for a minute or two before pausing to lean forward and scrutinize her face, which was flushed, wet with tears and very sweet. Laura's emotionalism touched Hugo. He turned her over on his lap and embraced her, kissing her mouth first, then lingering about her soft throat and velvety ear lobes. When he pushed her gown aside to nuzzle and lightly bite her smooth, white shoulders Laura whimpered.

"Get up," Hugo told her and stood up as well. He took her by the shoulders and made her kneel on the sofa with her bottom to him and her arms leaning on the back of it. "Face that way," he said, pushing her down with a gentle hand on the small of her back, positioning her ideally to be taken from behind. He raised her skirt to her waist and pulled her panties off.

"Don't move, young lady," he told Laura, removing his finely tailored suit jacket. She turned around to look and was promptly rewarded with a smart slap on the upper thigh. "Eyes front," Hugo told her, unbuckling and snapping off his belt. He doubled it and cracked it a few times for effect. Laura flinched each time he did this but could not resist craning her neck around to measure the length of the strap just once before turning away. This act of shy defiance earned her one sharp stroke of the belt, which made her cry aloud and called forth a fresh torrent of tears.

"I don't want to have to tell you again," Hugo said coolly, but momentarily put the strap aside to come around in front of her and mop her face with a pristine handkerchief. There was also time to kiss her again, run his hands through her fine brown hair and take her ear lobes softly between his teeth. Laura sighed, sobbed, and melted. This way he had of punishing then petting her kept Laura's tummy fluttering as it hadn't done since the early days of her marriage. Meanwhile Hugo was finding Laura so charmingly responsive that he was more inclined to cover her with kisses than red marks. Then he remembered how long she had made him wait for this evening, and this recollection hardened him just enough to make it exciting for Laura. He straightened up and threw the handkerchief aside. He showed her the belt.

"You're getting a strapping. Understand?"

"Yes," she replied meekly before lowering her expressive eyes and leaning over the sofa back with adorable resignation. "And there isn't going to be anything playful about it," he advised her, stepping behind her, placing one hand on the small of her back and delivering a sharp, stinging lick with the belt across the middle of her bottom. Laura gave a little cry and put one hand back to rub her bare behind.

"Can't stay still, can you?" Hugo picked up the discarded handkerchief. He went around in front of her again. "Give me your wrists, Laura," he said and when she obeyed with startled eyes, he tied them together with the handkerchief. "If you'd held your position properly I wouldn't have to do this." He gently pushed her back down so that the back of the sofa supported her tummy and her bound wrists were in front of her.

Hugo took up the strap again with a sigh. "Who would have thought it would have come to this, my having to resort to restraints to make you mind me," Hugo's tone conveyed profound disappointment.

"I'll mind you," Laura replied softly, while waiting with trembling for the next stroke to fall.

"Is that so? I'm pleasantly astonished, but why should I believe you?" Hugo stroked her pink tinged bottom with the palm of his hand.

"Because I say so," Laura murmured.

"Yes, well we both know that your word isn't worth the paper it's written on," he rejoined. "A true change of attitude has yet to be effected in you, my little gypsy." He clarified this point by flicking the strap across her buttocks a half dozen times, sharply and in rapid succession. Laura cried out with a startled little, "Oh!" each time the leather stung her bottom.

"So you're going to mind me, are you? That's sweet," he paused in the whipping to slip his left hand under Laura's tummy and press his palm against her silky, cream soaked pubic curls. Tucking the strap momentarily under one arm, he used his other hand to probe her, getting each finger wet in turn inside her snug, pulsating sheath. Hugo masturbated Laura gently, but firmly for some time, slipping his middle finger into her pussy as far as it would go, then pulling it out again, then putting it back again, very slowly and carefully, until her entire muff was frothy with her essence. Ten times in those ten minutes she felt herself on the brink of climax, but it always slipped away. She had the sense that he was controlling even that.

Hugo took his hands away and picked up the belt again. He said, "You're getting a dozen of the best now, Laura Random, after which you are going to pledge, in all sincerity, to forget about Michael

129

Flagg."

The first two strokes were briskly delivered, causing Laura to cry out in pained surprise. Hugo continued, "You will stay away from Detective Flagg and not upset our dear Marguerite." Two more licks of the strap followed, falling one above the other across the upper then the lower half of her bottom. Red marks appeared immediately.

"Your disloyalty to your own sex is shocking!" Hugo scolded. Two more times the strap came down, now across her tender upper thighs, which brought fresh tears to her eyes. "And speaking of loyalty, how do you think William would feel knowing that you made blatant advances to Michael in front of the rest of us tonight?"

"Oh, he doesn't care who I sleep with!" Laura protested.

"Is that so?" Hugo paused in the strapping, but only long enough to let her catch her breath.

Two more cracks of the belt quickly followed, robbing her of it again.

"How many was that, young lady?"

"Eight," Laura replied at once.

"Eight what?" Hugo sounded impatient. "Eight... Sir?" she ventured timidly, daring to look around at him for a moment.

"That's better. You know, I like a bit of formality between dominant and submissive. In your case, courtesy and respect are lessons which obviously need to be relearned." Hugo furthered the instructional process by administering two more licks with the belt.

"How many does that leave, Mrs. Random?" he demanded, rubbing his hand across the hurt part and leaving a tingling in its wake.

"Two, Sir," Laura returned, keeping her eyes properly front this time.

"Now, you're going to feel these," he warned her, before delivering two more smart whacks. Laura sobbed aloud at these, though they were only a bit harder than the others. Hugo threw down the belt.

"Knees apart and arch your bottom higher," Hugo told her, unzipping his grey flannel trousers and allowing his large, pulsating erection to escape. Guiding the knob of his cock into her snug, wet portal, Hugo smoothly and deliberately plunged all seven plus inches into her pussy at once.

"Oh!" she cried, pierced to the core. She would use the exclamation repeatedly over the next quarter hour. Fastening his hands upon her slender waist, Hugo commenced thrusting into Laura and continued with this intensely pleasurable activity for a good fifteen minutes without either of them uttering an articulate word.

The moment he began to drive into her, waves of liquid excitement began to course through Laura's body. He pinched her ear lobe smartly, then carefully freed her breasts entirely from the front of her gown to firmly handle them, never pausing in the rhythmic assault of his cock on her glistening pink glove. Everywhere he touched Laura thrilled her.

"Thirteen months you've kept me at bay," Hugo charged, pausing in his thrusting, while still buried to the hilt, to slap her right buttock hard. Laura gave a shocked cry at the unexpected resumption of her spanking, especially at that moment. "And now you admit that William doesn't even care about who you sleep with!" Hugo gave her another hard spank, this one on the opposite cheek and Laura cried out once again. "Now, I want to know exactly why you've been avoiding me all year," Hugo slapped her several more times to impress her with the extent of his curiosity.

"What's the use?" Laura wailed; "You won't believe me!"

"I will if you're telling the truth," he murmured soothingly, continuing to possess her now without the accompaniment of smacks. She was aware of both his hands on her hips now, pushing her from him and pulling her back up against him as his engorged cock pistoned rhythmically into her wet, velvet pocket.

"I do find you very attractive," she began, haltingly, having to catch her breath every few seconds as she came closer and closer to a delirious climax while he pumped her. He slowed down his thrusting to listen.

"You've captured my attention, continue," Hugo urged, slipping one hand under Laura to press upon her flat, satiny tummy while continuing to plumb her clinging depths.

"I... don't know what else to say," Laura stumbled.

"Really!" Hugo snorted. "Well I don't consider that an adequate explanation. Either you're for me or you don't give a damn."

"I'm for you!" Laura cried, squeezing her pussy around his cock hard.

"And I suppose you thought that denying yourself to me for a year was a good way of expressing this fondness?" He spanked her five times in a row on her right cheek. "I don't think so!" Then he spanked her five more times on the left one and each smack was hard enough to make her give a little yip of hurt surprise. But it was enough to also send her over the edge. So intensely stimulating was his firm hand striking her bottom while his hard cock thrust inside her to the hilt that Laura enjoyed a shuddering climax before many more minutes had elapsed. Moments later Hugo joined her.

I've been afraid of having an affair with you." Laura admitted, reclining on the sofa after having her wrists freed.

"And why is that?" Hugo demanded, standing over her to put his belt back on.

"Because I think I like you too much," she explained, every fiber of her sex still athrob. She almost came again just looking up at him, for his looks were quite appealing to her.

"If you like me that much, why be afraid?"

"It might wreck my marriage," she replied, with a sobriety which indicated that she had given this problem a great deal of thought.

"Really!" Hugo's expression was pleasant as he slipped his suit jacket back on then deftly adjusted his tie in the mirror.

"Hugo, you almost look as though you like that idea!" Laura accused, shocked by the enormity of the concept.

Hugo merely smiled at her serenely and said, "Let's just say the wrecking ball has arrived."

Chapter Five

Go West!

It was 9:00 on a Friday night at The Keep, Hollywood's best-staffed B&D club. Remedios was sequestered in the tiny, stuffy dressing room when the bell rang. She smoked while touching up the lipstick that richly delineated the contours of her full red mouth. She was a petite brunette who had that evening poured her stunning little body into a gleaming, black PVC mini jumper. Her long fingernails were dark red, her ankle strap heels 5" high and the seams of her black-tinted stockings precisely straight. A slightly strained expression compromised the beauty of her clear skinned heart-shaped face; she was tense, with an accelerated heartbeat.

When the bell rang Remedios remained in place. She had already done sessions that day. If a submissive were required, she would be summoned to assemble with the others for the client to review. She was often chosen to give the tour, as she was very lovely, with large, dark eyes full of emotion.

Heavy female footsteps approached the doorway, which was curtained from the hall, and Rayanne entered the room, furiously puffing a cigarette, her firm, young, broad hipped body squeezed into a leopard print sheath, her pale blonde hair pulled back in a severe ponytail to further accentuate her high cheek bones, her strong feet breaking down the sides of a pair of high heels.

"There's a customer out there," Rayanne softly revealed, eyeing herself in the mirror and pushing back a pale stray hair. "He wants to see a submissive," she continued, tossing Remedios a sidelong glance, dragging on her cigarette, picking up someone else's lipstick and touching up her wide sexy mouth. Rayanne was anything but submissive herself. "Be careful, I think he's a cop," she added in her characteristically hoarse, smoker's voice. Remedios crushed out her cigarette and slid off the stool.

"A cop!" the dark haired girl's heart began to pound even faster. "Is Hildy around?" Remedios referred to the unflappable young mistress of the house.

"She's doing a three hour session in The Woodshed," said Rayanne, referring to one of the upstairs dungeons.

"Can't he see one of the others?"

"He wants to see all the submissives before he decides. Don't worry. Just be careful," Rayanne counseled, picking up someone else's brush and taking it to her hair.

When Remedios emerged into the main parlor, which was furnished in black leather and pink hand-carved rugs, with framed Nagels and Ertes on the walls, she did a quick runaround the room with her gaze. It was a full house that night at The Keep.

Alice, tall, slim and bosomy, with straight brown hair almost to her waist, in a Chinese red silk dress with a stand up collar, was lacing up a pair of red thigh high boots and displaying a marked disinterest in the new customer. Like Rayanne, Alice had worked in B&D for several years as a dominant switch and also knew a cop when she saw one.

Sitting in a corner by herself was Park, the only girl in the club tinier than Remedios, a Korean beauty in her early 20's, dressed in an elegant white satin corset, her jet black hair loosely pinned up, her elfin feet encased in a pair of scarlet red high heeled pumps. Her eyes were downcast, either through shyness or self-absorption. She seemed not to wish to be scrutinized. Or perhaps she was simply above trying to attract a man with her smile or her eyes. Park was a Palos Verdes girl who had run away from home to play at punk and B&D in Hollywood and in spite of her achingly vulnerable appearance, she could be quite the willful brat. Like tall, willowy Alice, diminutive Park had already been featured in a half dozen bondage and spanking videos.

Kneeling before an arm chair, deeply engaged in conversation with the portly, ruddy client it held, was blonde, blue eyed Ronnie, one of the best known bondage video actresses in America, who showed up at The Keep once a month to make herself available to her fans. Fetching in a powder blue satin corset, white stockings and heels, Ronnie looked up to acknowledge the client with a vague though pleasant smile. As she was already engaged to do her next session with the gentleman at whose feet she knelt, she turned away from the newcomer almost at once.

Cleone was visible through the doorway to the inner parlor, parading around bare breasted, in a 19" waist cinch and 6" high heels, her silky mane of blue-black hair brushing her milky shoulders and a luscious pout adorning her generous mouth. Cleone, like Ronnie, was an internationally known bondage model. Whenever asked what she did in a dungeon, she replied, "What ever I like." Remedios classified Cleone as a dominant switch. Like Ronnie and Rayanne, Cleone had a big, voluptuous bottom for her slender torso and quite a bit of it showed beneath the hem of her richly brocaded black satin corset, which reached only to the top of her hips. The scrap of black satin bikini afforded only a shred of modesty to Cleone, whose mouthwatering buttocks it clung to. But the bondage star seemed oblivious to the effect that her spectacular semi-nudity might be having on the various denizens of the Club. She was dressing for a session and hadn't a thought for anything else. Another self-absorbed young lady was Cleone.

Bouncing up and down in an inexpensive lace combination, trying to attract the attention of the newcomer, was cute, plump, bouncy Cherry, a copper haired, blue eyed 19 year old imp whose ingratiating ways made her a favorite with most men and caused most women to reserve for her the most unpleasant thoughts. For once, however, her cuteness was being cordially ignored by the tall, tweed suited gentleman, who now seated himself on the sofa, with a smile on his fair complexioned face, beside slim, dark haired Carrie, the only young lady in the room who was fully dressed. She looked smart in a pencil-slim grey wool skirt, crisp white blouse, 4" black high heels and seamed hose.

The editor of a national spanking magazine, Carrie was popular at the Club, with clients sometimes making special trips to L.A. just to see her. As Remedios teetered into the room on her own high heels, she heard the possible cop say that he had been reading Carrie's columns for years and was delighted to meet her. In most cases, when Remedios heard these words, she would turn around and head back to the dressing room, assuming the client would be doing his session with Carrie. This time she knew he would want to see her first before deciding.

Carrie, who was quite articulate, had introduced the newcomer to all the other girls and as Remedios entered, she performed the introduction for her as well. Remedios stood with burning cheeks as she heard Carrie guilelessly inform the stranger of what an excellent submissive Remedios was, how she took a real spanking and looked devastating in bondage.

The tall, fair-haired man got to his feet and looked Remedios over coolly. Remedios' face burned as she met his eyes. Her heart was pounding violently now and her mouth felt bone dry. Finally he spoke.

"You're all so attractive, it's hard to decide," he said, turning his back on Remedios and smiling at Carrie, "But I know I'm not leaving Hollywood without spanking Carrie Eastern."

Remedios didn't know whether to scream, laugh or faint as Carrie jumped up to lead him upstairs. She rushed back into the dressing room to try to compose herself. She was immediately joined by Rayanne who demanded a cigarette and asked her whether she thought the customer was indeed a cop.

"Yes," said Remedios, "I think he is one,"

"We'll have to warn Carrie when she comes down with the money," said Rayanne conspiratorially. "You know how she gets with the good looking ones." She leaned out of the fitting room to listen with one ear to what was going on in the hallway above. This was where all the bondage equipment and spanking implements were kept and Rayanne could hear the client and Carrie selecting a variety of toys to take into their dungeon. In a few minutes, they had chosen a room to play in and Carrie came tripping down the stairs with the session money, which she gave to Cherry while she asked to be "started in 5 minutes." Carrie needed at least that long to slip into the dressing room, fix her lipstick and take a few hits off a joint.

The moment Carrie Eastern entered the small, smoky room Rayanne pounced on her.

"Carrie, be careful with that guy. He's a cop."

"Really?" Carrie hastily put away her supply of pot and fished in her locker for her breath mints instead, which she duly passed around to the other two. "But he's a real spanking person," Carrie pointed out; "He's been reading my stuff for years. He's got to be okay, even if he is a cop. Besides, he's from back east. This isn't even his jurisdiction."

"Just be fucking careful," insisted Rayanne." I mean control yourself."

"Okay, okay!" Carrie took a small orange packet containing a Rough Rider condom out of her skirt pocket and threw it into her locker behind a stack of stocking boxes.

"Of course," thought Remedios, "He picks the one who fucks!"

"He didn't say anything about sex. Just spanking. That's all he's into," said Carrie blithely, adding, "Isn't it great? He's so handsome!"

"He's still a cop," warned Rayanne.

"Well, so what? He's a cop into spanking. Cops have to recreate too, especially when they're far from home. See ya!" and Carrie was gone, calling out for them to start her session on the clock.

"You got a cigarette, Remy?" Rayanne asked, giving Cherry a hostile once over as she bounced into the tiny fitting room and began pawing through her locker for some necessary item. When Cherry squatted down her plump rear was fully exposed by the tiny poly-satin bikini, which girded her hips. Remedios exchanged a smile with Rayanne.

"Here, keep them," Remedios handed Rayanne a full pack of Kool Milds. When Cherry had bounced out of the dressing room with a pair of rubber tipped nipple clamps clutched in her chubby hand, Remedios asked Rayanne whether it was really true that Carrie Eastern made love to her customers. Rayanne grinned.

Remedios wandered out to the main parlor and waited, seated on the edge of a sofa, answering phone calls, until a half hour had passed. There were several spanking sessions in progress at that time, not only Carrie's but also Ronnie's, as the blonde video model had also gone up to a dungeon with her companion and Remedios could not distinguish from the sounds of the smacks coming from above which young lady she was overhearing getting spanked at any given moment. She was seated close to the doorway to the inner parlor so that she could listen to Cherry call up to Carrie's dungeon on the intercom to let her know her time was up. When Cherry did so Remedios was unnerved to overhear the crackly response that they were going to "extend for a half hour."

During the next half hour, Ronnie came down from her session, so that the only spanking going on in the club during that interval was the extended session Carrie was doing with the cop. Remedios sat and listened to the crisp volleys of rapid fire spanks with increasing anxiety. Park kindly asked her if anything was wrong and offered her a cigarette. They smoked together, quietly chatting. Remedios knew that so long as the noises were coming from the dungeon, Carrie and the cop could not be having sex.

Remedios went out to the kitchen and forced herself to drink water. She opened the back door into the yard and looked out into the small parking lot and tiny side garden. Even out here she could still hear the sounds coming from the dungeon above. It was awful, simply awful! Why was he doing this to her?

She knew why. To punish her! A large, late model Cadillac pulled into the lot and from it emerged an extremely neat and well-groomed young Japanese-American businessman who adored tickling Remedios. Oh no, Ken, not tonight!

Putting Ken off was difficult. He almost begged her to let him tie her up and tickle her. Instead she took him into the parlor and kept him by her side while they talked. They talked a great deal during their sessions anyway. Ken didn't have a girlfriend and needed someone to listen to him.

Finally Cherry went up to do a session and passed the login clipboard to Alice, reminding her to call let Carrie know when her time was up. This time when warned that there was only five minutes remaining to her session, Carrie came down almost at once. But the gentleman remained upstairs in the dungeon. Carrie was flushed as she handed a wad of cash for the second half of the session to thin, long faced Lester, the bouncer who took and put away the cash for Mistress

Hildegard throughout the day and night. He lived at the club, generally sleeping in a cage and none of the girls enjoyed being around or interacting with the heavy smoker.

Remedios looked up at Carrie, asking, "How did it go?"

"Oh, great! What a fabulous man. He wants to see Ronnie now," replied Carrie. Ronnie jumped up, patted her hair with a glance in the mirror and mounted the stairs, thinking one more session would round out the evening nicely! Remedios felt dizzy with disappointment.

A few minutes later Ronnie came tripping down the stairs with her money, handed it to Lester, told Alice to start her now for a half hour session with the possibility of extending to an hour.

Remedios followed Carrie into the fitting room.

"Well? What was he like? Was he hard? What did you do?" Remedios couldn't help herself.

"Look," said Carrie, pulling her grey gabardine skirt up to her waist and pulling aside one leg of her pink silk-satin tap pants to reveal one extremely red cheek. Carrie pressed one finger against her flesh and a white spot appeared against the red, then was absorbed into the redness, as with the after effect of a sunburn. "He had a hard hand!"

"Did he hurt you?"

"It was pretty hard but he was so sexy I hardly noticed the pain," Carrie admitted.

"Did he tip you?" Remedios asked out of practical curiosity.

"Yeah, he gave me forty bucks," replied Carrie, giving her hot pink bottom one last glance in the mirror before dropping her skirt. "Wow, what a nice way to end the night. I'm going home."

"Carrie," began Remedios awkwardly, "Did you fuck him?"

"No!" Carrie laughed. "I mean, he's a cop, so why would I? "

Remedios accepted the denial at face value. Carrie had no reason to lie, not knowing of Remedios' particular relationship to the client with whom she had just spent an hour.

Remedios now relaxed to a certain degree. If Carrie was notorious for her spontaneous passion, Ronnie, with whom the gentleman was now playing, had a reputation for only engaging in pure B&D. That meant spanking, whipping, bondage and role-playing but nothing that even came close to penetration.

It was the shank of the evening and busy but Remedios was refusing all comers. She answered phones, she paced, she went out into the yard to smoke, she went back to the fitting room to fix her hair and lipstick 20 times. As with his previous session, the visiting spanking enthusiast decided to extend to an hour. It wasn't every day he got to play with video stars.

Finally Remedios heard Ronnie's light tread on the stairs and the blonde girl was calling her name.

"Remy, he wants you next," said Ronnie, handing Lester the extension money for the second half hour.

Remedios felt her knees go rubbery. It was time. He wanted her now.

"What dungeon is he in?"

"Hades," Ronnie replied. "And he gave me the money for the first half hour so you don't have to come down again."

"Oh," said Remy, adding, "How was it, Ronnie?"

"I liked him," Ronnie said with her sunny smile. "He was a nice man," her words were counter pointed by the redness of her bottom, which was clearly visible beneath the lace-trimmed hem of her exquisite blue corset.

"Start me right away, Lester, okay?" Remedios said to the keeper of the cash. She then went straight upstairs, her heart pounding out of her chest.

She didn't knock on the door, but opened it softly and slipped inside.

The interior of Hades was dark red, with mirrors on two walls, a brick red tiled floor and very low light. The room contained a whipping post, a pillory, a leather upholstered bench, and a straight-backed chair; it lead off into a smaller room with a barred window, a tiny cell for prisoner fantasies.

Leaning against the whipping post, his suit jacket still on over his crisp white shirt and silk foulard tie, with his arms folded and a noncommittal expression on his face, was Michael Flagg.

Flattening herself against the door that she had closed behind her, hesitant to even draw a breath, she regarded her husband with trembling and awe.

"Well, Remedios," It was he who broke the silence. "I hope you haven't been too impatient waiting for your turn!" She dropped her eyes to focus on the tips of her shiny black patent leather ankle-strap heels. "Come over here and let me look at you," he said. But she couldn't move. "I've come 3,000 miles today, young lady," he said with some annoyance; "Don't you think you could manage the remaining five feet?" She covered her face with both hands and emitted a sob.

"Damaris," he said in a tone of deep reproach. She dropped her hands and raised her fine dark eyes to meet his cool blue ones. Her agitation registered upon him. Seeing she was rooted to the floor, he crossed the dungeon to her, took her in his arms and very gently crushed her to his chest. "I'm not surprised you're embarrassed," he whispered into a cascade of thick soft black hair; "to be tracked down by your husband in a place like this."

The words "your husband" sent a thrill through her, not to mention the luxurious sensation of being pressed against the strapping 6'3" muscularity of her Celtic hero. He felt her shiver and held her at arm's length to scrutinize her.

"You know you're lucky your girl friends were around to take the edge off my irritation," he told her in a way that let her know that he still had plenty of irritation to spare.

Damaris bit her lip, feeling her face burn with shame.

"You look very thin," he accused.

"No I don't," she replied, trying to avert her gaze from him again.

"Give me your wrist," he said, seizing it in his cool, firm hand. "Your pulse is racing," he declared.

"With you showing up like this, of course it is," she replied.

"H'm, it's true that you are in big trouble. But I'll bet that's not the only reason your heart is pounding."

"What are you doing here?" she demanded suddenly.

"I missed you." The declaration, although rather stiffly delivered, took her pleasantly by surprise.

"Damaris, sit here," he took a seat on the leather bench and patted a place beside him. She perched warily, suspicious of his quiet tone and the gentle way in which he took and held one of her soft, small hands in his large ones. "You're usually such a sensible girl," he began, patiently, as though he were lecturing an unmotivated schoolgirl; "You're not generally given to sudden caprices. Didn't you realize how annoyed I would be by this little escapade?"

"I... wasn't sure you'd even notice I was gone," said she, with some sarcasm.

"Have I really given you so little reason to believe that I would miss you?"

She did not answer. He had gone to a great deal of trouble obtain this interview. Arranging the time off must have been very difficult. And it had obviously cost a good deal as well, money he could ill afford with the expenses of the remodeled cottage still looming over them.

"Haven't you been mostly happy this last year with me?" he pressed her. She nodded and dared to meet his eyes.

"Haven't I provided you with a proper home?"

"Yes," she agreed, feeling genuinely guilty for the first time since packing her bags and leaving Random Point.

"I'm fully cognizant of everything you've done for me!" she cried, somewhat resentfully. This included his exemplary behavior toward her the year before, when he'd caught her selling contract bids for drugs. Not only had he not arrested her, but he had rescued her from loneliness, insecurity and sexual frustration by marrying her. His campaign to rehabilitate her had been mostly successful, though she'd been backsliding in Hollywood.

"I might believe you were sincere, if it weren't for that insolent letter you sent me!" Michael's tone became a bit sharper. "I received it this morning, so I was able to mull it over all the way to L.A.," he added.

It had been an insolent letter; not even in character for Damaris, who adored Michael Flagg in spite of his infidelities.

"Oh, the letter," she breathed fearfully, pulling away from him instinctively.

"Yes, the letter," he replied, standing up and removing his jacket. He tossed it on the straight-backed chair, loosened his tie and began to roll up his sleeves. "Get that dress off. You're getting a whipping. Right now."

Damaris trembled as he selected a martinet from atop a side table. The small, black leather-thonged whip had been used on her earlier that day during her bondage session, though not severely.

"You're going to whip me?" she rose to her feet slowly, her hand reaching back to unzip her tight, shiny black dress, as though she had been hypnotized.

"Yes, I am," he told her, lowering the suspension bar opposite one of the mirrors and motioning her over to him. When her dress had fallen to the floor she kicked it away and stood before him with her perfect breasts bare, in a pair of black Calais lace briefs, a matching lace garter belt, her sheer, black, seamed hose and breathtakingly high patent leather ankle strap heels.

"Come over here, I said," he ordered, motioning her to him again with some impatience. When she came to him he seized first one, then the other wrist and cuffed her into leather wristlets, the metal loops of which he then attached, using simple boat hooks, to the iron suspension bar that hung above her head. By means of a pulley to one side, Michael raised the bar, thus pulling her arms up above her head. She was loosely cuffed, in such a way that she could hold onto the bar with both hands.

"This is for the letter you wrote me," Michael casually informed her, shaking out the martinet and cracking it. Damaris trembled visibly and caught her breath. He came around in front of her, wound one hand in her long, thick, black hair and bent down to kiss her full on the lips. A hot jet of excitement seeped into her panties at his touch. He looked good and his scent excited her still more. He had come far to find her and his indignation thrilled her. He was acting like a husband who cared and this touched her. Then she realized he was going to whip her and she suddenly became afraid. She looked up at him with huge, tear-filled eyes, frightened to sobs at what was to come.

"Who do you love?" he demanded, lifting her chin to scan her tense, pretty face.

"You, Michael," she whispered. He stepped around behind her and began to feather her back and bottom with the whip, wielding it lightly, with a quick, circular motion, to produce the effect of a rather stinging massage, stimulating and seductive. This was the way experienced floggers often began. It was tempting to relax into it, but anxiety at what was to come forced her to remain taut.

"Haven't I treated you well?" he paused.

"Yes," she softly replied. He pulled back and administered one sharp stroke across her shoulders. She gasped and sobbed. It scared her more than hurt her, but the first stinging kiss of the lashes alerted her to the fact that the serious portion of her chastisement was now underway.

"Then why don't you respect me?" he surprised her by sternly demanding.

"I do respect you!" she protested, craning her head around to look at him.

"A woman who respects her husband does not send him a letter bragging about the attentions of other men!" Michael declared, administering a half dozen deeply stinging lashes across the black lace briefs that encased her well-rounded bottom. Damaris cried out loud at each one and the tears spilled down her face. The pain inflicted by the lashes of the martinet took a moment to fully penetrate after each stroke, which came about five seconds apart. The after-sting shocked her in body and mind, causing her to feel terribly sorry for herself all at once, to the point of contemplating begging for mercy from him.

"Please, Michael, please!" she whimpered helplessly. "It hurts so much!"

Flagg paused to pull down her panties and examine the damage. For a young lady who had been working in pro B&D for a couple of weeks, she had a remarkably white, smooth and unmarked bottom, save for the red marks which he himself had just striped her with.

"I don't care," he told her, holding her about the waist with one arm while raising the whip hand again. "You deserve this and much more for being a brat, a show off and I shudder to think what else while you've been out here!"

Holding her in the circle of his arm, he applied the whip again, this time to her bare bottom, which stung even more keenly. Twelve strokes, evenly spaced and quite stringent then fell, covering her cheeks from hips to thighs with red whip marks. This treatment flooded Damaris with ambivalent feelings. The pain was quite insistent and frighteningly harsh for someone used to firm hand spankings and a strapping now and then, but being held so close by him, almost cradled in his arm while he was punishing her, infused her with melting sensations which all but mitigated the pain.

"So you're not coming back till spring!" he accused, paraphrasing her letter. "You're coming back home with me tomorrow. Do you understand me?"

"Yes, Michael! I'm sorry!" And she truly was. Even now she could hardly believe that she had written so boldly to him. Four more times the martinet lashed her unprotected bottom, this time assaulting the tender juncture between buttock and thigh and leaving a score of whip marks in its wake.

"Not coming back till I appreciate you, are you?" his tone was derisive as he recalled how much that particular remark in her letter had irked him that morning before driving to Boston to board his plane.

"Smart letters show a want of respect, Damaris," he told her, administering a final six stokes, each of which drew a desperate shriek of anguish from the dark haired girl. "I never want to receive a letter one like that from you again. Do you understand?"

"I understand," she sobbed. He threw down the whip and undid the wristlets. Hot tears were rolling freely down her face. Her knees felt weak and her breath came out in gasps, and yet on one level, she felt more relaxed than she'd been in weeks. Her heartbeat slowed as she submitted to his handkerchief mopping her face dry. Letting her body go limp she leaned against him and dared to put her arms around his waist. He pulled her closer to him, so she could feel the enormous erection she had given him. The notion of placing her on all fours on the bondage bench opposite the mirrored wall and giving her the fucking of her life appealed greatly to Flagg, but he remembered the rules of the club and decided to practice patience until he got Damaris to his hotel. "Go downstairs, gather up your things and say goodbye to your friends," Michael told her, rolling down his sleeves and putting his jacket back on.

Damaris got into her dress fairly quickly and shyly asked him to zip her. Once he'd done so he couldn't resist giving her one resounding smack on the back of the shiny black PVC skirt. "I always liked that dress on you. Now hurry up!" he warned.

She turned at the door before exiting and said with actual mischief in her eyes, "No tip for me?" She did not remain to see whether her tiny joke amused him, but went carefully down the stairs of The Keep for the last time.

In the fitting room, Damaris was all thumbs as she hurried to change from her B&D gear into a pair of snug, black, pegged jeans, a white cotton blouse with a small collar and a short cropped oatmeal wool cardigan. She replaced her hose and heels with thick oatmeal wool sox and a tiny pair of black leather oxfords. As she was putting her hair in a long, thick pony tail with a beige grosgrain ribbon, Lester came in with her session money for the night.

Rayanne entered as Damaris was zipping up her garment bag with her PVC dress and a corset.

"Remy! How did it go?" Rayanne demanded, offering Damaris a cigarette, which was declined.

"I might as well tell you, Ray, he's my husband," said Damaris.

"Homegirl!" Rayanne was stunned.

"I have to go now. I'll call tomorrow to say goodbye to everyone," she briefly hugged the blonde girl who was still reeling with amazement.

Carrie Eastern, who had been persuaded to do one more session before departing that night was coming down the stairs as Damaris emerged from the dressing room to join Flagg in the main foyer.

"Going home, Remy?" Carrie said to Damaris, smiling at Flagg over her shoulder. "Did you two play?"

"Yes," said Damaris, unable to help herself. "And now Michael is taking me home."

"How nice!" said Carrie, who would have enjoyed going home with the good-looking detective herself, at least for a couple of hours.

Outside in the parking lot Michael handed Damaris into his rental car and put her garment bag in the trunk. He got in beside her and asked her where she had been staying. She gave him an address on

Franklin, which she then directed him to as they traversed the seedy back streets of Hollywood.

The Amour Arms was large, imposing, decaying and put Michael immediately in mind of the sprawling 19th century tenement in Emile Zola's L'assomoir. The halls were monuments to peeling paint, graffiti and stained, threadbare carpeting. Bare white electric bulbs lit the way and more than one unsavory Hollywood character lingered in them as Michael and Damaris made their way to her room on the fourth floor. The elevators were both out of order, so they walked up the four flights of stairs, passing miscellaneous zombies, gang members and punks along the way. Flagg's expression grew stonier as he observed every facet of the environment in which his wife had willingly placed herself these past two weeks.

Finally they reached her room, the lock of which was a poor joke. The door, Michael noted, might have been pushed open by a vigorous 3 year old. Inside the room it was shabby, dingy and sad, with more peeling plaster, an ancient wrought iron bedstead with a thin mattress and a new blue comforter, which Damaris must have purchased upon her arrival. A bunch of lilacs in a green cut glass vase had been placed upon the bureau.

"I can't believe you've been living here," he said, truly horrified, the moment he had closed the door behind them. "Are you out of your mind, Damaris? Have you seen this door?" he gestured toward the toy lock with contempt.

"It does get rattled three or four times a night," she admitted, pulling her suitcase out from under the bed and beginning to gather items from the dresser to fill it. The room let off into a tiny, unspeakable bathroom which even Damaris' zeal for cleanliness had not rescued from slum status. It was as clean as she could scrub it, but there was no counteracting the impression left by broken tiles and a particularly large species of black beetle, which had turned the leaking shower stall into a wading pool in her absence. Michael fancied he felt his blood pressure rise as he surveyed it all.

The club, with its denizens and implements and implications had not upset him. He'd entered in a somewhat dark mood, which was immediately lifted by finding himself surrounded by his favorite spanking video stars. By the time he had done his sessions with Carrie and Ronnie, both of whom were warm and real, he had almost felt excited for Damaris' sake. What a uniquely educational experience for a girl into B&D this must have been!

Although he had pretended to be outraged by her sassy little letter, he clearly understood that it had been motivated by her feelings of jealousy about his indiscreet ongoing affair with Marguerite Alexander back in Random Point and accepted the major portion of the responsibility for his wife's rebellious flight. But this unspeakable place did make him angry. That door! The idea that night after night his wife had resided in a den of dopers, derelicts and impoverished teenage runaway hookers made his proper Bostonian blood boil.

"I'm ready," she said, snapping her valise shut.

"Are you sure you've got everything?" he pulled open the top drawer of the battered wooden dresser before she could think of an excuse to stop him. In that drawer there was the remains of a tiny stash: two neatly rolled joints, a fresh pack of rolling papers, and in a small box of safety matches, a straight edged razor in a brown paper wrapper. Michael undid the safety wrapper and examined the razor with a practiced eye. It was dulled from several usages, with a light rusty cast along the edge, as if a chemical had caused it to oxidize. He sniffed both paper and razor and looked at Damaris, whose knees had turned to water for the second time that night.

"I knew you were looking unnaturally thin," he said coldly. "Well? What have you been doing? Coke? Crystal? Ice?"

Damaris looked down at the shiny rounded tips of her neat little shoes.

"Crank," she replied in a very small voice. There was no point in bothering to lie, he could always have the blade analyzed by the police lab.

"I knew it!" he practically snarled, grabbing the joints out of the drawer and disappearing into the bathroom to flush them down the toilet.

"I knew that this whole thing was about drugs!" he declared with disgust and marched out of the hotel room with furious haste. Damaris ran with her suitcase to catch up with his long strides as he seemed to cover the distance between fourth floor hall and ground floor landing in seconds flat. Indeed she flew down the stairs behind him so fast that she almost tripped and fell. As they emerged the oppressive old residential hotel and Michael made a beeline for the car Damaris stopped short with her valise.

"Maybe I shouldn't come with you after all," she ventured timidly, sad to the depths of her soul and terrified of having to go back into the Amour Arms Hotel by herself. She wanted nothing more right now than to leave this unreal and endless summer behind and return to her snug little cottage in the pines.

He opened the passenger door of the car and said, "Get in. I'm not in the mood to hold a debate here."

"But if you hate me..." Damaris said pathetically, hot tears welling up in her beautiful eyes for the second time that night. It had all been going so well. Even the whipping had been an affirmation of his love, but now this had to happen! Damaris noted the change that had come over him with positive despair. And there was nothing, absolutely nothing she could do about it. There was no way to get through to him now, not when his eyes had turned to blue ice and his mouth to a thin line of stone. She dissolved in a pool of tears, right in the middle of Franklin Ave., under a yellow streetlight, while the pale white creatures of the Hollywood night crept by them. She sat on her suitcase and burst into sobs, fully convinced that the next sound she heard would be that of a car door slamming and that same car driving away. Instead, she felt herself being pulled roughly to her feet by her arm and tucked under her husband's. He picked up her bag with the other hand and hauled them both over to the car, throwing Damaris in the front seat and the valise in the back. Then he got in beside her and they took off.

Damaris sat still and quietly wept as Michael stared straight ahead and took Sunset to the beach. It was a long, lovely drive at midnight, with very few cars sharing the road. He hadn't put the top up though it had grown quite chilly. When he noticed Damaris pressed against the door and shivering he turned on the heat to warm her feet.

"Don't you have a jacket?"

"I guess I left it at the club," she admitted, trying to get control of herself.

"We'll stop by on our way to the airport tomorrow and pick it up. It's cold back in Boston and you'll need it when our plane gets in."

His terse words calmed her sobs. She looked up at the stars and half moon, at the mansions and lush stands of towering pineapple palms as they glided by them. If he still planned to take her back with him, he couldn't really hate her. Damaris wished that Sunset Boulevard would never end, for she dreaded what would happen to her when they finally reached their destination, a splendid hotel on the Santa Monica beachfront.

They exchanged not another word until he pulled up in front of the imposingly elegant art moderne facade and Michael handed the keys to a smartly uniformed valet. He grabbed her suitcase in one hand and her own small hand in the other and briskly marched her into the spectacular vaulted lobby.

Damaris, who was keenly sensitive to her environment could not fail to make comparisons between the modern gothic hell from which she had just been plucked and the stylish retro hostelry through which she was now being led. They strolled passed indoor pools and saunas, sweating behind bottle green glass walls. Damaris eyed these longingly, weeks of tension still cramping her shoulders and neck.

They reached the elevators, which ran up the outside of the building facing the beach, and rode up ten floors. For a few moments Damaris got lost in the dazzling view of the Pacific.

Michael used his key to open the door to the impressive cream and mauve suite, which would be paid for by months of future moonlighting. He locked it again when she entered and immediately went to the wet bar, under which he found a refrigerator stocked with everything. He opted for vodka on the rocks. Remembering her preferences, he wordlessly mixed her a Bloody Mary and handed it to her. Then he drank and paced, divesting himself of jacket, tie and shirt as he did so.

Damaris quietly sat on a sofa, with her valise so annoyingly close to her that he was impelled to seize it and fling it into a closet before many more minutes had passed. She took large gulps of her drink after that, grateful for the quick burn and subsequent warmth that followed.

Emboldened a bit by the alcohol, she gazed wistfully at his muscular chest and broad shoulders. She'd missed those arms.

After his first drink, Michael's anger began to abate. The sight of her sitting there like a frightened schoolgirl did much to soften his mood. She was bad, but she was very dear to him.

Another few gulps of his drink and he looked at her again, taking notice for the first time that evening of just how stressed and vulnerable she looked. It was that vulnerability which had first attracted Michael to Damaris the previous year. This evening in fact, reminded him in some ways, of the first night they'd ever spent together. In the capacity of a private investigator, he'd caught her in a rather sordid little white-collar crime and subsequently decided to rehabilitate her himself. That process had included marriage.

Observing the tightness in her small shoulders and the sad, resigned look on her fine face he felt suddenly ashamed. Why was he doing treating her like this? Had he always been so pompous and self-righteous, or was this something he had picked up lately? This was supposed to be a game!

"Want another one?" he asked her, seeing she was coming to the end of her drink. The potion was restoring color to her face. She nodded, daring to raise her beautiful eyes to him.

What was he making such a big deal about, he wondered, finishing his drink. So she had taken some drugs. Wasn't that to be expected in that milieu, with temptation all around her? Everyone should be allowed to backslide now and then. And it wasn't as though she was puffing away on a cigarette in front of him. She still had that much respect. Once he got her home, she would be good again. He'd make sure of that.

"Crank!" he suddenly snapped aloud, in spite of his more humane thoughts. "Don't you realize they use that stuff to clean out industrial refrigeration units?" Damaris trembled, hung her head and looked miserable.

"Young lady, when was the last time you ate?" he asked, handing her a second drink.

"Earlier today," she lied.

"Or possibly yesterday, from the look of you!" He picked up the phone and ordered a meal for them from room service. He kept his eyes on her while he gave the order. It was almost one a.m.; she hadn't eaten all day, she'd taken drugs, she listened to him play with other women for hours. She'd taken a smart little whipping. He was willing to wager she was utterly exhausted, but because of all that had gone on that evening, she sat before him like a wound spring. Was this as well as he could take care of her? He put the phone down.

Remembering the condition of her bathroom at The Amour Arms Hotel Michael went to the hall closet and took down a fluffy white terry cloth robe, furnished by the hotel, and tossed it at her.

"Take a bath. You have time before the food arrives," he said. She jumped up at once, thrilled at the notion of luxuriating in a spotlessly clean, richly appointed bathroom. As she passed by him he pulled from his pocket the two joints he had taken out of her drawer at the hotel, the ones that she thought he had flushed. He put them into her hand.

"Here," he told her. "I want you to be able to sleep tonight."

Damaris almost fainted. She looked up at him, overwhelmed by this sudden and completely unexpected kindness. "Go on," he said. "You'll feel much better after a bath."

As Damaris closed the door behind her, stripped off her clothes, lit the joint and ran the bath she wondered what had happened to soften him so. When she looked in the mirror to examine the marks on her bottom she was stunned to note that except for several very small purple marks on her right hip and several more on her left inner thigh, they had all but disappeared. The whipping had felt so severe at one point that she expected to be confronted by a network of black and blue welts. Her bottom was no longer even pink.

Moments later, grasping a large cake of expensive French milled soap in one hand and her cigarette in the other, Damaris felt like Sara Crewe on the morning she and Becky awoke to a real wood fire, quilted bathrobes and fresh baked scones. She lay back in the large, milky green tile tub, covered in soft, creamy suds. And the best part of all was that Michael was waiting outside.

When she finally emerged from the bathroom, wrapped in the terry cloth robe and her little oatmeal colored ankle sox, she was warm and pink from head to toe. The sandwiches had arrived and Michael was already seated at the table. He motioned her over and she sat down opposite him.

"I want to see you make a happy plate," he warned her sternly as she shook her napkin out. "It's shocking how much weight you've lost in a few weeks!"

"Don't you like me slim?" she asked, biting into the French dip sandwich with a good appetite.

"No, I do not," he firmly rejoined. She made no further comment as she ate, being possessed of good manners. He watched with satisfaction as she consumed three quarters of the sandwich, half a baked potato and some salad before wiping her mouth with a napkin and pushing her plate away.

"Good girl," he said, and called room service to remove the dishes. When this service had been performed, Michael locked the door, folded his arms, leaned against it and looked at her.

"Feel better?" he asked.

"Much better, thank you," she replied.

"You look much better."

She accepted the observation without comment. For a time neither said a word but simply gazed across the room at each other. It was he who finally broke the silence.

"I'm not happy about the way you've been living out here, you know that, don't you, Damaris?"

"Yes," she answered softly, dropping her eyes.

"How many men have you let make love to you since we were last together?"

"None!" she replied with vehemence.

"So except for the drugs, you've been a good girl," he stated.

"Yes."

"I'd have rather you been a bad girl with other men than with drugs."

"I know," she replied, adding to herself, "That way you wouldn't have to feel guilty about Marguerite!"

"I'm sure you made more than enough at the club to stay at a decent hotel."

"Yes," said Damaris with a sigh.

"But that would have been out of the question with grams costing $120 and lids twice as much. Am I right?"

"Yes, sir."

"Don't you realize that you were putting your very life in jeopardy staying at that crumbling roach palace? Suppose someone with AIDS had broken into your room and raped you one night?"

"I never thought of that," she admitted, terrified in retrospect.

"That's always been your problem, not thinking."

"Yes, sir," she agreed, with a blush, recognizing the familiar formula. She knew very well when he crossed the room to sit beside her on the comfortable sofa exactly what was about to happen.

"Damaris, you need a good paddling," he told her, taking her by the arm. But instead of allowing him to pull her across his lap, Damaris pulled back from him and resisted.

"No!" she cried rebelliously. "You do!"

"I do?" Michael was so surprised by this declaration that he aborted the spanking. "How do you figure that?"

"You've been a bad husband," she accused, trembling at her own audacity. He waited for her to continue, releasing her arm. She sprung to her feet, not wanting to be within grabbing reach while she had her say.

"You've been cheating on me, continuously, with Marguerite. And don't try to deny it!"

Michael opened his mouth, then shut it again. His face grew warm.

"Ha!" Damaris cried. "There's not much you can say, is there?" She paced, burying her tiny hands in the deep pockets of the robe.

"I married you," he finally said.

"But you're in love with her!"

"I'm fond of her."

"You love her more than you do me!"

"That's not true."

"You can't stay away from her more than a couple of days. I can always tell when you've been with her. I can smell her perfume on you!"

"I'm sorry," he said uncomfortably. Being forced to acknowledge one's own bad behavior is never pleasant.

"I believe you," she replied. "You wouldn't have taken the trouble to follow me out here if you weren't sincerely interested in holding on to me. But that's not enough to compensate me for the insult! "

Michael was impressed by her sudden determination to take control of the situation. However, her defiance made him doubly determined to turn her over his knee before many more minutes had passed.

"What is then?"

"I've been a conscientious wife," she said, ignoring his question. "I've cooked, cleaned, held down a full time job, contributed to the household expenses and unlike you, I've been completely faithful. Have I not?"

"I guess you have been a model wife," he admitted, rather abashed. She was certainly winning this round.

"Michael, I love you, and I think you have deep feelings for me too, but we're going to have to get a divorce."

"A divorce!" This was getting out of hand.

"That way you'll be free to see both Marguerite and me as much or as little as you like," Damaris explained, patiently, reasonably and confidently enough to thoroughly exasperate him.

"No, it's out of the question!" he declared.

"All right," she conceded serenely, "since you're reluctant to give up an excellent housekeeper, I'll make an alternate suggestion. We'll stay married, but I'll see other men as well."

"You'll do no such thing!"

"I will!" she stamped her tiny foot.

"Other men like who?"

"Do you really want to know? There are any number of men in our town who would be interested. My manager at work has been making passes at me all year. Then there's the Latin dance instructor in Woodbridge. He's been begging me to come and work for him giving Cha cha lessons!"

"Cha cha lessons? How do you come to know a Latin dance instructor?"

"I took advantage of a free lesson and we had tea one afternoon.

His name is Armando and he asked me to leave you that first day."

"What do you mean, that first day? Have you seen this joker since?"

"I take a dancing lesson from time to time," said she with a challenging toss of her hair. "Of course, I haven't let him touch me. Yet."

"And you're not going to, either!"

"Oh yes I will. Him and anyone else I fancy while you're servicing the red head!"

"And who else do you have on your list of possibles, just for my interest?" Michael demanded, getting up to refill his glass.

"Well, let me see...Hugo Sands is one. You look surprised. Didn't you know I knew him? Oh yes, the typing bureau sent me to him several times this last month. He's a very sexy man and I can tell he liked me."

"I'll just bet!" Michael fumed, sloshing vodka into his glass.

"There are others of course," said Damaris airily.

"Are there!" Michael was still brooding about the dance instructor. How dare she go and have private dance lessons with an oily gigolo behind his back?

"Oh yes, and if I exhaust the locals I can always place a personal ad in The Boston Phoenix," she said practically, at which Michael looked so pained that she almost felt sorry for him. "Oh, don't worry," she laughed, "I'm a good month away from even having dinner with Armando. You've got plenty of time to time to start behaving like an honorable husband if you choose to do so!"

Michael was momentarily bereft of speech by this emphatic pronouncement. Someone had been teaching her to be a dom! He'd never seen her so determined to get her own way.

Draining his glass in moody silence, Michael reflected on what she had revealed. No one took Cha cha lessons anymore. The phrase was obviously plucked from his wife's earliest childhood memories of New York. If there were a dance studio in Woodbridge, it would be of the aerobic variety. Michael was relieved to realize that Armando was a fabrication, invented to make him jealous. He marveled at the ease with which Damaris had lied to him.

"I think I'll have to have a talk with this Armando," Michael said at length.

"I hope you're not thinking of trying to intimidate him. Armando is Columbian and well connected," Damaris cautioned.

"That does it!" Michael slammed his empty glass down on the bar. He crossed the room to her swiftly. She backed away but he stalked her, caught her around the waist, hauled her over to a well-upholstered sofa and put her across his lap. "I happen to know, Damaris Flagg, that there is no dance studio in Woodbridge!" He informed her before spanking her soundly.

The first few hard smacks took her breath away. She leaned up on her arms momentarily, looked back and shuddered at the descent of his formidable arm. She wished very much to kick, scream and cry in response but remembered where they were and kept her verbal responses to a series of woeful whimpers. Truly he had a hard hand! She bit her lip and buried her face in her arms. Time stopped. Nothing existed but Michael's lap, the strong arm holding her in place across it and the hand that was punishing her. There was a good deal of righteous indignation coming through here, she realized. The thought of her planning a dinner date with another man had upset him!

Meanwhile, this was the first time in months she had been turned over her husband's knee and of all men, he was the still the one who made her swoon. She had to face it; she was in love.

Since he was so tall and imposing, it was not difficult for her to feel like a very little girl whenever he took her in hand. She felt that way now as he spanked her, pausing only to pull up the skirt of her robe and bare her to the waist.

"There isn't any Armando!" he declared. A flurry of sharp smacks followed.

"Maybe not, but there could be!" Damaris cried defiantly.

"There could be, but there won't be!" he told her firmly.

"I'll make that decision for myself !" she declared stubbornly and was rewarded with a half dozen stinging smacks hard enough to bring fresh tears to her eyes.

"I don't like impertinence!" said Michael.

"Who cares?" she mustered defiantly.

"You will, when I get through with you," he promised, spanking her harder.

"No! Let me go! I want a divorce!"

He stayed his hand, resting it on the crest of her luscious, bare bottom.

"I told you I don't want to hear that word, young lady," he warned her.

"Then you'd better be nicer to me!"

"I can do that," he said, turning her over and taking her in his arms. He held her and kissed her and buried his face against her smooth, bare, perfumed throat. "I don't want you to see other men."

"I don't want you to see other women," she replied, encouraged by his ardor.

"All right, I won't," he vowed. She had never had him promise her anything before and thus did not know how to judge the sincerity of his words, but the fact that he had uttered them at all was most encouraging.

"You'll stop seeing Marguerite?"

"Yes."

The wonder of winning left Damaris dizzy. She submitted to his kisses in a daze. So Laura Random had been right. It really did take leaving one's husband to make him act correctly.

"Now, what more can I do remove this divorce brainstorm from your mind?" he took both her hands and brought them to his lips. Before she could reply he added fondly, "You know, you were the prettiest girl at the club tonight. I was proud that you're my wife."

These guileless statements brought a charming blush to her face. She had received many compliments during the past few weeks, but these were the only ones that had any meaning for her. She responded to the soft words in feline style, butting her head against his chest and almost purring.

"I think you need a climax to make you feel loved," he declared, parting her robe and covering her silky black public curls with his hand. Damaris was too shy to answer but her silence was eloquent. Michael turned her over on his lap so that she was once again in the spanking position. He raised the skirt of her robe and began to caress her bare bottom. It was lightly tinged with pink and extremely smooth. He stroked her from the backs of her knees to the tops of her hips with the palm of his hand, gently but deeply. She wriggled across his lap, pressing her moist pussy hard against his thigh.

Then she felt him separating her legs to gain access to her sex. Holding her firmly by the waist, he slowly inserted his middle finger into her girlishly tight, wet slit. He got three fingers soaked with her juices as he worked them in and out. When she was sopping wet he used her own fluid to lubricate the division between her cheeks. Realizing what was coming, Damaris caught her breath.

His long middle finger slipped into her bottom easily. She died of shame and hid her face. He moved his other hand down to hold her by the curve of her hip while firmly, slowly masturbating her. There was nothing she could do but be taken and respond. With his large, inescapable hand holding her in place and his broad, smooth thigh to grind against and his artful fingers probing her more deeply every second, what choice did she have but to submit to the thrilling sensations her husband was providing for her.

She liked to think of this as discipline. It made it more exciting to think that this was the treatment reserved for bad girls. Of course, it felt sublime, but the humiliation of being invaded and probed in this way, made it seem another sort of lesson to her. The urge to have this confirmed by her husband impelled Damaris to ask, "Is this part of my punishment?"

"I think you know it is," he said, quickly tumbling to her mood and finding her submissiveness adorable. "You haven't been punished like this in a long time and it's exactly what you need," he told her, reinforcing his statement with a couple of sharp smacks on either cheek. Now he began to alternate between fingering and spanking her, burying his finger inside her snug, clenching bottom for a few seconds, then pulling it out to spank her for a few more, then back again and so on, until after several minutes of this, she was in a positive frenzy of excitement. Several times, when he felt her grinding most furiously, he stopped her and made her lie still. "Don't you dare come yet," he warned. Not that he cared when she came, but all of this was so enjoyable visually and physically that he wasn't above attempting to prolong her ordeal by any means available to him. After she had calmed down he began to spank and masturbate her again; this went on a number of times while she alternately humped and lay still across his knees.

"You're getting punished again as soon as I get you home," he promised. "In the bathroom of our playroom," he added. She knew what that meant. Before they had moved to the cottage he had administered a bathroom punishment to her and she had often wondered whether he would ever do so again. Now they had a perfect and pristine blue tiled bathroom with all manner of clever and diabolical built-ins, designed by their architect friend William Random, with discipline in mind.

"No!" she murmured helplessly, envisioning herself bending over the cold, custom-built marble bench set into a special bathtub, which had been fashioned for the purpose of ritual cleansings. It hadn't happened yet and they'd been in the cottage several months, but she'd anticipated it often enough.

"Oh yes," he said, "we're going to have to rid you of all of these terrible controlled substances you've been choking your poor little body with these past few weeks. As soon as I get you home, you're getting as many enemas as it takes to leave you sparkling clean."

"No!" she protested weakly, madly in love.

"I'm not going back to work until Monday so we've got plenty of time. You've got a good deal to answer for, however, by the time I'm through with you I expect a truly humble and repentant young lady."

"But...you don't really want to do that to me!" she charged.

"Don't you think so?" he spanked her rather harder for doubting him. "Once a week wouldn't be too often for a bad girl like you." He noticed her intake of breath and took pleasure in her excitement. "It really is the most effective form of discipline for you. I realize that now," he told her, finally taking her over the edge with his actions and well as his words.

Damaris ground, came, whimpered and went limp. He kissed her and held her until her spasms subsided. Then he laid her on her back, fairly ripped off his trousers and revealed the enormous throbbing hard-on that had been vaguely troubling him all night. Finally after all these hours of teasing and temptation he was deep inside his snug, warm, wet, clinging, little wife, plunging into her to the hilt over and over again. She was so soft and small, so smooth and fragrant, so tremblingly responsive to every sharp, deep thrust, that he could not help but feel intensely satisfied with his day's efforts. She loved him and wanted to come home. He'd rescued her before the fast lane was able to inflict lasting damage on her fragile little body. And he'd done it bloodlessly. True, he had tormented her a bit by playing with the other girls at the house and he had also been his typical harshly critical self at the unspeakable hotel, but on the whole he felt he'd exhibited remarkable restraint in apprehending his errant wife. He also intended to behave like an adult about Marguerite from now on. Damaris had been perfectly correct about him being a bad husband and he knew he had to fix that.

Allowing herself to be taken, Damaris felt as happy as she had ever been. Being made love to by her husband was always special, there was something quite perfect about the way he took her, something about the rhythm or the velocity or thrust, or perhaps it was the duration. He always gave her quite a long, hard ride, one she could get lost in, could dream in, could muse on the awful punishments he'd threatened her with in. He never finished quickly. He always took her with him on the ride, bringing her to a high pitch of excitement five or six or ten times during the 20-30 minutes in which he remained inside her. Since they were so well suited to each other, he always prolonged the encounter. To her it was the time when she felt that she belonged to him most deeply as well as the way sex should be.

Finally they put off the light and went to bed properly. But Damaris was still excited and asked Michael whether he really intended to give up Marguerite. He told her that he truly did. She asked him whether he was really going to do those dreadful things to her when they got home.

"You just wait and see," he promised, pulling her against him in the dark.

Chapter Six

Hellfire Club

It was midnight and drizzling lightly on that pleasant April evening, when Anthony Newton's silver Bentley glided to a stop in front of an unmarked black door on 14th Street, in the dingy and nearly deserted meat-packing district on the West side of New York.

The immaculately suited Newton got out of the car, telling his driver to wait, then entered the dark, overheated atmosphere of the Hellfire Club.

Paying twenty-five dollars to a bear-like, leather vested cashier, Newton casually descended the pair of rough black stairs leading down into a modern facsimile of Dante's Inferno.

So this was where Susan spent her Saturday nights, Newton observed with interest, as he skirted the bar, which didn't serve alcohol and billiard table, where no one ever played pool, to suddenly find himself in a long, narrow room, leading into several other rooms, each of which swarmed with hungry men, many masturbating, on their knees, to the handful of urban goddesses who confidently strode through their midst, strikingly clad in black leather, PVC and thigh-high boots.

Glancing around, Newton now agreed with Susan's assessment that any woman visiting this strangely enchanted fleshpot, might soon be drafted, in spite of herself, into playing the role of Mistress to its worshipful male denizens. And this apparently included his own pony tailed girl, whom he spotted almost at once, seated on a little chair against the far wall, in a pair of black cotton trousers, an indigo blue cotton shirt, white ankle sox and tiny black work boots, both of which were now being adoringly cradled between the hands and lips of two

162

kneeling males, each 10 to 15 years Susan's senior. A circle of men surrounded these three, each one with his cock in his hand, with one or two venturing forward to furtively touch or attempt to fondle and nuzzle the small blonde's cotton-trousered calves and dainty, booted feet.

Susan pouted at her fawning suitors like Scarlett O'Hara at Twelve Oaks, smoothly retaining control of her group with the subtlest of gestures and looks. Newton was impressed when Susan ordered them to come for her and half a dozen instantly complied by shooting a shower of liquid tribute into the air. His little girl was growing up!

Anthony moved in closer. She was about to allow one of the kneeling slaves to unlace her high collared boot and possibly even remove one of her snowy white socks to reveal the aching beauty of her satiny, size 5 foot, when Newton caught her eye.

Susan felt a thrill as she met her lover's gaze. She'd never expected him to come looking for her here. He folded his arms and waited. She jumped to her feet, pushed through her circle of admirers and threw her arms around Anthony's waist, snuggling her head against his snowy shirtfront.

"Very nice, I must say!" he declared, "What are you going to do for an encore, suck the doorman off?"

Not a bit put off by his sarcasm, Susan smiled up at him.

"Anthony, you came to the Hellfire Club! I'm honored beyond words! Come on, let me show you everything!" Susan took him by the hand and began to lead him through the palpably moist catacombs of the club with the excitement of a child skipping through a doll shop with her favorite uncle.

"You're quite the little dom," he commented, momentarily distracted by a tiny blonde mistress, with a high teased pony tail, who'd been poured into a leather jumpsuit, buck and pitch upon the back of an athletic young man, stripped to a harness, with a saddle on his back.

"That's Danny the Wonder Pony," Susan pointed out, adding enigmatically, "And what you just observed was a purification ritual. After what I've been through today, drastic measures were necessary to restore my self-esteem."

Coming out into the furthest room of the club, Newton and Susan observed two scenes already in progress. On a raised platform at the far end of the black-walled room, two slender, pale, brunettes, one in a black leather teddy, the other in a black lace bustier and tight toreador pants, both in stiletto heels, were simultaneously whipping and shoving their crotches into the face of a kneeling, middle aged white male in a studded jockstrap. One of the pretty young women flogged her slave like a vindictive child breaking her toys. A semi-circle of males, penises in hand, were making the most of the performance.

In another area of the room stood a pillory, into which had been locked a voluptuous blonde in her late twenties, nude except for a g-string, garter belt, fish net stockings and thigh-high boots. Behind her, wielding a martinet with precision was a tattooed master.

The one remaining play area in the room, a raised stage equipped with a leather bench, stood vacant. Newton and Susan exchanged a look.

"I have a good mind to take you up there and spank you," he told her.

"You mean for ordering so many men to come for me?" Susan laughed. Being the lover of a sophisticated man 20 years her senior had given her poise.

"For being so proud it," Newton declared, pulling her up the steps by her slender wrist. He then seized and turned her over his knee with graceful ease.

The twenty or so spectators who had been devouring the whippings, immediately defected to watch this unusually attractive pair take the stage. No one had ever seen a meticulously groomed gentleman in an Armani suit spank a Carol Linley look-alike at Hellfire.

Newton, an accomplished showman, immediately began to play to the voyeurs. This was, he realized, with a thrill, the first time in his fifteen-year theatrical career, that he had ever administered a spanking in front of an audience. And what an audience! Every one an appreciative enthusiast. He was performing a public service to the B&D community, spanking Susan like this.

Susan kicked and squirmed across his lap, attempting to wriggle free, but Newton held her fast and spanked her soundly. She limited her verbal responses to a muffled miscellany of inarticulate noises, refusing, out of pride, to argue, beg or sob aloud before the benevolent zombies who panted up at them.

He spanked her continuously, at a steady, measured clip for at least ten solid minutes before letting her up. It was such a thorough spanking that Susan could feel the warmth and deeply penetrating sting of it for at least an hour afterwards, in fact, all the way home and beyond.

Only one of the transfixed observers was a genuine spanking enthusiast, a young tourist from New Hampshire, who'd been deeply regretting descending into this particular circle of hell, when the over the knee spanking commenced. Now he stood and stared, enraptured, unreservedly loving New York, especially the Hellfire Club.

After the first five minutes, Susan grew exhausted from struggling and became more passive. Newton easily restrained her across his lap. Presently the audience around her became a soft blur and the harsh monotony of his hand impacting repeatedly against her bottom began to awaken a tingling response between her legs. Susan was aware that Anthony was showing off for the crowd; but the romantically possessive way he held her, and controlled her so confidently, she accepted as a personal gift. When Newton finally released his girlfriend she couldn't help but rub her bottom with both hands.

"Aren't you going to thank me for not pulling your pants down in front of your slaves?" he asked her, getting to his feet to follow her out of the room.

She did thank him, at least mentally, for preserving at least some of her dignity.

Ten men wistfully stopped masturbating as the couple stepped down from the platform, carelessly breaking the spell.

Susan claimed her nicely broken-in black leather bomber jacket at the coat check and ran up the stairs to the rain-misted street. The Bentley purred at the curb and Dennis, the young English boy who was driving for Anthony these days, jumped out to open the door for Susan.

Dennis, 23 and nearly innocent, was often asked to drive his employer's young lady around late at night. He worshiped Susan, whom he believed to be the most perfect creature in the world. Yet even he disapproved of her visiting this neighborhood.

Susan smiled at Anthony's driver as she got into the car, but once Newton joined her in the back seat she forgot all about Dennis up front. Newton tapped on the partition and Dennis slid it open. He instructed his driver to take them home the long way, by the river. At this hour, in the rain, traffic was thin. The big sedan surged forward.

Susan tucked her heels underneath her as small girls do. Newton folded his arms and leveled an indignant glance at his fiancée.

"So this is why I can never find you on a Saturday night when I want you."

"I'm just gathering data for my graphic novel, you know that!" Susan assured him.

Susan Ross, now 20 and a sophomore at Barnard, resided with Anthony Newton, a composer of musical comedies. Since inviting Susan to live with him, he had dropped all his other attachments. Susan adored him and he grew fonder of her every day.

"We'll return to the impropriety of your behavior in that surreal pit of perversity momentarily, meanwhile, tell me about what happened today to rob you of your self-esteem?"

"Oh, Anthony, it was awful. I did something bad, really bad," Susan confessed. "Shall I tell you?"

"Please, I'm agog."

"Well, I know it was a bozo maneuver, but it was something I'd been thinking about doing it for a long time, part of my odyssey into the scene."

"Susan, you didn't get a tattoo!"

"No, I didn't."

"You didn't go and get yourself pierced, did you?"

"No, no, nothing like that."

Anthony looked relieved. "Well, what then?"

"I did a scene with a Master."

"Oh?"

"He had an ad in an S&M newspaper. I'd been looking at it for months. Well, I finally called him."

"And today was the day that you met, is that it?"

"Yes," Susan sighed. "And it was all wrong. I knew it was wrong the second I walked into his apartment, but once I'd committed myself to playing I couldn't think of any diplomatic way to extricate myself from the situation."

Even if Newton had been the jealous type, the desolate tone of Susan's confession would have neutralized his ire.

"Tell me!" he prompted her.

"Well, to begin with, he wasn't my type. Not even close."

"I never knew you had a type," Newton smiled.

"My type is cute and hot and sexy," she explained, taking the hand that had just warmed her bottom so thoroughly and bringing it to her lips. "Master Ollie looked like a marshmallow in a Hawaiian shirt who had sold his soul to the devil."

"Master Ollie?"

"That's his name. When it came to the scene, I hated just about everything he did to me, and he did it all too hard."

"What did he do?"

"Lots of whipping, mostly on my back, my breasts and the bottoms of my feet."

"Let me see if you're marked." Anthony unceremoniously pulled her down across his lap and pushed up her jacket and the oversized blue shirt, hit the overhead light and examined her back. It was smooth and unmarked. Obviously, the marshmallow was competent with a whip. Newton rolled her over and pushed up her shirt in front. In the way of college girls, Susan wore no bra. Her small yet voluptuous bosom appeared in perfect condition as well, though the nipples, normally a dark coral hue, appeared unnaturally pink. On closer examination of her peach-shaped, blue-veined breasts, Newton discovered a few tiny purple spots on the undersides, apparently left by the lash.

"Your nipples seem slightly irritated. Did he put clamps on them?"

"No, I didn't let him. But he pinched and squeezed and whipped them quite a bit," Susan reported.

"I know you don't like that," Newton remarked with a frown, pulling her shirt down and letting her up. Dennis, who had been watching them in the rear view mirror, tried to ignore his aching erection. The driver had never expected to be allowed a glimpse of Susan's exquisite bosom. Newton and Susan behaved as though he wasn't there.

"They hurt," Susan said, with a pout, rubbing her chest through her shirt with the heels of her hands.

"What else? I have a feeling I haven't heard the worst."

"You're right. One of the most bizarre aspects of the scene was Ollie's insistence that I keep my mouth open and my tongue extended the entire time, while I simultaneously played with his nipples."

"And how'd you do with that challenge?"

"I resented the hell out of it, but I did what he told me to do."

"What else?"

"Well, when he wasn't musing out loud about how much he could sell me for, he was berating me for all the things I wouldn't let him do, such as gagging me, collaring me and suspending me off the ground. He said I was a tourist and not really submissive because of all the things I wouldn't do. He guilted me in to letting him shove an enormous dildo up my pussy, from which I'm still sore. And I... gave him a blow job."

"You gave a stranger a blow job, in this day and age?" Newton did not have to pretend to be horrified at this. Susan hung her head. He drummed his fingers on his knee, then leaned forward, slid open the partition and told Dennis to proceed homeward.

Susan said, "I didn't like being a slave."

They drove along in silence for some minutes, Susan mostly staring out the window at the rain washed streets while snatching momentary glances at Anthony. He gazed back at her sternly, causing her tummy to contract.

"Girl, are you gonna get it when I get you home," he promised.

They arrived at the house, a narrow, 3 storey building in red brick, 75 years old and fully restored. When Susan started up the stairs that led to her studio he caught her by the wrist.

"Where do you think you're going? Don't you realize I have immediate plans for you?" He led her through the ground floor rooms to the back of the house at which there was a service staircase.

"Where are we going?" she asked as he led her by the hand three flights up.

"A room I've been keeping in reserve for you," he told her as they came to a halt on the third floor back landing, in a chestnut painted foyer, which framed a heavy oaken door.

"Just for me?" Susan watched him search his pockets for the key. She had never known him to lock a door in his house. The evening was continuing along its Gothic path.

Newton found the key and opened the door, flicking on the light as he did so, into a long, narrow room, paneled in squares of polished oak. The furnishings and appointments suggested a turn-of-the-century examining room, with its padded table, dentist's chair and tufted couch, all upholstered in chestnut leather and riveted with heavy brass studs. Tall wooden cabinets with glass doors containing medicinal paraphernalia, artfully arranged, lined one of the walls. Susan noticed a mortar and pestle, cotton gauze, blue glass bottles filled with alcohol, aspirin and other innocuous items. There were also more exotic clinical aids, including a number of syringe bulbs with nozzles as well as an antique clyster pump with the logo of an 1890 patent medicine company gaily painted on its side.

Along another wall, set below an enormous mirror, a double marble sink, gleaming with porcelain fixtures, assured the would-be patient of consistently fastidious care. Newton folded his arms and watched her face as she took it all in.

"I'm not ready for this," she announced, with the air of a light-footed girl about to flee down three flights of stairs.

"I'll be the judge of that," Anthony commented, locking the door behind them. "There's no need to panic," he remarked, going about the room to turn on a few additional lamps before dimming the overhead light. The result was a softer, more intimate ambiance. "You wanted a scene and now you're going to get one."

"I've had my scene for today."

"No, you had Ollie's scene. This will be your scene. Sit down, young lady. Let me explain something to you," Newton motioned to the leather sofa. Susan curled up in the corner with a little shiver. He noticed and turned up the heat by means of unscrewing the cap of an old silver radiator. In a very few moments the comforting scent of steam heat filled the air with its accompanying hissing sounds.

"Susan, your behavior clearly indicates that you've been bored."

"I haven't been!" she protested.

"It's partially my fault. I've been such a perfect gentleman, so faultlessly polite that it's no wonder you forgot that I'm supposed to be your dominant!" For the first time a tinge of annoyance creep into his tone.

"I didn't forget," she replied, though meekly.

"The fact remains that you went out looking for something today that you had in your own back yard. Just look around you. Did the dreary little apartment you visited this afternoon possess these capabilities?"

"Of course not. It was horrid."

"Fact number two: Your actions today clearly indicate to me that you occasionally have the desire to relinquish control. You do not need to have your breasts whipped until you cry in order to achieve this."

Susan was only half paying attention. The crotch of her panties became soaked as she contemplated the examination table.

"Fact number three: I do intend to discipline you." He sat down beside her on the leather sofa and turned her to look at him. "Do you understand why?"

"I guess so," she murmured, trying to avoid his gaze, which was making her uncomfortable.

"You know I'm not the jealous type, don't you, Susan?"

"Yes," Susan replied, without actually knowing that to any provable extent, but it seemed most expedient to agree with whatever he said now.

"Then tell me why you're about to be punished."

"Because I blew that guy," she replied guiltily.

"That's a good reason, but not the main one. Your most serious mistake today was allowing a person you didn't even find appealing, to bully you into participating in a number of activities which you do not enjoy. Why were you a jellyfish today?"

"Since I went to his place like that and expressed an interest in B&D, I felt as though I owed him a certain measure of obedience."

"Did he earn or deserve such extraordinary favors?"

"No."

"Did he make the slightest effort to please you?"

"No."

"But you still felt you had to comply with his wishes."

"It was awkward. Once I'd agreed to play, I felt honor bound to proceed," she explained.

"This honor-among-submissives thing is quite a phenomenon," Newton observed; "It seems to serves as the justification for a good deal of unnecessary pain."

"I'm sure you're right," she agreed softly, meeting his eyes.

"It might be argued that if a so-called submissive is so proud as to brag about her honor, she deserves to have it tested to the limit."

"In my case it wasn't so much pride as simply not wanting to hurt his feelings," Susan admitted thoughtfully.

"I hope you understand that for that alone you ought to be thrashed."

"Is that what you're going to do?" Her look almost melted him.

"Oh, Susan!" he took the point of her chin in his hand and kissed her on the mouth. "At your worst, you're adorable." She looked relieved as he got to his feet. "No, I'm not going to thrash you. But I am going to teach you a lesson."

"What sort of a lesson?" she asked him when he rose, divested himself of his jacket and rolled up his sleeves.

"Young lady, I intend to introduce you to a form of discipline so effective that I probably won't have to repeat it again for a year," he informed her. "And it won't involve a great deal of pain, unless you prove uncooperative."

"Define cooperative," she said, shrugging off her leather jacket as it had warmed up considerably.

"Cooperative means you do what I tell you to immediately and without argument."

"Oh," said Susan quietly.

"I notice you've been eyeing my examination table. Suppose you climb up on it right now," Newton suggested. Susan hesitated. "Susan, I said now," he ordered. She approached the table, contemplated it, but made no move to mount it. Impatiently he strode across the room and lifted her to sit her on the edge of the table. They gazed at each other momentarily and he looked very grave.

"I'm sorry that I have to humiliate you like this," Newton lied, "but it's for your own good. Now lie down."

The moment he rolled her over on her tummy all resistance left Susan. The situation was out of her control. She buried her face in her arms. She had a pretty good idea of what was about to happen and this knowledge made her throb. When Anthony pulled her cotton trousers down to her thighs, the throb became a tangible ache. What if she came, she mentally fretted, before he even began? She ground against the tabletop to mitigate the ache.

"What do you think you are doing? Lie perfectly still till I tell you otherwise," he warned, patting her bottom sternly before pulling her high cut white cotton bikinis down to her mid-thighs as well.

All the pinkness from the spanking at the Hellfire Club had faded by now and her shapely bottom was pristine. He ran his sensitive pianist's hand across its girlish contours, charmed almost to distraction by its smoothness. Susan suffered through this exquisitely. It shamed her deeply to be placed face down on a table and have her panties pulled down, exactly as though she were a child of five, visiting the doctor's office, perhaps for the first time. She remembered her childhood doctor distinctly, an authoritative German who was not exactly scary, because he never hurt her, but who always seemed determined to place her in this humiliating position in order to have his way with her bottom. Could he have even been dimly aware that he was creating an anal-erotic submissive when he took her temperature in her bottom, for what seemed like the longest time?

Susan realized that she must have confessed her perverse preoccupation with examining rooms to Anthony, for he said he'd had this room done just for her. She dared to cast him a look over her shoulder. He'd begun to remove her lacing boots and was pulling them off when he noticed her looking at him. She quickly hid her face again.

"That's right, you hide your face," he recommended. "You've

been a very naughty girl." He pulled off her cotton trousers and tossed them aside. Her pretty legs were well rounded and gleamingly smooth. Several tiny purple marks marred the perfection of her white inner thighs, reminding Anthony that Susan had been whipped that day. It astonished Newton that the dominant she had met that afternoon had shown so little interest in her bottom.

"Stay just as you are," he told her firmly, then went to wash his hands at one of the marble sinks. She peeked at Anthony from above her folded arms and saw him remove a jar of petroleum jelly and a 4" rubber plug from one of the cabinets. The mere sight of this intrusive device caused her face to flood with color as she gave a little gasp and said, "No," in a tiny voice.

"Oh yes, Susan. All that and more before I'm done with you tonight," he promised, returning to her with these two objects. "Now then, please elevate your bottom and bring your knees to your chest." He helped her to achieve the new position with gentle efficiency, separating her little white socked feet as much as possible, so that when he was done arranging her, she was comfortably kneeling head down, in a classic widespread, knee to elbow posture, with her buttocks uppermost and slightly divided.

Beneath this pulchritudinously feminine display, her dark blonde pubic curls were perceptibly dewy. He pressed his palm against her moist, pulsating labia.

"Aren't you ashamed of yourself for becoming wet so fast?" he demanded.

"Yes," she confessed, hiding her face again.

"I don't think you understand you're being punished," he pointed out, slapping her smartly on either cheek a half dozen times.

"I understand," she whimpered, trembling in an agony of pleasure as he fully lubricated her anus, probed her deeply with a slender, middle finger, then slowly inserted the slim, cold, rubber plug as far as it would go up into her rectum.

"Remain in this position," he ordered, wiping his hands on a clean, hot towel, which he furnished himself with from an ample supply in the cabinet below the sink.

"Please!" she cried, "I'm afraid it might pop out."

"Be afraid, be very afraid," he advised, but spared her this possible additional embarrassment by pulling her panties back up between her cheeks like a thong and surrounding the base of the plug which depended from her bottom with the soft, snug, white cotton of her bikinis.

Susan's heart pounded fiercely as he casually walked away, turned to observe the picture she made from a distance, then busied himself at the sink with his back to her. She was grateful at that moment that she was no longer face down, with her crotch pressed against the table, as the foreign object now lodged in her bottom would have surely made her climax instantly. As it was she was in grave danger of coming, such was the erotic power of this tenderly invasive treatment.

"Do you know, Susan, that there are about six different kinds of enemas? I personally feel that the syringe style is the most appropriate for a naughty little girl."

When Newton returned to Susan it was to place a white enamel basin of warm water in front of her on the table. He showed her the black, rubber, pint-sized syringe bulb and let her watch him first squeeze out the excess air in the bulb, then insert the 6" nozzle into the basin and fill the syringe with clear water.

"It's much more intimate than a bag with a long hose attached," he pointed out; "And with this modest size, I should think that even a diminutive girl like you would be able to accommodate four or five of these."

Placing the bulb back in the basin to keep it warm, he went behind Susan, pulled her panties off and withdrew the retention plug with care. He took his time in retreating to the sink to thoroughly wash and sterilize the plug with alcohol before laying it aside to dry on a snowy white hand towel. Fairly swimming in her own excitement by now, Susan was still able to detach herself enough to appreciate his meticulousness. Although she nearly died of shame when he made a point of using one of the hot towels on her bottom after withdrawing the rubber plug from it.

"Aren't you going to thank me for being so thorough?" he said, as if reading her mind.

"Thank you," she whispered.

"Do you see this?" he showed her the lengthy nozzle, as he lightly coated it with Vaseline. "This is going in you momentarily. The water will feel very warm, but it won't be anything you can't handle. I expect you to take it like a good girl. Understand me?"

"Yes," she replied with her eyes tightly shut.

"As I said, this is for your own good," he reiterated. "It might feel slightly uncomfortable at first, but it really shouldn't hurt."

Spreading her gently apart with one hand, he inserted the tip of the nozzle into her tiny, pink anus with extreme care. She gave a little moan as he did so, her clit throbbing violently. Holding her cheeks firmly open, he pushed the nozzle in inch by inch. When at last it was buried in her bottom to the hilt, he supported the full bulb of water in the uppermost position and began to squeeze it.

As embarrassing as all of this was, Susan had never felt more excited in her very young life. The warm water gushing into her bottom was exquisitely stimulating. And yet as much as she reveled in the sensation, she did feel truly punished. When he placed one hand under her tummy to hold Susan firmly in place, she almost drifted over the edge. Had he even grazed her clitoris she might have climaxed then, but he was careful to avoid doing this.

"You really are mostly a good girl," he informed her, "which is why I'm being so lenient with you." The first bulb was finished. He withdrew the nozzle, wiped it clean with an alcohol soaked towel, wiped the alcohol off with another hot towel, then refilled the bulb in the basin. Susan didn't say a word, but merely waited breathlessly for the second pint. He took great care to pat her bottom cleft completely dry, then lightly re-lubricate the tiny pink portal that divided it before every reinsertion. She found this treatment touchingly considerate, particularly after the nonchalant manner in which the stranger had used her that afternoon.

Slowly reinserting the long nozzle into her bottom, he administered the second syringe.

"Even though you're mostly good, you were mostly bad today," he told her sternly. Her pussy throbbed as her tummy grew full. "You let a stranger tie you up, which was insane; you allowed him to subject you to inappropriate forms of discipline and most disturbing of all, you had unsafe sex. Is that correct?" The second bulb was drained.

"Yes," she gasped, positively transported by the sensation of the warm water filling her through the long nozzle lodged in her rectum.

"You're too inexperienced to know this, but idiots like the one you met today are almost always more submissive than they are dominant."

"They are?"

"That so called master of yours is probably the most degraded slave in Manhattan when he's really being himself."

"You think so?"

"I'll bet he wears a pink full slip, takes it up the ass from dominant queens and goes to sleep with his face in a shoe."

"Oh, my god!"

"File this for future reference: 9 out of 10 hardcore sadists are masochistic sluts," Newton further instructed.

"Thanks for... filling me in," she replied, pleased with her joke.

"Honey?"

"Yes?"

"You'd better be taking this seriously."

"I am! I swear I am!"

"Are you sorry for what you did?" Anthony asked, once more withdrawing the syringe and patting her dry with a towel.

"Dreadfully sorry!" she swore, feeling horribly afraid that she might have an accident now. Susan looked so spectacular in this position, with her bottom spread and thrust into the air, that Anthony was tempted to mount her from behind and give her the benefit of his large, throbbing erection, but he remind himself that they'd essentially only begun and gained a simpler form of contentment by finally removing her indigo shirt.

He handled her firm, perfectly round breasts, whose nipples were stiff, rosy peaks. Then he let a hand stray to her belly, which was silky smooth and slightly swollen now.

"We're half way there" he told her, refilling the syringe from the basin, then going behind her again. "Two more bulbs will make two quarts, which is just about right for a girl of your size."

"That seems like too much," she protested.

"I'll be the judge of that," he told her coolly. She was in no position to argue as the long nozzle penetrated her deeply once more. At any rate, there was something perversely delightful to Susan in contemplating the prolongation of this intensely exciting treatment. "Although you are free to let me know if it becomes too uncomfortable," he advised her.

This time, as he administered the third full bulb, he kept his palm pressed hard against her lower abdomen. She squirmed between his hand and the nozzle, unable to ignore her aching sex.

After the third bulb he increased her helplessness and confusion by making her lie flat on her full tummy and pressing her thighs together, then strapping her down to the table by the waist. The effect of having her muff flush up against the cool leather tabletop at last was maddening to Susan.

"Just one more to go," he told her, filling the syringe for the fourth time in front of her. She whimpered and twisted and tried not to come as he pried apart her bottom cheeks and pushed the nozzle up her yet again. But it was absolutely no use trying to resist the inevitable. The combination of being flat on her belly, with her legs pressed together, the nozzle up her bottom and the warm water gushing in sent Susan spasming into a climax.

"Bad girl!" he exclaimed, noticing her shudder with a frown. "Did I give you permission to climax?"

"I'm sorry," she panted. "I couldn't help it."

"I'm sorry too, but the treatment must continue without interruption to prove effective. I suggest you calm down and lie perfectly still right now."

Anthony made sure she'd received the full measure of the fourth syringe before withdrawing the nozzle completely and dropping the spent syringe into the basin. Once her spasms had subsided, she was able to lie perfectly still, just as he'd suggested.

"Now then, young lady," he told her, "in case you were worried, there's a perfectly splendid W.C. off this room which you will be allowed to escape to in due time. Meanwhile, wait for me." With this he left the room with Susan still strapped down to the table. She had no doubt he would return to release her before she experienced discomfort due to the enema. In their entire relationship he had never shown her cruelty and she knew he was not about to begin.

Only a few minutes passed before he returned, having visited her quarters on the same floor as this secret room to provide her with a pretty change of clothes. He laid the Victorian style blue velvet dressing gown and slippers aside as he undid the strap that bound her to the table.

"Put that on," he told her, taking the plug from the marble sink top and waiting for her on the tufted leather sofa.

Susan pulled her panties back up and hurried into the beautifully fitted robe, which had collar and cuffs of pristine white eyelet and was fully lined in the same material, so that when the skirt of the dressing gown was pulled up, the effect was of a lavish petticoat. She slipped the little velvet mules over her socks and knotted the dressing gown's sash around her waist.

Anthony motioned her to him and when she came he pulled her down beside him on the couch.

"Shouldn't I go to the bathroom now?" she blushed as she asked.

"Did you forget you're being punished?" he asked, pulling her gently across his lap.

"No, sir," she replied, respectfully. This was not a title he had ever demanded, but to hear her say it now and then was touching to him.

"This device that was in you before is called a retention plug." He held the object in front of her face to let her examine it afresh. "I'm going to insert it again and then you're getting a spanking."

He pulled the skirt of her dressing gown up to her waist and pulled her panties down to mid-thigh, as before.

"You're panties are sopping wet," he scolded, lubricating the tip of the freshly sterilized butt plug with her own creamy essence, with which her labia was saturated, then slowly inserting it into her bottom again. Then, clasping her firmly about the waist with his left hand, he raised his right and began to spank her.

"This isn't going to be a very hard spanking, just a very long one," he promised, striking each cheek firmly with his flat, open hand.

Susan wondered how it was possible to feel so deeply humiliated and still be enjoying herself and yet she was. The palm of his hand stung her lightly as it fell on either cheek, but she was much more aware of the slim rubber cock which he'd inserted to help her retain. In spite of her hopes and best efforts, she felt the plug begin to slip out.

"Don't you dare," he warned her, spanking it back in, which action stimulated her greatly. Thereafter he spanked each side once and the middle once in his measured rotation of smacks. Presently he enhanced her delirious torment by slipping his left hand under her very full tummy to press against her freshly throbbing sex.

"This is what you get for giving strangers blow jobs," he advised her, spanking her soundly. It happened that this was a quite hard spanking. She realized this the next day when she ached in her muscles there; but while it was happening, she was only aware of a bittersweet pleasure in submitting to him. "Until they find a cure for all sexually transmitted diseases, you are never, ever to do that again. Understand?"

"I promise, Anthony!" she cried, much more angry with herself than he was with her for taking such a foolish risk.

"And no more adventures with pompous, demanding dominants, right?" he prompted, pausing to stroke her deeply pinkened cheeks.

"I swear it," she replied, breaking out in a sweat as the pressure in her tummy began to send a message to her brain.

"Good girl," he commented. "Now, I'm going to let you up. But don't run away just yet."

He carefully pulled her up off his lap before arranging her on her knees on the sofa, facing the back of it, with her bottom toward him. In this position she was able to comfortably lean her arms upon the sofa back and even turn her head to look at him while he unzipped his trousers to release his ravenous cock.

"Anthony!"

"Hush, this won't take ten minutes," he promised. After an hour of unremittingly voluptuous foreplay he doubted very much he would be able to last much longer than ten seconds.

Her pussy was so slippery wet by now that he slipped his large cock into it in one smooth gliding thrust, penetrating her to the hilt painlessly.

Susan buried her head in her arms and allowed the new sensation to overtake her. Between the butt plug in her bottom, the warm water still in her tummy and this big, new invader plunged into her to the root, she soon felt a second climax shuddering though her small frame.

Always mindful of not giving her a baby, Newton pulled out one second before an enormous load of semen spurted gaily from his cock. It shot into air then fell upon her bare behind. He didn't allow her to move or rearrange the costly dressing gown until he had blotted up his liquid offering with his handkerchief.

At last she was dismissed and not a moment too soon.

Chapter Seven

Random vs. Random

Everyone who knew them was disturbed by the idea of the Random divorce. Perhaps this was because William and Laura were one of the first couples brought together by the local scene and had seemed to have the ideal marriage.

William had ruled her quite firmly at first. Later on, he indulged Laura more. But there was never any question of who the dominant was. There were rumors of unfaithfulness on both sides; never the less, everyone believed them to be deeply in love, or at least as deeply in love as two extremely attractive and unabashedly selfish individuals can ever be with each other.

Anthony Newton, the musical composer and Laura's future brother in law, had been away from Random Point for several months when he finally returned to the Cape late that August and found Laura encamped in his house on the cliff. It was then that he heard her version of the story.

According to Laura, until he turned up the previous week, she hadn't seen her husband for eight months. He'd departed in the winter for a mountain climbing trip in the Andes that was supposed to have lasted for two weeks to a month. Instead, a whole season passed before Laura received a letter explaining that an interesting engineering project had materialized and that he would remain in Peru until its completion. As summer followed spring, Laura wondered whether her architect husband had been kidnapped by the Shining Path and was currently being forced to work as a techno slave. Her second theory was that William had suffered a Mosquito Coast-style nervous breakdown and had set himself up as a sort of engineer god in a primitive village. A third possibility was that he was simply in the mountains taking drugs, in which case she truly resented not being invited to join him. Twice he had wired for money and supplies, and there had been one more brief letter about how he hoped that Laura would take care of the business in his absence, which she had done, rather smartly. Other than that he seemed to have completely forgotten his wife's existence, until resurfacing again, nearly unrecognizable, in Random Point the previous week.

Laura was suing for abandonment and seeking a settlement of eight months executive wages for running Random Construction in William's absence and a written apology for the humiliating assault upon her person, which she alleged William had perpetrated, on the evening of his return.

Lawyer Sherman Cooper was staying at the Bone and Feather Inn because Laura had asked him to represent her in court. He was a special friend of her sister's whom Laura also deeply admired. Newton ran into Cooper in the bar of the inn on Saturday night and immediately asked for the lawyer's perspective on the divorce.

"Laura is determined to tell the world that William lost his temper and spanked her!" Sherman Cooper uttered with significance.

Anthony agreed with Sherman that leveling such a charge in a court of law was absurd coming from Laura, who for years had been an illustrator in the scene. That Laura would use spanking as a weapon against her husband in the divorce seemed unworthy of her as well as an insult to the community that had nurtured her.

"The way I understand it," Sherman said, sipping whiskey, "William Random returned without warning one afternoon last week, after being away for eight months. He simply showed up in Laura's kitchen, a travel-stained hobo, with an untrimmed beard and very long hair.

According to Laura, she bolted upstairs for the gun, thinking a dangerous derelict had broken into her home. William had raced upstairs after her, reassuring her that she really did know him. Laura calmed down, but only slightly, so appalled was she by the sight of him. She claims the assault occurred later that night, after she refused to satisfy him," Sherman concluded, hating the notion of having to present such a sordid concept to a judge.

"I'll bet she refused if he was looking as good as all that," Newton snorted.

"She's not charging abuse, nor is she seeking damages. Obviously, she simply wants to embarrass William in court."

"She seems to like you, Sherman, why don't you try to talk her out of this divorce thing?"

"But I'd like it if Laura were divorced," confided the boyish Cooper. He was attractive in all ways, well groomed and reserved, with an Ivy League education and a partnership in a successful New York's law firm to account for his untroubled outlook on life.

"Sherman, am I hearing correctly? You covet my future sister-in-law?" Anthony was not as surprised as he pretended to be.

"Laura has permitted me the pleasure of her company several times since William's been away," Sherman modestly revealed to Newton, who knew Laura well enough to know that this meant that Sherman had had her.

"You seem to have quite a weakness for the Ross girls, Sherman," Anthony observed, causing the fair-haired, bespectacled Cooper to color.

"It's okay," Anthony assured the young Manhattan attorney, picking a small mote of lint off Cooper's lapel and straightening his handkerchief; just to show he cared; "I've known about you and Susan from the start. I don't mind." Newton smiled pleasantly.

"Really?" Sherman asked, daring to feel relieved.

"Really, Sherman. I'm not the jealous type," Anthony assured him truthfully; "And I like you."

"Thank you," Sherman replied; greatly reassured. He then excused himself to meet with Laura while Anthony remained in the bar, waiting for other denizens of Random Point to quiz about the divorce.

Hugo Sands walked into the bar a few minutes after Sherman Cooper departed. He concurred with Anthony and Sherman in his disapproval of Laura's dragging the volatile subject of domestic discipline into a court of law. The way she was acting lately, it was almost impossible to believe that Laura Random had ever been submissive.

"It's William's fault. He never should have left her in charge of the construction company," Hugo stated with conviction; "He empowered her."

Lt. Michael Flagg, of the Random Point police department, was the next to join the quiet little drinking party in the red leather booth at the rear of the bar. As recorder of the official police record, which the Randoms' domestic melee had enlivened the previous week, Detective Flagg was also shocked by Laura's hypocritical behavior, and was happy to share his feelings with Anthony Newton and Hugo over a beer.

"As far as I'm concerned, she has another spanking coming, for seducing my wife!" Flagg commented sensationally.

Newton and Sands stared at him.

"What's your wife to Laura?" Newton asked him.

"Damaris has been Laura's Gal Friday in the office while William's been away. She used to be his secretary a long time ago. One day last week I came to pick Damaris up and got a glimpse of them together through the window. Laura was dressed in trousers, a shirt and a suit vest, with her hair pulled back and her sleeves rolled up, very butch. She looked cute, by the way. She had Damaris backed up against a filing cabinet and they appeared to be engaged in an act of frottage," Flagg revealed with the casual candor of a man who has seen it all and which nothing shocks.

"You don't say so!" Hugo was impressed.

"And how did you feel about this?" Newton interviewed Flagg.

The tall, sandy haired detective thought for a moment before replying, "Annoyed! I wanted to spank them both."

"And rightly so," Hugo stated. "Our Mrs. Random, appealing though she is, has obviously lost all respect for the male sex. She needs to be taught a lesson."

Newton said, "You almost sound as though you think one of us should do it."

"All of us should do it. For the honor of the scene. Besides, she needs it. And if the evening goes according to plan, it should also help to bring the Randoms back together," the urbane erotic magazine publisher revealed, lighting a cigarette.

"Just what are you proposing?" Flagg asked.

"That we do Laura," said Hugo, with decision.

"What, the three of us?" Anthony demanded, accepting a cigarette, ordering another cocktail and feeling like Dorian Gray.

"We could invite Marguerite along as a chaperone," Michael suggested casually.

"Should we have Susan there too?" mused Newton.

"Susan is essential to my plan," Hugo pointed out. "After all, someone has to run and get William when things get out of hand."

"You mean like somewhere in between the caning and the birching?" Anthony grasped the brilliance of the idea.

"What if William doesn't come?" Flagg asked.

Hugo said, "Wouldn't you rescue your wife from a dangerous B&D gang who were taking advantage of her?"

"Sounds like my last trip to Hollywood. However, you don't really expect me to allow you to kidnap Laura Random, do you?" the policeman asked.

"Come on, Michael," Anthony protested; "You know it's only for her own good."

"That might have some relative meaning if she were truly one of us," Michael pointed out; "But is she? The divorce proceedings would indicate otherwise. And P.S., you should hear what you guys sound like."

"I know Laura," Hugo said, "she's still one of us all right, she just happens to be rebelling at the moment. But I see your point, Michael. We can't have you involved in anything improper. Don't worry, I'll get her to consent beforehand. I'll call her right now. Come on, you jokers," Hugo led the way to a pay phone in the lobby of the inn. He dialed Anthony Newton's number. Laura was at home and answered immediately.

"Hi, sweetheart, what are you doing?" Sands sounded pleasantly innocuous.

"Hugo? Oh, I was just expecting Sherman. We have to go over a few things about the divorce. It shouldn't take long. Why? What are you up to tonight?" Laura's voice held the warmth one reserves for the closest comrade.

"Anthony Newton and Michael Flagg are with me at my house and Susan and Marguerite are about to come over. Why don't you come by? We'll have fun."

"Sure!" said Laura brightly. "I'll be there as soon as I'm done with Sherman."

Hugo hung up with a smile. "See how easy it is when you know how to talk to women? Did she not agree to have fun?"

On departing the tavern Michael hesitated in the street.

"I can't go," he said.

"Why not?" Anthony asked, his hand on the door of his Bentley.

"Marguerite's going to be there."

"So?" Hugo was puzzled.

"I haven't gone near Marguerite in nearly eight months because I promised Damaris I wouldn't pursue her anymore."

Hugo shook his head sadly. He could remember a time in the not so distant past when a dominant male could keep a wife as well as a girlfriend without having to put up with the slightest bit of nonsense from either of them.

"That's very touching," Hugo commented, "But we won't tell if you don't. Besides, inviting Marguerite was your idea, so you might as well derive some benefits from it."

Not surprisingly, Michael gave in. He agreed to meet them at Hugo's house within the hour.

Hugo called Marguerite next, but found her a bit harder to persuade. She felt it would be disloyal to her ex-Bennington roommate to abet three men in bullying her.

"Marguerite, I was talking to William's lawyer today," Hugo lied; "You'll be interested to know that if Laura drags the spanking thing into the case, the attorney has been instructed to make a very big deal out of the pro B&D sessions she did with you a few years ago in New York. Your name will be mentioned in the capacity of procuress." In actuality Hugo hadn't the slightest idea of whether William even had a lawyer yet.

"My God, she can't talk about those sessions in court!"

"Then you'd better join us tonight. And bring Susan along.'

Marguerite explained to Susan what was about to take place at

Hugo's as she went through her wardrobe to choose an outfit. The notion of confronting Michael again, and under these circumstances, made her heart beat fast. For one moment she was actually dizzy with pleasure. Obviously Michael was taking the night off and for once she was going to be there.

Meanwhile the petite blonde Barnard junior was immediately doubtful that anything like this should happen at all and made her misgivings known.

"Marguerite, are you saying that Anthony, Hugo and Michael propose to take turns disciplining my sister, while we watch? It sounds like an Ironwood book!" protested Susan Ross.

"Doesn't the prospect interest you, even on an artistic level?" Marguerite selected a pair of cream colored riding pants, a white linen shirt and chestnut riding boots. "If your intent is to chronicle the scene, you ought to be anxious to observe the rituals of play," Marguerite advised the younger girl.

"Laura is entitled to divorce her husband for whatever reasons she feels are valid," said Susan firmly; "Who are they to decide what my sister can or can't tell her lawyer?"

"Susan, you don't understand," said Marguerite coldly, "I can't have descriptions of she and I doing sessions together coming out in court. My family are rigidly correct Bostonians. I would be disowned."

"If you ask her not to mention you, I'm sure that Laura won't," Susan said.

"In case you haven't noticed, Laura has become very stubborn lately," said Marguerite, refusing to acknowledge Susan's moral quandary, brought about by being asked to participate in the public humiliation of her sister.

Yet on one level, Susan was excited at the prospect of seeing Hugo again and finally meeting Michael Flagg, whom she had heard so much about. Marguerite approved of Susan's outfit. Susan was a well-proportioned small girl, clad in a pair of cut-offs and a sleeveless white cotton shirt that was knotted at the midriff, tiny black leather shoes and white sox. She wore her thick blonde hair in a ponytail and her only make up was the berry lipstick that adorned her voluptuous mouth. She had very nice teeth, intelligent blue eyes and a highly developed sense of ethics that caused her to continually process, weigh and reevaluate scene related data.

This evening Susan was uncertain as to what her attitude should reasonably be. Like Hugo, Michael, Marguerite and Anthony, Susan agreed that Laura should not drag spanking into her divorce for no good reason. But unlike the others, she questioned their right, as an unofficial group representing the scene, to avenge its honor, in this positively gothic way, upon her sister's person. She presented these feelings to her red headed mentor in the car, the result being that the moment Marguerite got her to Hugo's house, the tempestuous book seller determined to let the men know that Susan was being difficult and might actually attempt to obstruct the plan for the evening's entertainment.

Susan was suitably impressed by her first glimpse of the legendary Michael Flagg. In fact, each of the men devastated her in turn as she viewed them ranged around the corners of Hugo Sand's splendid den.

An old film buff, Susan mentally assigned each man a silver screen alter ego. Michael Flagg was Joel McCrea, impossibly attractive but a bit scattered. Hugo Sands, although fair rather than dark had always reminded her of the cynical, charming and definitively sophisticated Warren William. Anthony Newton, Susan's lover, was Don Ameche, impulsive and engaging. Yet in spite of the sartorial elegance and physical appeal of the group, Susan knew that they were all potentially dangerous to her. She was in a room with three different men who all thought it proper to spank young ladies. She felt suddenly warm and dropped her gaze.

"Susan!" said Hugo sharply, the moment after Anthony exited the room with Marguerite for a private conference. Susan jumped.

"I want to talk to you," he declared, seizing her by the forearm, in the manner of a grown-up about to correct a very small girl. Leading her into the center of the room, which was furnished with a leather sofa and chair grouping, Hugo clearly communicated what was about to happen.

"So you think you'd like to start an insurrection, do you?" He didn't wait for a reply but sat down on the sofa, pulled her directly across his lap and administered a dozen sharp, stinging smacks to the seat of her shorts. Then he paused, saying, "Did you really dare to venture an opinion on a subject which has already been decided by Anthony, Michael, Marguerite and myself?" Another dozen hard spanks warmed Susan's bottom thoroughly and caused her shapely little legs to kick.

"I just don't know if this is right," Susan whimpered, overwhelmed by the enormity of arguing with three men and Marguerite, yet guilt ridden over conspiring against her sister. In his present mood, Hugo daunted her. She had no wish to defy him, yet her principles compelled her to do so.

"Who cares what you think? You're just a little girl." Hugo spanked her again.

"I know, but... "

Hugo didn't let her finish. "I'm not interested. First of all, you're too young to have anything of interest to say. Secondly, I can see that you too have lost all respect. Understand this, you are not to question." He delivered another volley of smacks to the rounded seat of her cute Guess shorts. "Repeat that, young lady."

"I am not to question," Susan replied smartly, anxiously wishing this ordeal would conclude before Anthony came back.

"Do you think that I would plan anything for Laura that wasn't for her own enjoyment, knowing how I feel about her?" Hugo paused in the spanking to ask her,

"No," Susan gravely replied, though in point of fact she had only a vague notion of how Hugo felt about her sister.

"Are you going to behave yourself as befits a privileged guest this evening?" his hand pressed firmly on her waist as a prelude to further smacks regardless of the answer.

"I'll try."

"Oh no, you won't," Hugo said, rather fed up, reaching under her lithe little body to unsnap the top of her cut-offs, pull the zipper down and then yank her shorts down to her knees. "You will not simply try," he advised her, spanking the seat of her white-on-white patterned cotton panties smartly. When he pulled them down a moment later he was pleased to see the color pink suffusing the incomparably smooth texture of her twenty year-old skin. Now his hand came down hard on

189

her bare bottom at least two dozen more times.

Michael watched spellbound. Susan was so sweet in her distress, so perfectly positioned, so humiliatingly exposed. What a jewel, thought Michael.

Hugo released Susan, who was amazed to realize that she had tears in her eyes. He folded his arms and looked at her. "You know, I still don't believe this one is convinced," Hugo directed this remark to Flagg.

"I'm convinced!" Susan cried, pulling up her panties and shorts. The last thing she was needed was to be handed over to that tall, muscular man for additional persuasion. For one split second, the moment Hugo let her up, she and Michael had gazed into each other's blue eyes, and the subtle knowledge of a future relationship flashed between them.

"Very well," Hugo said, "give me a kiss and say you're sorry," he held his arms open to her. She obeyed with a grinding in her tummy. "Anthony doesn't realize the mistakes he's making with you," he lamented. "Now sit over there and be quiet." He indicated a comfortable leather love seat opposite. Hugo continued to frown sternly at Susan for a moment or two, reminding her that disloyalty to the party line would not be tolerated this evening.

Susan meekly climbed onto the love seat with lowered eyes and didn't dare look up at Anthony when he returned with Marguerite and they took up positions, she in a chair and he leaning against the large, brown and rose marble mantelpiece.

Michael had gone behind the wet bar to prepare drinks. Hugo went outside to await Laura's arrival, upon which, shortly thereafter, he led her in by the hand.

Laura was suggestive of Gloria Grahame that evening, Susan thought, with her slim torso turned to perfection in a dark blue 50's style cotton halter sundress, with a fitted bodice and tight skirt that flattered her bottom; her 4" ankle strap sandals were dyed to match and displayed her dark red painted toe nails and bare pink heels provocatively. Her sleek brown hair was down around her shoulders. Gold hoop earrings gave her a Hollywood-style island look while gold slave bracelets adorned her upper arms. Her eyes were dark, soft and wide and her lips very dark red.

Laura knew that something unusual was about to happen when Hugo brought her into the room, which immediately fell quiet. She looked quizzically at Susan, who wouldn't meet her eyes, then at looked at Marguerite.

"Yes, dear," Marguerite said, "something is going on here."

"The truth is, Laura, you've become impossible lately," Hugo stated.

"I have?" Laura appeared startled by this pronouncement.

"Future sister-in-law," said Newton, taking Laura by the hand and depositing her in an armchair facing them. "By dragging the scene into your divorce in this absolutely frivolous manner, you dishonor your husband and yourself."

"Is this some sort of tribunal?" Laura looked around the room.

"If you stay of your own free will," Hugo explained, "and accept your punishment, you may eventually be forgiven. Though disloyalty is the thing I find hardest to forgive."

"Taking this all rather seriously, aren't you?" Laura casually tossed off, marching up to the bar and requesting a Vodka and tonic. Michael looked at Hugo who nodded.

"You might as well drink," said Hugo. "Since we're all taking turns with you." He offered her a cigarette and even lit it for her. "Except for Susan."

"Sounds like you're lining me up for a gang bang," Laura stared at Hugo boldly.

"Zesty idea but we'll save that for a day when we're happy with you," said Anthony Newton.

"Laura, they plan to thrash you!" Susan suddenly burst out. Hugo turned on her with irritation.

"Susan, go stand in the corner," he told her. Susan blushed to the roots and shot Anthony a panic stricken look. Newton did not countermand the order. Lacking the courage to tell them all to go to hell, Susan looked around for an empty corner. Laura was sorry that Susan had tried to warn her.

"She's very badly behaved," Hugo complained of Susan to Newton.

"Thoroughly spoiled," Newton agreed, regarding the straight little back of his small darling facing the wall.

"If she were my fiancée I'd spank her twice a day," Hugo continued, still amazed at Susan's impulse to defy him even after he'd spanked her. He now deeply regretted not having spanked Susan very much harder and made a mental note not the make the same mistake when he finally got Laura in position.

"I blame her sister mostly," Anthony complained, while admiring Laura's figure in the seductive dress.

"As her brother-in-law to be, Anthony, you ought to be exerting more of an influence over Laura Random," Hugo suggested.

"Laura, come over here," Anthony took her by the wrist as he said this and led her to a leather upholstered bench, on which he sat before pulling her graceful form across his lap. "As almost a member of the family, I get to spank you first."

Once Anthony had Laura comfortably settled across his trousered knees, he gently tilted her head up so that looking straight ahead she could not avoid gazing into the cool blue eyes of Michael Flagg, who was leaning his arms on the bar with his chin on one hand and staring straight at Laura. She had had a crush of sorts on the good-looking detective for several years.

"What has he got against me?" Laura asked over her pretty bare shoulder while pointing in Flagg's direction.

"He'll address that when it's his turn," Anthony informed her, smoothing down the paradise blue skirt over her slim, shapely bottom. "Right now we're discussing family matters. Such as the dreadful example you're setting for Susan, your sister and my future wife."

"I am not!"

"Quiet!" he smacked her hard, once across each oval buttock. "The disloyalty you're showing towards your husband on a frivolous whim sets an appalling example for a girl like Susan." He proceeded to spank Laura rapidly and hard, causing her to wriggle and kick.

"When your husband goes away you should be happy to tend to his business. Isn't that right?" Anthony appealed to the voyeurs.

"Even Benjamin Franklin left his wife in charge of the print shop when he traveled abroad," Hugo declared helpfully.

"If it was good enough for Mrs. Franklin, it ought to be good enough for you, dear," Anthony informed Laura, raising her skirt to reveal a pair of luxurious, dark gold, full cut, pure silk-satin panties. Newton recognized Loire of Paris lingerie. Merely running the palm of his hand across the curve of Laura's bottom encased in this lavish material was an erotic experience.

Anthony caught Hugo's eye and motioned to Susan in the corner. He wanted his fiancée to see this.

"Nice you've been making little economies while William's been away," Newton observed, reverently patting the silk panties, which held the sheen of a golden pearl.

"I have the right to spend anything I like!" Laura retorted.

"Is that so?" Each word was punctuated by an emphatic smack.

"Ow!" responded Laura. Hugo had meanwhile pulled Susan out of the corner and sat her in a chair at a good vantage point.

"Susan," Anthony looked up for a moment, "I hope that was the last outburst we may expect from you this evening."

She did not reply but rather timidly lowered her eyes.

"Now, Laura, I want you to admit that you've behaved abominably." Having said this, Newton proceeded to spank her in such as way as to convince her to comply. Laura didn't realize that Anthony could spank so hard, being under the impression that he took great care not to roughly use his pianist's hands.

"I will admit no such thing!" Laura replied with spirit, flashing Newton a mutinous look over her shoulder.

Newton pulled her satin briefs down to her knees to survey the deep magenta coloration with which his hand had stained her flawless white cheeks.

"William had no business trying to play with me like that his first night back, before he even got a hair cut or shave or did anything nice that I'm used to!" she continued, breathlessly, trying to put one small hand behind her to fend off any further attack; this he immediately pinned to her waist by the wrist.

"Laura," Anthony said, administering several hard smacks to her bare bottom, "You know damned well that on the day of your husband's return you threw a Class-A tantrum."

"How do you know?" she twisted on his lap.

"Because that's what bad girls do."

"I might have uttered some ill-advised remarks that night, but considering the way he'd neglected me for eight whole months, he ought to have borne them meekly. He never even apologized!" Laura complained of her husband eloquently.

"Laura, the issue here is not postcard etiquette, it's respect." Newton told her. "But for now, you may get up."

Laura was off Newton's lap and setting her clothes to rights in an instant. A dusky blush suffused her entire face as she looked around the room at her friends. It happened to be a moment when Michael Flagg and Marguerite Alexander were exchanging complex looks and this made Laura smile in spite of the spanking. Rubbing her bottom through her cotton sundress, her gaze then fell on Hugo Sands, whom she favored with a defiant toss of her head. He regarded her coolly.

"You men," Laura said; "are so ridiculous!" This sally was delivered with such loftiness that for a moment all three of them felt the truth of her words.

"Better finish your drink, Laura," Anthony advised, "we're just getting warmed up here."

She strode boldly up to the bar, still unconsciously rubbing her bottom through her dress. Anthony's hand left a warm, sexy sting behind. Taking a sip, Laura looked steadily at Marguerite, her best girl friend.

"You don't honestly intend to participate in this kangaroo court, do you?" Laura asked her.

Marguerite had to force herself to concentrate on Laura's question, so wholly focused had she been on Flagg's face.

"I've been asked to do the bondage," the redhead replied. "Won't that be fun?"

"Am I not to be trusted to hold a position without restraints?" Laura fixed Hugo with a solemn gaze while continuing to rub her bottom, which endeared her to him slightly.

Hugo shrugged and said, "You know that restraints serve as a natural adjunct to the application of certain instruments." Laura noticed for the first time how unusually cool Hugo seemed toward her.

Susan was herself troubled by what seemed to be happening and questioned her own purpose at remaining as a passive observer. Could that not also be interpreted as conspiring in this unfair attack on her sister? Susan was unaccustomed to the degree of obedience that Hugo seemed to expect and did not understand its purpose.

Susan wanted to ask Laura truthfully whether she was enjoying this strange situation or merely enduring it. But she could still feel the imprint of Hugo's hand on her bottom and understood that he would not tolerate further interference from her.

Anthony was apparently on their side tonight and could not be looked to for support while Michael Flagg seemed even more inaccessible. She couldn't compromise Marguerite by asking for her solidarity, not when Hugo was around. Marguerite's obedience to him was fairly absolute. Was there no one whose sense of fair play she could appeal to?

Meanwhile, Michael could not remove his eyes from Marguerite's expressive face, which was currently adorned by a full-lipped pout. Now that he was seeing her up close again, he was astonished at how much more tempting she was than he remembered, with her tawny hair down on her shoulders and that impossibly tiny waist dividing the most magnificent curves on the Cape. The sculpted muscles of her calves so handsome in the boots and her shapely thighs so stunning in the perfect riding pants, all conspired to leave Flagg breathless. And that wasn't even taking into consideration her glorious bottom or those wonderful green eyes. The more Flagg gazed at his erstwhile lover, the more urgently he desired to remove her from this place and spend the next six hours making love to her.

Finally he tore his gaze away from Marguerite long enough to catch Laura Random staring at him with something like a smile. Laura was a very charming girl herself and always seemed to flirt with him in a most improper way. Flagg intuited that this might be the reason for Marguerite's pout.

"Don't worry, Laura," Michael told her, with masterful diplomacy; "I have no intention of spanking you. I'm simply present to witness the event."

"Suppose you detect an impropriety?"

"If it falls under my jurisdiction, I'll correct it."

"Hugo, I'm going upstairs to get what I'll need," Marguerite told her patron as she exited the parlor. Michael followed her out and they climbed the stairs in silence. Finally, in the upstairs hall, Marguerite turned to him and said, "It's nice to see you again, Michael." Her cool civility annoyed him. He reacted by pulling her against him and kissing her. She pulled away and slapped his face resoundingly and with enjoyment.

"How dare you?" she demanded.

"I'm sorry," Michael colored and in an uncharacteristic gesture, caught the hand that had slapped him and pressed his lips to its palm. She snatched her hand away.

"Am I supposed to be impressed?"

Marguerite proceeded into the master bedroom where she went to a magnificent bureau to search for the required disciplinary aids. She knelt opposite the bottom drawer and pulled it out to reveal a truly excessive collection of wooden and leather corporal punishment implements, including paddles, straps, whips, tawses, canes and switches, arranged upon a liner of blue velvet. Michael knelt beside her. She smelled of cinnamon.

"You don't love me in the slightest!" she accused.

"You know that isn't true," he swore; "You're always on my mind." When he ventured to place his hand on one creamy linen shoulder; she shrugged it off with irritation.

"Go to hell," she told him.

"You're right, of course," he sighed.

Michael knew he had no right even to speak to Marguerite, yet he wanted her more than ever.

"You seek my favors, as before?" Marguerite imperiously asked, as they rose to leave the room with the equipment she had gathered.

Michael smiled at the antique phrase, bowed his head and humbly replied, "I seek your favors."

"You renounce your promise to your wife to avoid my company?"

"I do."

"Very well then, as proof of your sincerity, you will kneel and beg my forgiveness for eight months of neglect, kiss my foot and call me

Mistress."

"The hell I will!"

"Oh? Then go to hell!" she turned on her heel and marched out of the room. He followed, highly irritated.

"Marguerite really!" he protested. "I am sorry, very sorry I've neglected you for such a long time," he stopped her with his hand on her arm, "But there are limits!"

"Thank you for making that clear," she said, smiling sweetly and continuing on her way.

"Marguerite, can't we compromise? I mean, need I be quite so abject?"

"Would it kill you?"

"No, but —"

"Oh, forget it. Don't even bother your silly boy head with it anymore, because that option has now ceased to exist. The new rule is if you want to get anywhere near me again you'll have to take a whipping from me while locked into the town pillory!" she announced, leaving him speechless at the top of the stairs as she quickly ran down to the parlor.

Michael followed, shaking his head.

When Michael reentered the parlor Marguerite had begun to tie Laura Random face down, to the saddle of a large, antique hobbyhorse that occupied one corner of the room.

Susan, accepting an eggnog punch from Anthony, noticed how firmly Marguerite fastened the straps around Laura's wrists and ankles as well as her waist. Before even straddling the wooden pony Laura's panties had been coaxed off by Marguerite. Laura's tight skirt had been pulled up to her waist, revealing the totality of her charms as they were so prominently displayed upon the saddle.

Once Laura was bound in position, Marguerite blindfolded her securely with a white handkerchief.

Caressing Laura's bare bottom, which was still pink from Anthony's spanking, the redhead addressed the room, "I thought before moving onto the more serious portion of tonight's entertainment, I could have some fun with my crop and in the process, we could force Laura to climax for us."

"No!" cried Laura, jerking on the pony.

"It's not up to you," Marguerite informed her; "but I will require assistance," she looked around with a mischievous smile.

"I'll volunteer," said Anthony.

"Laura, please understand," explained Marguerite, stroking her friend's smooth dark hair and slender neck; "that we hate to have to do this."

Marguerite had brought a very old black leather riding crop with a square slapper at the end. Pulling Anthony to her lips, Marguerite whispered several suggestions in his ear. He nodded and began to fuss with Laura's skirt, making sure it was completely pulled up. Laura's body rather arched to his touch, in spite of her resolve not to cooperate with their decadent plan. In the split second that her tummy left the saddle, he slipped his hand in under her abdomen, so that when she lowered back down, it was to settle her sable muff into the palm of his hand; to which Laura cried, "Oh!" With his other hand, Anthony lightly pressed down on her waist to hold her in place for the crop.

"This could take some time," Marguerite informed him seriously.

"How dare you?" Laura twisted across the horse but could not escape the velvet clutch in which she lay. She almost sobbed with shame when the first stroke landed with a smack on her left cheek. It was obvious that every time the flat, square slapper impacted against her bottom that her Venus mound would be driven against the palm of Newton's hand. Almost immediately, Laura's sex began to ache. Again the crop fell sharply, this time on the other buttock. Laura tried to hold still but it was no use. She was sandwiched between his hands, restrained, with her bare bottom upturned when the crop began to fall rhythmically.

"Laura," Newton scolded, "Don't make such a fuss."

After Marguerite had administered at least two dozen sharp strokes, each of which elicited a separate cry or groan from Laura Random, she stood back and gave Newton a nod. Laura was by this time fairly palpitating under the attention, which had left her buttocks bathed in an all-over pink glow.

Newton then placed one palm on each of her buttocks and gently divided them. "No!" cried Laura again.

"Oh yes, my love," promised Marguerite, taking extremely careful aim before bringing the crop slapper down directly across the tiny aperture between Laura's cheeks. Laura caught her breath then sobbed.

Anthony said, "Shouldn't we be videotaping this portion for William's lawyer, for when she introduces spanking into her suit?" In so saying, he continued to press her buttocks apart with the heels of his hands so that Marguerite could apply the spanker to Laura's anus, now so explicitly revealed for all to see.

Susan felt very warm as she watched and was aware that the crotch of her panties was becoming saturated with her excitement. She felt every stroke vicariously and squirmed as they fell.

It was almost too much. Susan forced herself to turn away, but immediately collided with the amused gaze of Michael Flagg. He had been watching Susan watch her sister being disciplined, fascinated by her fascination and thoroughly delighted that two such sisters could exist outside of fiction.

He was now seated on a leather sofa and motioned to Susan to come to him. He made her sit beside him and took her hand. Leaning towards her he said very softly, "Are you okay with this?"

Susan stared at the large hand that had swallowed her tiny one, feeling terribly embarrassed and excited.

"Thank you for asking," she noncommittally replied, looking up at him. He immediately relinquished her hand, which disappointed her.

"I'm getting a bit hot under the collar, are you?" he whispered. Susan blushed and nodded in sincere agreement. And sitting next to this extraordinarily good looking 6'3" male into spanking only added to the almost painful state of arousal Susan suddenly experienced.

Susan saw that every time the flat, square spanker impacted against the tender division between Laura's buttocks that Laura ground against the saddle. If they kept it up, she would surely come and the concept of a forced climax thrilled Susan.

The tableau was quite attractive, with Anthony suave in his well-tailored suit and Marguerite devastating in her riding pants and boots. Hugo, savoring the scene from the bar, noted with amusement how

Michael Flagg had apparently adopted Susan Ross over the last few minutes.

Susan began to relax more with the scene. If things got out of hand, Flagg might possibly intervene. Had he not just been extremely considerate towards her?

"How about that Laura? Shall I get the camcorder?" Hugo asked.

"I don't give a damn if you video tape me having five orgasms, I'll say whatever I want in court!" Laura maintained staunchly and was rewarded quite sternly by Marguerite with twenty hard swats on either cheek.

Hugo sighed as Laura sobbed, "You're all a bunch of bullies!"

"Oh dear," said Anthony, "And I thought we were being nice."

"We were being angelic," Marguerite assured him. Then Marguerite untied Laura for the caning, which required an entirely different position.

Laura tore the blindfold off and left the horse dizzy, lubricated and challenging. She pulled down her skirt at once.

"I'll say anything I like in my divorce!" she reiterated.

Hugo took up the slender English school cane and called Laura to him. Susan squirmed when he took Laura by the ear lobe and led her to a pretty little writing desk, which was the perfect height for bending a young lady over and also gave her something to hang onto.

"Laura, I never expected you of all people to be so disloyal," Hugo informed her, smoothing her dress down over her buttocks, pressing down on the small of her back for a better tilt of her bottom upwards, while instructing her to straighten her legs.

"Laura, this is the only time I will ever cane you and you're going to remember it," Hugo promised.

Laura, who had been caned only once before, and then quite carefully, by Marguerite, as an entertainment at a party, shuddered at these words.

Hugo placed the cane on the table in front of Laura while raising her skirt and lowering her panties. Then he took it up again and briefly let it rest across both cheeks midway down. The room was very still as he pulled his right arm back but slightly to deliver the first stroke.

The snap of the stroke was all in the wrist. Laura felt two distinctly different sensations as it fell: first the initial sharp, frightening bite of the cane impacting against the surface of her flesh, then the dull, heavy, secondary slash of the rattan as it penetrated down into the tissue. Laura cried out, seared by the pain, unable to conceive that Hugo was starting out this hard. Tears immediately flooded her eyes and spilled onto the desk. Laura tried to hide her face but Susan noticed right away.

Susan was deeply shocked by the appearance of a serious red mark across Laura's bottom when Hugo stepped back with the cane. Next Susan watched the red line pale to white. A welt on the first stroke? That couldn't be right. And Laura was bitterly crying as well. Susan looked around the room.

Michael was sitting in an armchair, riveted. Marguerite was leaning against the mantelpiece, dividing her attention between the caning and Michael's handsome profile. Anthony was casually disposed on a leather sofa, thoroughly absorbed in the spectacle. She'd often seen him in holiday moods, as his temperament inclined towards the sunny, but Susan had never seen Anthony appear so blissfully entertained as at that moment. "You debauched monster," thought Susan, "my sister's sobbing her heart out and you're enjoying the hell out of yourself!" She didn't appreciate Marguerite's complicity either. All of them were scaring her badly. Had the body snatchers replaced all of her friends with B&D creatures from hell?

Anthony Newton, who had been playing for almost as many years as Susan had been alive, felt privileged to witness the caning of a beautiful submissive woman. The rush of tears didn't surprise him. When you caned most girls, they cried. The marks raised by the first and second stroke did not shock him terribly. A real caning would necessarily leave marks. Laura's reactions were exquisite from Anthony's point of view. The way she moved, the sounds she made, her expressions, were all intensely stimulating to him.

Michael Flagg shared Newton's aesthetic appreciation of the entire situation and additionally approved of Laura being caned on general principle. He had always thought her fresh.

In most cases Hugo himself did not advocate caning for girls, but this was one of those times when it was called for. And while he realized that Laura Random might not speak to him for months after this evening, the prospect didn't stop him from carrying out his task.

"That was two out of six of the best," he told her, kneeling in front of her and patting her face dry with his handkerchief. "After that, two sets of twelve will follow."

Laura blinked at him in disbelief. Did he really expect her to take 28 more strokes? Even Marguerite was shocked. Like Michael and Anthony, she considered at least one good caning a necessary part of every well bred young lady's development and was not about to faint at the sight of a few marks on her best friend's pearly flesh, but the proposed count of strokes seemed unduly harsh for a light-to-medium submissive like Laura, who had only ever been caned once before, and then with great restraint by herself. Marguerite didn't relish the notion of opposing Hugo, but neither could she allow him to inflict thirty strokes of the cane on Laura.

"I can't take that many," Laura sobbed.

"Oh yes you can," Hugo replied coolly, rising to his feet again and going behind her. The third stroke was the hardest so far and fell across the juncture between buttock and thigh. It caused Laura to scream for the first time and look back at Hugo with anguish.

"Eyes forward, please," he told her, pointing with the cane. Laura dropped her head and sobbed. The next time Hugo looked around the room he noticed that Susan Ross had disappeared.

Seven minutes later, in his house in the cul-de-sac at the end of Shadow Lane, William had just dropped off to sleep, fully dressed on the playroom sofa, with one cat on his chest and another on his head. All three slumbering creatures were startled into tumbling off the couch together at the shrill ring of the telephone.

William was surprised to hear from his sister-in-law Susan at that hour and calmly asked her what was going on. Susan, somewhat breathless from running the three quarters of a mile down the moonlit lane, explained that she was calling from the Dutch, a neighborhood bar between his house and Hugo Sands' and asked him to meet her there right away. She said that some people were hurting Laura and he had to come and save her. William thought Susan meant some drunks at the Dutch and hung up immediately.

He went out to the garage and jumped in the 1956 midnight blue Cadillac convertible he'd been rebuilding before his prolonged sojourn in Peru. It surged to life instantly even though it hadn't been warmed up in eight months. Duly proud of his ability to give tune ups, the athletic young husband in exile roared down the road to rescue his wife from bullies.

His adrenaline was pumping by the time he got to the tavern, envisioning himself having to pull one or more belligerent specimens of late summer tourist trash off Laura. He was getting a hell of a break, William beamed to himself as he barreled along. And he had that nice little Susan to thank. How smart of her to think of him to call. But when he pulled up to the front of the quiet pub minutes later, only Susan was waiting outside.

"Susan, where's Laura?" he asked, jumping out of the car. "Have they taken her somewhere?"

"No, get back in! Start the car. They're at Hugo's house," Susan explained, jumping into the front seat. "Go there immediately!"

"Hugo's? I don't understand," he started the car and shot down the road.

"Hugo's caning Laura at this very minute. They seem to be taking revenge on your behalf because Laura threatened to drag the scene into the divorce. They've taken it upon themselves to punish her, Hugo, Anthony, Marguerite and Michael. When I left she was already marked and in tears!" Susan explained, in an animated rush.

"Okay, Susan, calm down. We're going there right now," William assured her, enthralled.

"Will you stop them?"

"Of course I'll stop them. Where do they get off?"

"You should see how hard Hugo's caning Laura!"

"Really?" William couldn't help smiling.

"He's welting her!"

William stopped smiling. "That's not very nice," he said angrily. "I hope she doesn't think I put them up to this."

Hugo had just administered the tenth cane stroke to a sobbing young lady, whose once pristine bottom was now thoroughly marked. By an unfortunate chance, the tenth stroke fell directly across a previous and the combined severity of the two strokes upon the same narrow strip of skin resulted in a tiny bit of speckling; meaning a minuscule pin prick of blood had appeared. This dramatic visual, accompanied by a nerve shattering scream, met William Random's gaze when Susan ushered him into Hugo's den exactly 23 minutes after she had escaped it.

Everyone turned at their entrance, including Laura, who stood up at once, let her skirt fall, and gazed at her husband with extreme surprise while dashing the tears from her eyes. Her ragged sobs instantly subsided as she saw that she was saved.

"I couldn't believe what Susan was telling me," William snapped at Hugo. "Have you all gone nuts?" He scolded them, pulling Laura into his arms. "How much more were you going to cane her?" William gave Laura his handkerchief to dry her face.

"She knows how to say mercy," said Hugo, disappointed that Susan had brought William back so soon, for he had been getting the most sensational reactions out of Laura during the last several strokes.

"And you think her not saying it makes this carnage okay? I'm taking Laura home," William told them. "All right, Laura?" She nodded, clinging to him for balance. She was ready to faint with relief at not having to take the remaining 20 strokes of Hugo's horrible sentence, while the pain of the ten she had taken left her weak.

Laura felt exhilarated driving off in the convertible beside her husband. "I'll take you back to Anthony's place, okay?" William asked deferentially.

"Okay," she replied agreeably. She noticed he had cut his hair and shaved since their unfortunate encounter the previous week and looked quite like his old self. His extremely well defined physique was casually revealed in a pair of baggy khaki trousers and a black polo shirt. His eyeglasses gave him a scholarly look, which Laura found appealing.

"Hugo hurt me," she complained, gazing up at the clear, starry sky as the warm summer wind whipped through her hair.

"Why did he?" William reflexively put out his hand to gently pat her thigh through her dress.

"They didn't want me to mention certain things in court."

"I hope you don't think I had anything to do with this. I don't give a damn what you mention in court."

"I know," Laura reassured him. "Thank you for coming to save me," she smiled at him.

"What are ex-husbands for?" William smiled back.

Laura brought William up to the well-appointed bedroom suite that Anthony had given to her, on the top floor of the house. It had French doors opening out onto a balcony overlooking the cliffs and the ocean.

William made her change out of her dress and heels into a light cotton wrapper. He had her lie face down upon the blue and gold counterpane and pulled her wrapper up to examine the damage closely. Then he fetched a damp cloth and a pomander of aloe. Laura was in shock after looking in the mirror while changing her clothes and seeing that she was welted.

"So how do you like your good friend Hugo now?" William couldn't resist asking, while applying a cool compress to Laura's bottom.

"He's a sadist," said Laura thoughtfully.

"He certainly punished you much worse than I ever did," William observed.

"That's true. I never realized he had it in for me like that," she remarked, still awestruck by the marking.

"You just got to see the real Hugo for once," William told her.

"I wanted to ask for mercy," she admitted, "but I couldn't endure his contempt, so I let him continue to cane me. It was going to be 30 all together, then you came in and saved me. Did I thank you for that?"

"Yes, Laura," William smiled, "you're welcome. You should really thank your sister. She had the presence of mind to come and get me."

"What courage she had to stand up to them all!" Laura was thrilled by her sister's loyalty.

"Laura, I was wondering... "

"Yes?"

"If we might see each other."

"You mean, you want to take me out?" she asked, looking back over her shoulder at the operation in which he was now engaged.

"Yes," he replied, looking up at her.

"That would be acceptable," she said, then hid her face in the pillows as he continued to massage the balm into her bottom.

"Laura, I also want to apologize for approaching you so clumsily the other night."

"You? Apologize?" Laura looked at him.

"Am I that bad?"

Laura smiled at him.

"Laura?"

"Yes?"

"You're very wet."

Laura instantly rolled over and sat up, blushing deeply. She forced herself to say. "You should probably go now," very much the princess in her bedchamber dismissing an overly fond courtier.

William got to his feet and pulled her up with him. He hugged and kissed her and nuzzled her throat. This approach got him farther than words. Her soft body melted against his hard one.

He laid her back on the bed, unzipped his trousers and covered her body with his. Before she could protest, he covered her mouth with his. When he could feel her completely relax under him he reached down to guide himself into her. He said with a connoisseur's appreciation, "You took a real caning."

"It was horrid."

"They're mostly your friends," he reminded her.

"Go easy, okay? We haven't done this in a long time," she reminded him needlessly.

"But I'll bet you've been doing it with someone," he said, with academic curiosity, while nudging into her slippery glove.

"Not often," she admitted. "What about you?"

"Not since the last time I saw you."

"I'm ready now, but go slow," she instructed and for once, he was the one to obey without question.

William took infinite care that night, to please Laura. In fact, she had never known him to be quite so attentive to her needs. It made her wonder whether some Peruvian seductress had been training her husband over the last eight months. Little did Laura suspect that William had been, over the last few days, reading the concise little collection of female self-pleasuring books Laura had accumulated during his absence. The perennial mechanic, William had finally stumbled across the manual for girls and was gratified to note that the applications worked.

William went away extremely content with the evening's progress. Thanks to Hugo's cruelty and Susan's valor, he was well on the way to winning Laura back.

Michael insisted on seeing Marguerite home, going on foot through the village at her side. On the way, in the moonlight, they stopped in the square and Marguerite pointed out the three hundred year old whipping post, flogging block, pillory and stocks, which her Puritan antecedents had erected to punish miscreants.

"Want to go see how the equipment works, Michael?"

"Sure," Michael said, attracted to the block most of all. They approached it in the circle of light provided by a ring of old fashioned street lamps.

"I'll have you know that several cultivated men of my acquaintance have crossed oceans and continents to take a whipping from me in this square," she informed him.

"Marguerite," Michael's hand closed firmly on her wrist, "the only reason I let you bring me over to this morbid exhibition was because this flogging block seemed the perfect height for me to sit on and take you over my knee." And then he did just that, seizing her by one arm. A sudden flush of heat flooded through her at what seemed to be happening.

"What do you think you're doing? Don't you dare!" Marguerite found herself flung face down across his lap and restrained across her waist by a heavy arm.

"You've been challenging me all night," he pointed out, smacking her rapidly and hard through her snug riding pants, while alternating cheeks.

"Let me go! What if someone sees?"

"You should have thought of that when you brought me up here."

"Oh, go to hell!"

"You really do need a spanking," he observed and administered at least thirty more smacks to the seat of her breeches before letting her up. "That's what you get for even thinking about dominating me, Marguerite Alexander."

"Oh really!" Marguerite gave a little stamp with her foot. "Well you just wait, Michael Flagg, you'll beg me to dominate you some day."

Marguerite pouted till he kissed her. She encouraged him to undo a few of her shirt buttons, giving him access and leave to bite her neck and flawless shoulders. He cupped her bosom with one hand and drew her against him with his other arm about her impossibly small waist. She melted and whispered in his ear that they should go into the old graveyard off the other side of the square and have sex behind one of the seventeenth century headstones. Michael gave her a look and took her home.

Laura was alone and still awake when Anthony looked in on her an hour later.

"Where's Susan?" Laura asked.

"Hiding out at your husband's house, I expect. She's probably terrified that Hugo's out looking for her with a switch."

Laura said, "Isn't she brave?"

"She's a little pill and she's getting a thrashing next time I see her," said Anthony haughtily.

"No!"

"Oh yes she is. But let's talk about you. Are you all right? That was quite a caning you took."

"I know. I hate Hugo. But wasn't William divine? I fell in love with him all over again."

"I think the rescue could have been a good deal more dramatic. William might, for example, have punched Hugo," Anthony pointed out.

"I approve of his restraint," Laura protested; "it was dignified."

"After that caning you wouldn't have enjoyed watching someone deck Hugo?"

"Of course not. I like Hugo."

"You just said you hated him," Newton reminded her.

"After tonight, I certainly fear him," Laura admitted.

"You're a funny girl. Quite a good sport too."

"Thank you. But if you like me so much, why did you participate in tonight's auto-de-fe?"

"Because you were setting a bad example for Susan. Which reminds me, why don't you call your sister and make sure she's tucked in at your house for the night."

"Why?" Laura asked, her hand on the phone.

"I want to make sure she doesn't walk in while I'm comforting you."

"I do need to be comforted," Laura told her future brother in law, getting up on her hands and knees on the bed and pulling up her sheer, exquisitely embroidered Italian cotton nightgown to reveal her bottom to him. The satiny skin, which had been so pristine when the evening had begun, was now welted with a cluster of purplish parallel lines. Anthony ventured to touch one of the marks with the pad of one fingertip. Laura winced and gave a little sob in sudden recollection of the pain she had suffered during the caning.

"Didn't William comfort you when he brought you home?"

"Yes, very nicely," Laura told Anthony as he bestowed a kiss on her extremely bruised bottom. "But since I've been so severely punished," she said, "I think the world owes me an extra sin. I pick you."

When Marguerite emerged from the room-sized cedar closet off her bedroom, she was clad in a cream satin Fernando Sanchez nightgown and matching high-heeled slippers with marabou trim. Her long, smooth hair was down around her shoulders and her cleavage in the form fitting, bias cut gown was classic 1950's Hollywood regency.

She was taken aback to discover Michael kneeling beside the large, luxuriously dressed maple bed in his pleated, gray, wool trousers, stripped to the waist and showing off a breathtakingly "V" shaped back.

"What are you doing?" she asked fondly, running her fingertips across Flagg's broad shoulders teasingly. When she bent to nibble on his ear, her perfumed hair brushed his throat.

"I'm begging your forgiveness for neglecting you," he told her, kissing her hand then bringing her around in front of him so that he could also bestow a kiss upon her graceful instep. "Beautiful mistress," he added, with all due respect. Marguerite was gratified and blushed.

"How unexpected to see you on your knees after what you said," she smiled.

"As yet, here I am, fully prepared to humble myself to you. Will you permit me to serve you?" he asked her sincerely.

"Serve me? In what way?" Marguerite was highly amused.

"I don't know. What way would you like?"

Marguerite was touched by his clumsy though apparently sincere attempt at worship, which was so unlike him.

"Well…" she said, strolling over to her marble dresser top and picking up her cherry wood hair brush. "If you would like to perform a useful and soothing service for me, you may brush my hair." She handed him the brush and sitting on the large featherbed, with its creamy Egyptian cotton linen, patted a place beside her for him.

As he lifted Marguerite's thick russet mane to carefully brush out the underside first, Michael remembered with a pang of guilt that he also did this for his wife. Then, quickly putting Damaris out of his mind, as there was plenty of time to brood about his despicableness later, Michael kissed the back of Marguerite's neck while smoothly holding most of her hair in one hand. Then he began biting her shoulders and neck, remembering what this did to her. She ground back against him, wrapping both his arms around her waist so that they locked in front of her. "Harder!" she commanded, until he finally stopped, afraid he was beginning to leave marks on her alabaster shoulders.

"Harder!" she pouted.

"Marguerite, I'll leave marks on you if I bite you any harder," he admonished, letting her go and picking up the brush again to continue with the original task.

"This is a lovely hairbrush," he said.

"Yes, isn't it?" she calmed down a bit.

Looking straight ahead she could study his handsome reflection in an old nautical mirror facing the bed.

"I've never seen an oval one quite this large before," he commented.

"Go to hell, Michael."

"Why?"

"I know what you're thinking. That it's perfect for my bottom!"

"Just because I have a hair brush fetish and you have a ravishing bottom, why would I think that?"

"I didn't know you had a hair brush fetish. Why didn't you ever tell me?"

"You never asked," he continued to brush her hair gently but firmly and quite precisely. He had never felt so taken with Marguerite, but then he realized that he always felt this way with her.

"Michael, I have many beautiful, antique hair brushes," Marguerite informed him, as though patiently pointing out a positive character trait long overlooked.

"That's nice for you," Michael commented, brushing her hair carefully, while admiring its thickness, lush waves and gorgeous russet color.

"Would you like to use a hair brush on my bottom?" she asked needlessly.

"Very much," he replied honestly.

"But I don't like pain," she pouted.

"The spanking I gave you in the square tonight wasn't terribly painful, was it?"

"It certainly stung," Marguerite blushed, "but not unacceptably so."

"You see? I can make it nice for you, even with a hairbrush. You can trust me. I'd never leave a woman the way Hugo did tonight."

"Really?" Marguerite turned to look at him; "I thought the caning was sexy," she admitted.

"On one level I was enjoying it. At the beginning I even thought that Laura deserved a caning. But half way through I wanted to stop it. I'd never seen a caning in real life, only on video, and I didn't realize the results were so severe."

"They don't have to be. Hugo was being a swine. And your sentiments do you credit. Perhaps I will let you give me a little bedtime spanking with my pretty hair brush," said she, allowing Michael to pull her gently across his lap. Marguerite's smooth, taut, womanly bottom, so sleekly encased in the stunning satin gown, upturned in expectation of a large, oval, highly varnished rosewood hair brush was so sweet a sight that Michael simple gazed on it and stroked it lightly for quite a few minutes before beginning.

Meanwhile, Marguerite grew feverish with anticipation as she lay across his lap, with her bottom so vulnerable, yet so beautifully displayed, as he caressed her through the gown. Then he firmly took hold of her waist and Marguerite held her breath.

The brush began falling quite lightly at first, upon one then the other cheek. The strokes were hardly more than taps. But how quickly a tap can become a smack with a wooden hairbrush! A flick of the wrist can change everything. However, Marguerite had chosen wisely when handing her lover a hairbrush. The cherry wood brush was very light. Marguerite, who could take a very serious hairbrush spanking if she had to, did not stop Michael from starting lightly. She wanted to see where he would go on his own.

He soon began to spank her somewhat harder with the brush, making each swat sting. Then conflicting emotions made him stop and stroke her through her gown. First of all, he was not used to being invited to spank Marguerite. He was also so madly in love with her at that moment that he couldn't bear to hurt her. But then his overwhelming desire to use this perfect wooden hairbrush vigorously on her magnificent bottom reasserted itself and he proceeded with the spanking.

"I just remembered," Michael said sternly, "that you slapped my face tonight."

"Yes, don't you feel honored?" Marguerite gave him an extremely impertinent look.

Michael pushed the satin nightgown up to her waist to reveal her long legs and bare bottom in all their womanly radiance.

"Admire it," said Marguerite with confidence. The hairbrush through the satin had already made her rosy. Michael kissed every spot that was pink before picking up the hairbrush again. He was extremely careful with the brush because Marguerite's skin was so fair and delicate. He had never marked her before and shuddered to think of what her reaction would be if he did so now. Still, it gave him a great deal of satisfaction to be able to use a hairbrush on her beautiful bottom, even moderately.

Marguerite looked back over her left shoulder for a glimpse of chiseled masculine profile as he continued to spank her. Noticing her turn, he returned her look gravely. She gave a little sob of excitement, feeling her abdomen and her clitoris pulsate.

Rejoicing in the fact that he was obviously charming her, Michael momentarily lay the brush aside and keeping one hand fastened to her slender waist, reached under her bosom with the other, freed one full, round, cherry tipped breast and pinched the nipple firmly between forefinger and thumb. Marguerite caught her breath and ground against his thigh in deep contentment.

"Are you going to behave yourself?" he asked.

"No!" she replied, which was as good as inviting him to pick up the hairbrush again, which he did.

"Now you're gonna get it," he told her.

"No!" she cried, putting one hand back to shield her bottom.

"Sorry, you shouldn't have been so smart!" he said, pinning her wrist to her waist and applying the back of the brush to her bottom six times, hard. Marguerite then agreed that in this position, being smart was stupid.

But then the spanking was over and Michael let her up. She immediately went to a mirror to examine her bottom for marks. She found none save for an all-pervasive rosy tinge to her skin.

He pulled her back down on the bed and covered her body with his. He said, "I should have spanked you harder."

She unzipped him and freed him. Her fragrant, goddess body was totally accessible to him. Penetration was quickly achieved, but continued for a very long time. This evening would long be remembered by the illicit lovers as one of their most romantic encounters.

Hanging up on her sister Laura a moment after William walked into the downstairs hall, Susan rushed out to the landing and looked over the balustrade.

"I'm hiding here tonight," she explained, running down the stairs to greet him. He smiled up at the best little friend an estranged husband could have.

"Whom are you hiding from?" he took her hand and led her into the downstairs sitting room.

"Hugo and Anthony. I just spoke to Laura at Anthony's and told her I'd be staying here the night."

"You're staying here with me?" William asked.

"Is that all right?"

"It's splendid," he said, enjoying the surge of excitement, which accompanied the thought of taking Susan to bed. "Susan, what you did tonight was very thoughtful. It helped me to get back in Laura's good graces. She even let me make love to her for a while."

"I'm so glad!" Susan beamed and bounced.

"But after eight months of total abstinence, I feel like one large, aching sex organ. And I'm afraid that if you remain in this room with me for even a few minutes longer, looking as cute as you do right now, I won't be responsible for my actions."

Susan blushed quite deeply at this warning and boldly laid her hand upon the front of William's baggy khaki's only to discover an 8" lead pipe therein. She stared down at her little black shoes and confessed that she had always adored her brother-in-law.

William sat down on a leather chaise and motioned Susan to him. Making her stand in front of him, William unzipped her size 5 jeans shorts and slipped his hand inside the front. His fingers explored the cotton crotch of her panties and found it damp. He slipped one finger in under the crotch and up inside of her, where it was a warm, snug velvet vise.

William couldn't resist putting her across his lap and continuing to explore her charms in the over the knee position. She made a sort of "mmmm" noise as he pulled her tight shorts and white panties down to reveal her shapely bottom fully.

He deftly masturbated her with blunt fingers, relishing her look in this position, with her voluptuous buttocks upturned and her baby-smooth thighs spread. Susan buried her face in her hands and abandoned herself to the sensation of being handled.

"What an excitable girl you are, Susan," he scolded, freeing his hand momentarily to give her a couple of smacks.

"I did get excited," she agreed breathlessly. It was true that just then she had been longing for a spanking.

"You enjoyed watching your sister get punished tonight, didn't you, young lady?"

"William, you know I deplored it!" Susan protested, wriggling across his lap. He spanked her smartly, telling her to lie still.

"But there were some parts that you didn't deplore. I can tell because you're wet." William pointed out.

"I did find it exciting when Marguerite and Anthony were trying to force Laura to have a climax."

"I missed that part," William paused with his hand on her bottom. "But I'd be very happy to force you to have a climax right now," he offered.

Susan twisted around on his lap to look at him. "How would you do that?" she challenged.

"Are you kidding? I've been going through the cupboards in here this week and over the last eight months Laura's amassed an arsenal of vibrators. Plus I've been reading her books on female self-pleasuring, having nothing else to do and... believe me, I've absorbed enough knowledge to get you off in five minutes flat," he promised enthusiastically, like a child about to show off a tumbling routine. William unceremoniously dislodged her from his lap, tugged her jeans shorts back up and pulled her upstairs after him to the master bedroom.

"Look at this, Susan," he opened the doors to an antique armoire to reveal an impressive collection of vibrators and other sex toys.

"I don't think I'm into this," she demurred, turning away.

"Are you kidding? Sure you are," he told her, in a surprisingly authoritative tone; "Now look, why don't you leave it to me?"

"I don't like dildos," said Susan firmly.

"All right. But what about this?" William selected a long, disc-topped vibrator, about four and a half inches in diameter. "This one's powerful enough to get you off through your clothes. Totally zipless. Would you like me to demonstrate?" When Susan nodded William said, "All right, get up on the bed in the all-fours position." She complied without fear, but shyly.

In an almost clinical manner that aroused Susan greatly, William placed the disc top of the vibrator against her public mound without even taking down her shorts. He switched it onto low at it began to hum against her, immediately diffusing buzzing sensations though her whole pelvic region. For a few moments, he merely held the vibrator against her, just under her tummy. Then, with his free hand, he undid her zipper and slowly began to work her shorts down over her bottom. He stopped when they were only half way down. She was still bending over and he was still holding the flat-topped vibrator against her pussy through the jeans. Now he began to spank the exposed portion of her bottom. Then he paused to pull the shorts down a little more, revealing more of her bare bottom. Then he spanked her some more. Still he held the vibrator against her. She whimpered, moaned and wriggled and seemed on the verge of coming so quickly that he suddenly deprived her of the vibrator, sat on the bed and pulled her down across his lap. Now he pulled her shorts down completely and gave her a proper spanking.

"I'll bet," he said, smacking her bottom slowly, "that I could force you to have that orgasm just by continuing to spank you like this, if I do it long enough."

And sure enough, every time William's hand came down, Susan's pulsating sex was slammed against his rock-hard thigh. In less time than William predicted, he compelled Susan to come.

Having melted into a puddle, Susan slid off his lap and onto the floor. She leaned her head against his knee and William stroked her hair while she caught her breath.

"You're no trouble at all," he complimented her.

"I've always adored you!" she assured him, jumping up on the bed and pushing him down on his back, straddling his body and covering his face with kisses. William locked his arms around her waist and suffered these attentions with quiet contentment. "I hope Laura does divorce you now. Because I want you for myself!" Susan backed up these flowery declarations by deftly unbuckling his belt and pulling his zipper down. "And don't you dare even think about not fucking me now," she further warned, leaving William no choice but to lay his glasses aside and fully avail himself of her warmth.

Hugo fed his big black cat, locked up the house and went for a walk to the village, which was rimmed at its narrowest tip by the rocky coastline. He knew very well that he had been the bad guy that night. He could hardly fail to notice since he was the only one who didn't wind up with a girl. But he'd gotten William and Laura back together again, under romantic circumstances, which seemed like the right thing to do. He still wanted Laura badly, but the time was not still right for them yet. He didn't want to take her from William. He wanted her to come to him on her own, because she herself finally realized that they were meant to be together.

Hugo threw pebbles into the surf, smiling when he thought about Susan. She'd flashed him one fearful look upon delivering William into his drawing room, then lit out the door. Susan had rebelled rather spectacularly tonight and knowing her as he did, Hugo imagined that she was presently torn between exaltation and guilt. He could tell that it had pained her to defy him. But it was even more important for Susan to do the right thing. He would call her in the morning and let her know that in spite of everything, he still considered her mostly a good girl.

Hugo reflected that Susan, Laura and Marguerite no longer fit into the strictly submissive classification. One could spank them now and then and they were still sexually accessible, which was made them loveable, but when it came to playing, you had to do things their way or they got up and left. Hugo felt their scene was changing but didn't quite want to change with it. At least not yet.

Some of them still showed respect for the old ways when it suited them. Like Laura. The way she had taken her caning had been admirable. The tears pouring down her face were so exciting. She begged for mercy with her eyes and he ignored her. It was classic, gothic and real. She'd be marked for 2-3 weeks and would pout for as many months, but Hugo knew instinctively that the caning he had submitted her to would fuel Laura's imagination all winter. Whenever they encountered each other in the village or on the road, she would instantly remember his unemotional execution of the sentence and her utter inability to excuse herself from it.

Hugo and Laura were entering year four of their relationship. Sometimes she seemed to seek him out for thrills, when she was bored. Tonight she'd paid her dues for those thrills. Testing her hadn't been gallant, but that didn't mean he didn't love her. He had always considered her his, with her shallow marriage merely serving as the prelude to their deeper, longer lasting relationship. Setting it up so William could be a hero tonight had cost Hugo nothing. It also meant nothing. Sooner or later, Laura would belong to him.

When Hugo finally strolled back through the village, all of Random Point was asleep. The last shop he passed on Shadow Lane was the All Night Bakery. Hugo stopped in for some fresh pumpernickel and ran into Damaris, Michael Flagg's wife, feeding quarters into the ancient cigarette machine.

"This really is the only place in town to get cigarettes at three a.m., isn't it?" Hugo said to the very beautiful Mrs. Flagg, a pocket Venus with long, black hair and large brown eyes, which Hugo was surprised to note were glistening with tears as she turned toward the door.

"Hello, Mr. Sands," she mumbled, pushing past him and out into the street with her cigarettes tucked in the pocket of her fitted motorcycle jacket.

"Damaris, is everything all right?" Hugo followed her outside, forgetting his bread. She stopped with her hand on the door of her canary yellow VW bug.

"You want to hear what happened?" she sobbed, shaking out a Lucky and letting him light it for her

"Sure," he accepted a cigarette. She sat on the fender of her car in the manner of a New York City girl.

218

"I thought Michael was working late tonight. You know how he works nights half the time?" Hugo nodded. "Well, he's not working tonight. His car has been parked outside of Marguerite's house for the past two hours!"

"What were you doing driving past Marguerite's two hours ago?"

"I always drive past Marguerite's when Michael's supposed to be working nights," Damaris admitted; "But this is the first time in almost a year that I've found any proof that he's seeing her again."

"What are you going to do?" Hugo asked.

"I don't know."

"Why don't you come back to my house?"

"Your house?"

"It would teach Michael a lesson not to find you at home."

Hugo marveled at how quickly inspiration could come. Or was he just unusually lucky? Here was tiny, adorable, sexually submissive Damaris Perez Flagg considering him in the moonlight, with the wind blowing through her incredibly beautiful hair.

"Are you sure I wouldn't be imposing?" she let him light her next cigarette and appraised him like a girl out of a James M. Cain novel.

"No, I'd be thrilled to entertain you."

"It would be naughty," she mused with a smile. "Yes, I think I'll come!"

About the Author

In Random Point, everything is linked to spanking and this is true for the author of the Shadow Lane novels as well. Eve Howard has been writing and producing spanking erotica since the 1980's, when she began freelancing for one of California's largest fetish magazine publishers. While editing *Spank Hard* magazine (as Lizzie Bennett) in 1985, she was discovered by the video producer Nu-West and offered a chance to perform in spanking videos. In 1986 she published the first Shadow Lane story and the following year formed the video production company Shadow Lane with her partner Tony Elka. The Shadow Lane novel series, originally published by Eve in serial form in her magazine *Stand Corrected*, was brought out in paperback volumes by Blue Moon books beginning in 1992. There are nine titles in the Shadow Lane series and Eve is currently working on Volume 10.

Since 1988, Eve has written, directed and produced over 140 spanking videos, the vast majority featuring the same male-spanks-female dynamic portrayed in her novels. Female-friendly and designed to make people feel good, rather than guilty, about being into spanking, Eve suggests an irreverent alternative to the all or nothing B&D subculture portrayed in such beloved classics as *The Story of O*. Many spanking fans have discovered the real life spanking scene by following the same patterns of social networking as described in the Shadow Lane novels. And for almost twenty years, Eve's company Shadow Lane has been one of the primary social organs of the real life spanking scene. She lives with her husband Tony and three cats in Las Vegas.

Reader Reviews about the Shadow Lane Series

"I've become addicted to the "Random Point" series so much that I can't wait until the next chapter. I've ordered the first two Shadow Lane volumes and have re-read them over and over. I never tire of them. Eve is the only person I know who can make an enema sexy."

"I discovered Shadow Lane about a month ago via AOL. Prior to that time I thought I could write excellent spanking erotica. Then I ordered, "The Problem with Laura." This is just a note to commend Eve Howard's spectacular talent and to say thanks for an incredible erotic experience."

"I have just completed "Return to Random Point" and decided that I had to write about how much I enjoyed it. I have not been so aroused since reading my first discipline novel many years ago, about a girl raised in England and "coming of age" as I believe they put it. More recently I have enjoyed reading Grant Andrews' My Darling Dominatrix and Ann Rice's "Beauty" series. It seems that women, though, have the right touch when it comes to writing about this subject. Eve, especially, knows how to touch that erotic nerve and bring it to a pure, raw sensuality until one feels that he/she is near bursting with lust."

"I, for one, have always loved (and by loved I mean devoured... breathlessly) Eve Howard's novelettes. To read them... especially when I was just 'coming out'... was to feel completely validated. I truly identified with each and every heroine; the feisty, sassy ones, the shy, demure ultra 'subby' ones... the young ones, and the more mature. I loved the gentle yet firm "taken in hand" nature of the romantic variety of spanking D's that Eve always incorporated into the stories. I loved that the plots were not complicated... but, feasible nonetheless. I loved the depictions of sexual escapades after many of the spanking interludes. I appreciated that the girls were cherished and adored by the affably rogue-ish gents... that the submitting was willing and desired... that it wasn't like 'rape.'

I like the settings... having grown up in New England and living here almost my whole life. I LOVED the idea of the bookstore (which I always find sexy). Then and now. I could cite many passages too, but I fear I've rambled enough. Eve was/is always my favorite spanking author."

www.ingramcontent.com/pod-product-compliance
Lightning Source LLC
Chambersburg PA
CBHW020837260626

47169CB00003B/1028